Fellengrey

Scott Thomas

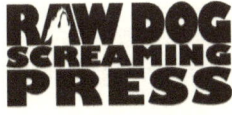
RAW DOG
SCREAMING
PRESS

Fellengrey copyright © 2012 by Scott Thomas

Published by Raw Dog Screaming Press
Bowie, MD

First Edition

Cover & book design: Jennifer Barnes
Cover Painting, Top: Thomas Whitcombe - Naval ships off Cape Town
Cover Painting, Bottom: a section of Miranda - The Tempest by John Willliam
Waterhouse

Printed in the United States of America

ISBN: 978-1-935738-23-7

Library of Congress Control Number: 2012952991

www.RawDogScreaming.com

For Dad, who was a Navy man

Burnshire, the Shrunken Coxswain

An Introductory Tale

Small Island

You'll be familiar, no doubt, with Fellengrey, that country comprised of twin kidney-shaped islands floating in the chill waters of the northern Gantic Ocean. It was off the western kidney, in the year of 1734, that Mill Burnshire rose, breakfasted and got about his duties as coxswain on the navy frigate *Bold Osprey*.

Autumn had come on, more noticeably inland, where the season put gold upon boughs and in windy fields of barley and rye. Here, out at sea, it meant the cold water was colder and days shifted more swiftly to darkness.

Burnshire was dressed for it. Beneath his dark cloak he wore the standard blue-green tailed jacket of his rank (single breasted, with notable white cuffs and a high stiff collar left open to show a pale linen stock). The waistcoat, breeches, stockings and shoes were black, as was the cocked hat atop the man's head. One of the flaps of the hat bore a decorative coin-sized medallion of brass with a tiny relief depiction of a navigator's sextant. He was a sharp-looking study, regardless of what the barber thought!

The man's hair could not be helped. It was unruly by nature, and always had been. As a boy his father had teasingly called him "shrub." Dark wavy curtains fell about his face and in back reached as far as the shoulders.

The man had great sad eyes with as much lid below as they had above, a look that made him appear either sleepy or wise, or perhaps both. The face in general was shaped of interesting angles, rather lean, and leading all was an impressive beak that had sniffed its way through twenty-five years of life. Today the nose took in the salty sea air.

Burnshire made his way to the quarterdeck of his floating wooden home and joined a small group of men gathered in the chill near the wheel. Lieutenant Allspice was pointing off portside while a sailor and two midshipmen went up on their toes and craned necks to follow the lead of his finger.

Burnshire plucked a telescope from under his arm and opened it with a snap, focusing before a word could leave his mouth.

"Women lacking garments?" the coxswain asked with a touch of the wry.

"Not lest she be a great dark woman with a blowhole what spouts water thirty foot in the air," Allspice came back.

Burnshire, swift with wit, was about to deliver a subjectively vulgar reply when he noticed something through his lens. Early light was on the water and the water was shifting, the light ever changing, the light cool-looking on the cold blue motion of the sea. Briefly, from that glittering, shifting surface, there flashed a large black fin and the slick ebon arc of a tail, though it dipped from view and was gone in a gulp of foam before the massive rear flippers could be seen.

Burnshire and the lieutenant pointed at one another at the same instant; both said, "*The captain...*"

Post Captain Bark had single handedly killed more men than any other captain in the royal fleet. A quiet, somewhat ominous man, he had been forced to go ashore when the bombardment of an enemy fort on the Vers-eh-sen southern coast went dreadfully awry. An accidental explosion in the forward magazine of his warship, compounded by enemy fire from two Vers-eh-senian three-deckers and the heavy guns of the fort, had forced his ship aground where an unfriendly battalion awaited.

Needless to say, Bark survived the ugliness that followed, but he did so by ending a good many lives. But *that*, he reasoned, was the business of war.

This morning, after being summoned from breakfast, he strode onto the deck, tall and lean in a longish dark green coat with double rows of buttons and golden shark silhouettes at the shoulders. His bicorne faced forward above the long rectangle of his solemn face. His age was a mystery, to look at him; he might have been twenty-nine, or he might have been forty-three. Whatever his age, Captain Bark squinted always, more so in sunlight and storm, and did so now as he nodded to the anxious men clustered at the wheel. He raised his telescope for a look.

"It's gone, I want to say," Allspice reported meekly, "but wasn't she a big one, sir?"

"There be not much for whale in these waters, commonly," Bark said in a grave voice, a hand on the handle of the sword that hung by one thigh. "Who saw it?"

"I," each man replied in turn.

Bark looked to Burnshire, whom he trusted more than the rest.

The coxswain, one of the most important figures on the ship, said, "Quite a large specimen, I'll give you that, Captain, just by the sight of her back-most fin. Too big for a hoof-head, and too dark for a milk whale."

Allspice nodded anxiously and pointed again to where the creature had made its brief appearance.

Bark nodded, said a curt, "Be keen about it," and returned to his breakfast.

Swift, sturdy and lying low to the water, the *Bold Osprey* was 118 feet long and 32 wide, her heavy black 9-pounders housed on a single gun deck. The three soaring masts were square sailed, their massive canvas sheets bulging roundly like bellies after a feast. In terms of color she was a sober sight, black from the waterline to just below the gunports and from there on up to the rails she bore a dim unpalatable green. Her trim was black around stern windows and railings and even on the balustrades which defined the poop and the forecastle from the middle of the ship. The proud figurehead of an osprey pointed the vessel on her way.

About her patrol for enemy Vers-eh-senian ships, the Fellengrey frigate came within view of the Drowned Horse Islands. The day had dimmed (more quickly now that autumn had arrived) and clammy vapor blew across the water. The sails were shortened and the men were so hungry that they actually looked forward to their salt beef and petrified biscuits.

Mill Burnshire dined with his coxswain's mate, an affable young fellow from the outskirts of Demmingsfife, who, like his helmsman master, bore responsibility for everything that had to do with the steering of the ship, the quadrants, sextants, compasses and the rest.

Following the meal, the mate, Woolbrick, paused before heading off to his hammock, and while he tried not to appear worried, his concern was evident.

"Not likely we'll run up against any Vers-eh-senians hereabouts, I should think. They shouldn't want for a base on the Drowned Horse Isles, cursed as they be, and shouldn't have cause then coming about. Not *here*, I mean, not off the Drowned…"

"Not at all likely. Sleep well, Woolbrick."

The mate smiled gratefully and closed the door.

Burnshire was not simply placating his nervous shipmate, for he himself took stock in the reassurance given. The enemy forces had nothing to gain from the Drowned Horse Islands, which, as young Woolbrick noted, were indeed cursed.

Each island was burdened with some sort of undesirable magic. To step foot on Cat Milk's Lapse, for example, was to risk having one's mind become precisely like that of a feline, which may, in fact, have been an improvement in some. Broken Mast not only boasted the rockiest shore of the bunch, but offered the singular disease known as mirror blisters, the symptoms of which were chestnut-sized welts that looked to be scrunched versions of the face of the person they appeared on.

And, of course there was Small Island, where a man could only remain for thirteen hours before shrinking to the size of a child. Once afflicted with *the shrink*, an inhabitant could only be off the island for thirteen hours, or suffer certain death.

Thirteen separate bodies formed the island group off the starboard side of the anchored *Bold Osprey*. They were arranged, more or less, in a horseshoe with the largest, Small Island, at the rear of the curve. The islands were vague above the night water, the moonlight just strong enough to define them as lumpy black objects.

Another lumpy black object reared from the deep Gantic some short distance away and headed toward the horseshoe, and the smaller object bobbing nearby.

Late in the evening Mill Burnshire reposed in his quarters, which weren't much, though he enjoyed more privacy than that afforded the average shipman who slept dangling in a hammock among crewmates and cannons on the gun deck. Burnshire poured the last glass from the last bottle from his stash of wine, kissed the empty vessel and said, "Goodnight, my dear," and set it on the floor.

Trugfield, the quartermaster, made it a habit of checking in with the officer of the watch before retiring. This night, like the rest, he tottered to the quarterdeck, his wide chest and round belly leading the way, his jowls jiggling with every step, the small gray tail of hair at the back of his tricorne bobbing.

"Well, a fine night," Trugfield puffed when he reached the midshipman at the wheel.

"Not a cloud nor drop of rain to be seen," the young fellow who was barely old enough to sport facial hair replied in a squeaky voice. "Though, sir, I care little for the chill."

The water was a glassy black, hypnotically strewn with a billion winking reflections of the moon. The men were looking out toward the islands when they heard the unique and horrifying roar of a soaring cannonball. They heard this before the report of the blast that sent it could reach their ears. After the ball struck, Trugfield had no ears for *anything* to reach. His head broke like an old apple, spattering the midshipman and everything else in the general vicinity.

Another low swoosh and another impact followed, though this one broke through the hull, rather than a man. Other balls came crashing, soaring metal meeting wood. The midshipman ducked down in a ball for what must have been minutes before abandoning his post and dashing for the open ladderway. He caught a glimpse of bright blooms spitting into the dark, distant eyes of light winking as the cannons of a vague ship released a broadside.

Mill Burnshire, his head full of wine, made the top deck on the heels of Captain Bark while the crews in the gun deck were scrambling to return fire. Both men had thrown on their uniforms in record time, though the coxswain had neglected his hat. It was treacherous going in the dark, for the deck was strewn with debris, lengths of broken rail, jagged pieces of planking and the odd body part. They paused when the foremast gave with a great creak and a groan. It seemed to take forever to fall, the web-like rope shrouds that had helped support it snapping, whipping at the autumn air.

The *Bold Osprey's* portside long guns began thumping, the smoke from their discharges a strange white against the night. Burnshire saw the captain standing like a ghost, a telescope to his eye, engulfed in the clouds that billowed back over the deck.

"Vers-eh-sen speeder!" the man called back over his shoulder.

A speeder, or a "spider," as Fellengrey sailors liked to scoff, was the Vers-eh-senian version of a frigate.

Captain Bark flew into the air like a child's doll as the sea came up through the middle of the ship—an upward burst of wood and water flung high as the remaining masts. Burnshire found himself sliding backward as the *Bold Osprey* smashed in two with a noise worse than anything. He hit the wheel hard, grunted and just glimpsed the massive black frontal lobes of a rump whale, a distinguishing split running the length of the tremendous head. It had rammed up through the craft with incredible force, the orbs like great cannonballs fired from below.

Men were shouting, screaming, toppling, grabbing for anything to hold to as the aft half of the ship moved beneath them, moved in a way that none had felt a ship move before. The ship, or that *half* of the ship, rolled toward one side, the port cannons dipping into the Gantic as the Gantic came up with a rush of hungry darkness.

Mill Burnshire got a grip of something and held to it, but with his eyes full of salty spray he could not see what it was. Felt like a man's boot. Yes, a man's slippery boot. The boot was on the foot of the quartermaster, Trugfield, whose broken bulk was wedged between lengths of rail. While Trugfield had been a big man, his boots had been oversized, and the blasted thing slipped off and Burnshire found himself sliding down the tilted deck into the cold night sea.

The Survivor

Daisy Milkbloom thought she heard thunder during the night, but in the morning when she looked out there were no puddles to be seen from the window, and the thatch of her cottage's roof was dry. Perhaps she had dreamed the thunder. If so, it might be expected to rain later on, for she often foresaw the coming day's weather in her sleep. At any rate, she put the thunder (whether dream or prediction) from mind and set about making breakfast.

Poor Stump, her tailless cat, was half mad with fleas. He sat by the fire waiting for a taste of what she was preparing, but his begging was interrupted by tiny biting monsters and he tilted his head, squinting, digging behind his right ear with a hind paw.

"There, my poor little Stump," the four-foot tall red-haired woman said with a look of woe, "those nasties will let you have no peace, will they?"

The cat—cream striped with marmalade—regained his composure for a moment but then was right back at it, head tipped, eyes squinting, digging, digging, digging.

The main living space of the Milkbloom cottage was half-timbered with clean whitewash between the stark angles of exposed wood. It was a simple room in a sturdy house, dominated by a tall wide fireplace with a hearth of pale green fern-slate. The furniture was severe, fashioned of fruitwood and oak—a settle, table and some skeletal hoop-and-spindle chairs.

This was the heart of the home, a place of utility and repose, cool enough in the summer for the closeness of the sea and not the worst place to heat in winter, for the beamed ceiling was low.

Two identical frowning uncles appeared in time for breakfast, which, by any standard, was a modest (if homey) repast. Hot porridge known as slush-apple along with griddle-oats. The men were old enough to have gray hair, scruffy hair down over the ears and necks, though little to speak of on top. One had a bushy beard and one had a muzzle of tight whiskers that proved impervious to shaving. The differing facial hair was about all that the average person could use to tell the sturdy fishermen apart.

Twilbin, the elder brother by a moment, who had a rectangular head on a square build, sat at the table in a simple white shirt and breeches. Grimacing, he twisted his left arm behind himself, the arm at an awkward angle.

"Flea," he noted stonily.

The other, Hobgrey, grimaced and twisted his right arm behind himself, the arm at an awkward angle.

"Brother to your flea," he said, scratching.

"Perhaps I ought try a spell," young Daisy offered, squeezing in between the uncles to take her place at the table.

Both men widened their eyes and uncharacteristically raised their voices.

"No!" they said.

Daisy looked at one and then the other. "And why not, might I ask?"

Twilbin, the more loquacious of the two, explained. "When we was boys an old Missus Skibbletwig tried hand at such a spell with result you shouldn't like to think upon."

That was the end of the story.

Daisy demanded more. "What manner of result did she come to?"

Twilbin sighed, took a deep breath to power a more lengthy verbalization than he was accustomed to, and then told how an elderly neighbor attempted a spell to rid her cottage of fleas, but instead wound up enlarging the pests to the size of cats.

Daisy made a face.

The militia of that time, which was little more than a handful of men with muskets, rallied to tend to the matter, but the creatures proved too much until local fishermen hailed the assistance of a navy ship and her crew.

"Perhaps I'll *not* try a spell to rid the fleas," the young woman said, bending an arm behind herself as she tried to scratch between her shoulder blades.

Uncle Twilbin looked up at the ceiling and asked, "Where is our Laurel?"

A sad look came to Daisy's face at the mention of her twin.

"She feels quite unwell, I fear, and wishes no breakfast."

The brothers looked at one another and frowned. Recently they had scolded the young woman for not eating. But she had been sickly following the sting of a peculiar bee with eyes that glowed like two little moons, and found her appetite lacking. Too weak to help with the many chores that now occupied Daisy, Laurel confined herself to the little upstairs chamber the sisters shared, doing little else but drawing.

Twilbin and Hobgrey brooded over their plates, their own appetites dissipating.

Twilbin, the more talkative of the two, said, "We are none of us safe, dwelling as we do on these cursed islands."

14

There was enough mist coming in off the sea, at the lower end of the South Road, to mellow the early autumn colors of maples and blunt the sharp tops of spruce that followed the winding track. The air farther inland was crisp, but here, so close to shore, the air was hardly ever anything that could be called crisp. When the village at Mullbatten Hill felt a snappish chill, the shore villages were clammy. When Mullbatten Hill got snow, the coastal homes were apt to see freezing rain. Thus, it was clamminess that accompanied the Milkbloom brothers as they made their way to their boat.

A small single-masted fishing vessel *Two Frowns* floated by a pier in dark cove water. The unpainted relief carving of a sea-moth, which no sensible fisherman would be without if he were at all concerned about good luck, called the eye to the bow. But something else drew the Milkblooms' attention. Both brothers stopped and stared, for a man (large in comparison to the locals) was onboard, apparently preparing to steal *Two Frowns*. He was a soggy man in white shirt and black breeches, with long dark hair and a notable hook of a nose.

"You there!" Twilbin, the brother with the stubborn stubble on his jaw shouted.

"Halt!" Hobgrey, the brother with a bushy beard called.

The thief, Mill Burnshire, looked up in surprise as two men the size of half-grown children thumped hurriedly along the dock. Burnshire dropped the tether he had been loosening and threw his hands up.

"Here, good fellows, I sought only to borrow—"

Burnshire's protest was cut short when Twilbin launched onto the boat and charged like a bull into the larger man's midsection. Burnshire was tossed back by the impact and his head struck wood. His mind went black.

A shady lacework of oak branches, seen from below, filled the coxswain's sight when he returned from his stupor. A green cloud hovered above him, branches like veins feeding the green, and an almost-blue sky bearing a bloom of vaguest sea vapor above that. A noose hung down from one of the lower boughs.

Three figures also stood above him, peering down. Children he thought at first, but as his eyes focused he saw that they were miniaturized adults. Burnshire suddenly remembered where he was and squirmed against his binds.

"Haste!" he cried, "Release me before *the shrink*! I must make off the island!"

Swellbrick Kibbinghen, sheriff of the Drowned Horse Islands, had been summoned and stood holding a flintlock pistol, which seemed almost comically oversized in his grip. He was younger than the other two, more round, more pale, more generously furnished with hair. His dress was as simple as the other islanders', good hardy garments made to last generations, fashion not being so changeable or esteemed as on Fellengrey proper.

"You might have thought as much before making to steal these fellows' boat," the sheriff said.

Burnshire had lost track of time. The ship had gone down in the night, but what hour of the day was it now? How much time had passed? In a more sensible state he would have applied his keen navigational skills and taken into account shadows and sunlight, but urgency has a way of obliterating rational thought. For all the man knew he might have been seconds away from reducing to the size of his captors.

Burnshire stopped squirming and pleaded, "Please, I must make off land or I shall shrink."

Twilbin rubbed at his stubble, looked to his brother and mumbled, "Should *the shrink* take him we shall need only dig a small grave."

"I am of the King's Navy, coxswain of the *Bold Opsrey*," Burnshire now tried to sound firm. "I demand my release!"

The sheriff squinted. "I see no ship hereabouts."

"She was lost in the night, assailed by a Vers-eh-sen speeder and attacked by a rump whale. Did you not hear cannon fire?"

Kibbingham countered, "I sleep as a rock. As for your rump whale, there be none of the kind hereabouts."

Burnshire had nothing to prove his story, not having worn a sword and he had lost his uniform jacket in the terrible night. A drowning crewmate had latched onto him and, in panicking, had clawed and tugged so that both men almost went under.

Burnshire was pulled from the buoyant wood he had gotten a hold of and his jacket was torn away by the thrashing sailor and lost along with the man. Fortunately Burnshire had managed to splash his way back to the floating debris, which eventually rode the tide to Small Island.

"Enough prattle," Twilbin rumbled. "Let's swing him and have about our day."

Burnshire tried his best to reason with the men, talking faster than he ever had before, with hardly a period between sentences, but his words, like his wriggling, had no effect. The twin brothers proved strong for their size. They hefted the captive to his feet and held him steady under the oak while the sheriff fitted the noose, drawing the scratchy lumps of the slipknot firmly against the back of Burnshire's neck.

The other end of the rope was fastened to the sheriff's cream-colored pony, who found this whole human business tedious. Kibbinghen waddled over and was about to clap the beast on the rump when he stopped, squinted and reached down the neck of his boot to scratch his shin.

"Oh! Something's bit me."

Just then Burnshire the coxswain felt a strange chill come over him, something other than the clammy air. The earth seemed to fall away beneath his feet and, with nothing supporting him, he found himself dropping, the noose's snare tightening around his thinning neck as he sank until the rope went taut and his toes touched grass. Just enough contact with the ground to keep himself from dangling.

The man's damp shirt flopped loosely about him and his breeches, which had been tight enough to demonstrate that his nose was not his *only* notable feature, slid down his legs and swallowed his shoes, buckles and all. *The shrink* had come on.

Two things happened then, one good, one bad. The good thing was this: a young rider from the village came drumming along the South Road, which passed the stand of oak where the hanging party had gathered, and hailed the sheriff.

"Ahhh, there you be, Sheriff, sir," the man said, breathing quickly, as if he and not his mount had been doing the work.

Kibbingham had a hand down one boot, grimacing. He looked up.

"Yes I am—oh! Bit me again, little fart! What *is* that? I am about my sheriff duties, hanging this boat thief."

The young fellow said, "Sheriff sir, there be bodies all about Densingbloom Cove, sir, navy men all."

The sheriff straightened, holding something between finger and thumb. He held it close to his eye for inspection and muttered, "*A flea.*"

"Bits of ship washed up as well, sir…an awful thing."

The twins, leaving the shrunken coxswain balancing on his toes, came over frowning. "Navy men?" one said after the other.

The words the young man had spoken finally made it from the sheriff's ears to his brain. "*Navy men.* Oh, dear."

The hanging party turned toward their prisoner, murder gone from their faces. They smiled awkwardly with about twelve teeth between them.

The bad thing that happened was this: Mill Burnshire realized that he was doomed to spend his life (but for thirteen-hour intervals) on Small Island, or else perish. He could never return to the world he knew, the brave sailing ships, his dear home village in Lower Spinning on the south-west coast of West Fellengrey, his mother and father and twin sister.

Suffering a numbing wave of despair, and squeezed by the fist of rope around his neck, the poor fellow fainted.

The sea was an elusive color, not quite blue, although blue whispered somewhere in the mix. There were light shades and dark, silvers and grays and other colors near-mystically intermingled. They would have seemed incongruous together elsewhere, while here the sea married them as only the sea can. It was altogether something one would not find in a rainbow.

More conventional colors held sway on land. The nourished green of the salt marshes, the yellowing fields, the feathers of goldfinch in the spruce, the turning leaves and the whitewashed cottages.

Thatched and seasoned, the Milkbloom cottage made home of a hill overlooking the strange-colored sea. A single chimney of plaster and stone rose from the center of the pitched roof, a comfortably unrefined monument to hearth and heat. The windows were smallish with small panes, the door a sturdy batten barrier against storm and cold and intruder. The place was pleasing in its simplicity, and to look upon it was to look upon the meaning of *home*.

Inside, Daisy made her way slowly up the tight staircase adjacent to the buttery. She had prepared a small something for her sister to eat and carried it on the pewter tray their father had purchased for their mother to use in bed while recuperating from the birth of twin baby boys. Sad little souls had only witnessed three days of life.

Daisy could hear the distinctive song of a gorse-wing out in the trees, its afternoon song, which was the creature's morning song in reverse. Gorse-wings were rare visitors to the island.

It was dark in the little plain bedchamber. A drawn-looking version of Daisy was propped in the bed they shared, hunched over her sketchbook. Laurel's color was poor, her cheeks and eyes hollow; even her red hair seemed drained by her malady. The hair hung in curtains at either side of her face, shadows from the curtains deepening the hollows of her visage.

Daisy stood in the doorway. "Something to eat?"

Laurel smiled weakly. "Oh, thank you, but I couldn't," came the weak answer.

"A bite or two, dear," Daisy insisted gently, "you *must* have something."

"A bite or two," Laurel conceded, putting her artwork aside.

Daisy placed the tray across her twin's lap then sat on the bed and picked up the sketchbook.

Laurel sampled her toast, which was generously spread with a nutmeg-sprinkled mash of autumn berries. She drank a little of the small-squall, a quick-brewed version of its hardy dark counterpart.

"Lovely work," Daisy remarked about the art, the work-in-progress being a gorse-wing on a branch. She could still hear the song of a gorse-wing coming from outside.

"Laurel," Daisy said, putting the sketches aside, "we have a visitor."

The word *visitor*, when used on Small Island, denoted someone from off the island. Laurel raised her head and her brows.

"A visitor? Who might it be?"

"A terribly sad man. His ship went down off the horseshoe, and were that not bad enough, he's had *the shrink*."

"Oh, dear!" The natives, generations of them born on Small Island, and many happy to be, still appreciated what a great misfortune *the shrink* was for someone from afar.

Daisy's face lit up and she stressed, "*A navy man.*"

Laurel, who was as unmarried as her sister, straightened, "A navy man? Is he fine to see?"

Daisy grinned. "Well, he has poignant eyes and a nice mouth, though his nose is rather great."

Laurel leaned back and sighed. "He sounds pretty!"

Daisy prodded. "Well, then, fly up from bed and come have look. It's so rare we have company."

Laurel shrank back, looked sickly again. "Oh, I couldn't. I dare not allow a navy man see me so. Perhaps when I am better."

Daisy understood. She did not push, as her uncles, who were less sensitively inclined, would have. Instead, she touched her sister's arm softly and said, "Yes, when you are better."

Daisy went to the door and looked back. Laurel seemed so small and worn just then, but she managed a smile as the door swung shut.

Daisy pinched her cheeks and fluffed her red hair as she went down the stairs.

The frowning twin uncles and the coxswain from the lost *Bold Osprey* sat in chairs by the fire, the cat, Stump, at their feet scratching. No one had a thing to say. Mill Burnshire looked far away, gazing into the flames, oblivious to the thrashing of a flea which was drowning in his tea. He was thinking about his dead crewmates, how they looked on the shore, the brave Captain Bark limp on the rocks, tangled in slippery arms of wrack. He pictured the young coxswain's mate Woolbrick tossed on the shore like driftwood. He wondered how many of his friends had drowned, how many died from the water's cold, how many had been crushed by enemy cannonballs, or in the teeth of the gargantuan rump whale.

Burnshire noticed the pretty young woman returning to the room and had mind to stand, the thing a gentlemen would do, a thing men on Small Island never did. Daisy blushed, the firelight in her green eyes.

"More tea, Mister Burnshire?"

"Thank you, no." Burnshire tried to smile.

Daisy sat on the settle, her wide skirt, with its pattern of moths and moons, flattening on the seat at either side of her hips. Her tatty shoes showed, but neither those, nor her humble country clothes could detract from her loveliness. Even in his despair Burnshire noticed.

The uncles lifted their white pipes to their mouths, Twilbin with his left hand, Hobgrey with his right.

Burnshire cleared his throat and said, "I am entirely determined to find some magic with which to reverse my...condition. Would there be someone skilled in magic about the island?"

Daisy thought of someone right off, but found herself silent. The thought of the navy man growing to his normal size and leaving, leaving her with no prospects beyond the loutish locals that sought to court her, brought on a sense of dread. She frowned when Twilbin made a suggestion.

"There be Widow Ducksbother up Mullbatten, she be skilled in magic and the like."

"Well, then," Burnshire said, "perhaps we might summon her come morning?"

Twilbin bit his pipe and nodded. Hobgrey bit his pipe and nodded. Daisy looked at the fire and clenched her little white hands.

In the morning Mill Burnshire helped bury the dead from his ship. The air was clammy, for a fine sea mist hung over the shore villages, ghostly air that smelled of salt. A good number of islanders had shown up to help in the grim task and they all proved kind to the stranger, rather impressed by his being a naval man.

Sea-moths circled in the air, sharing the air with gulls, the moths the color and size of pewter plates.

The graves were dug in a field of wild blooms, goldenrod and pungent spice-spark offering yellow to the bees. Burnshire noticed that the Milkbloom brothers were very skittish about bees.

All the world seemed odd to Burnshire, the bees bigger, the trees bigger, the ocean and its horseshoe of sibling islands bigger. But nothing was really bigger, it was only that *he* was now so much smaller.

Daisy brought tea up to her sister, but found Laurel sound asleep. A couple of gorse-wings were singing outside the window, serenading the sick woman's dreams. The sickly sister had completed her latest sketch, which, in fact, showed two gorse-wings, which mated for life. Daisy noticed a sheet of paper lying on the floor, poking out from under the bed. She put the tray down on a candle stand and bent to retrieve the artwork.

Curious. Boxes and dots. What did it mean? She studied it awhile before recognizing the layout of rooms; it was a simple floor plan of the Milkbloom cottage. The staircase and narrow buttery gave it away. She identified the downstairs bedroom her uncles shared; this is where the concentration of dots was.

"Fleas," Laurel said, sitting up, startling her sister.

Daisy turned to face her twin with an inquisitive look.

Laurel lamented, "I brought them."

"*Brought them*? How?"

"With *that*." She pointed at the drawing.

"I'm afraid I quite don't understand."

"Since that queer bee stung me, since the illness, I find I may conjure living creatures with my work. The gorse-wings, the fleas... But, I meant for them not to spread, and how terribly sorry I am!"

It wasn't so much the use of magic that surprised Daisy, magic was not the most uncommon thing, but the fleas, why the fleas? She inquired.

"Our uncles had been harsh to me, do you not remember, for I would not eat? They were very angry. So I thought to punish them."

Daisy lowered the artwork and sat on the bed. She took Laurel's hand. "Dear, they meant not to be cruel; their anger is for your condition only, not for you. It frightens them to witness you ailing."

Laurel nodded.

Daisy thought a moment, said, "You summoned the fleas, can you not have off with them as well?"

"I don't quite know."

Laurel took up her pad and once again made a floor plan of the cottage, but this time she left out the dots. All the fleas in the building died at that moment.

Daisy went off to check the cat, to see if he were still scratching. She didn't notice the drawing of a rump whale that had fallen, and floated like an autumn leaf, landing far under the bed. Laurel had not intended for the mammoth beast to cause any harm; she had only wished to watch it swim in the bay beyond her window, seeing as whales were so rare in that part of the sea, rump whales especially.

Laurel had neglected to mention how she felt herself growing sicker and sicker every time she used her art for conjuration.

In the evening the Milkbloom cottage had company aside from the unfortunate Mill Burnshire, who had been put up in a bed with the twin snoring uncles since his welcome into the home. Dusk was on the sky when a faint knock came at the door and Daisy rushed to answer it. An old woman was admitted, small even amongst her own and likely only as high as an off-islander's naval. She wore a patch over one eye; the remaining eye was the color of damp lilac blooms.

Daisy welcomed Widow Ducksbother and an underfed girl of twelve or thirteen, a granddaughter who had brought the crone down from Mullbatten in a farm cart. The girl, Pansy, bowed. She was pretty enough in her simple skirts and a passed-down day cap with yellowing lace. The elder Ducksbother scrutinized the surroundings, squinting her eye.

Daisy Milkbloom was all pretty smiles and thankful words, for the widow was not one to anger, strangely powered as she was. Even those who spoke ill of her behind her back found their tongues lumpy with warts.

Mill Burnshire, dressed in simple clothing loaned by the Milkblooms, in consideration of his new form, rose, bowed graciously, and smiled, as he had been instructed to do.

The old woman stood hunched, small and shabbily dressed, a bony hand on a bony hip, looking the man up and down. Her assessment was this: "Not so much for a navy man. Little more than nose and hair."

Burnshire reddened but bravely maintained his smile, which was more like grit teeth.

"I'm far more impressive in uniform," he offered.

The woman grunted skeptically and said, "Well, let's have done with it. Looks to rain and don't my bones quite hate the rain?"

The woman was swiftly provided with a chair and tea. Her granddaughter, a coy flower of a girl with small violet eyes under the winking flight of crow lashes, sat on the floor by the fire and petted the no-longer-itchy cat, Stump. Ducksbother had brought a small wooden box and now balanced this on her lap. She turned to gaze at Burnshire.

"Have you prepared your wish, young man?"

Burnshire, who sat just beside the magic woman, nodded eagerly. He had written his request (that being that he wished to be returned to his natural size) on a piece of paper and rolled it into a scroll. He held it out and the woman snatched it from his hand.

Ducksbother narrowed her purple eye at the navy man and warned, "*Asking the fire* proves a perilous doing, young man. There be risks, as you have no doubt heard tell."

Indeed Burnshire had. The Milkbloom brothers had strayed from their characteristic silence to give him an ear-load—examples of misfortune befalling those who dared *ask the fire* for guidance or cure. One man went blind, several men had their hair burst into flame, and a young woman from one of the fishing villages on the other side of the island found her breasts grown to the size of cooking cauldrons. For whatever reason, *asking the fire* only worked on the Drowned Horse Islands, but not many locals were comfortable indulging the custom.

Widow Ducksbother spilled some yellowish teeth out of a small cloth bag and handed them to Burnshire.

"Teeth of a dead man," she said. "Swish them about your mouth whilst you count thirteen in your mind."

Burnshire sneered. "*Swish them in my mouth?*"

"Yes, yes, in your mouth. You needn't fear; they shall not bite you."

Burnshire did as directed, but after the teeth were returned to the widow the man wanted to spit. He restrained himself and pretended to smile. The woman raised her cupped hands and muttered some antique words to the teeth then tossed them into the fire.

The others in the room observed with interest as the crone opened her little wooden box. A dead bird levitated out of it into the air and would have floated up to the ceiling if the woman hadn't caught it by a leg. The bird was an up-dead, a small, unremarkable thing of brown, no bigger than a sparrow. For reasons unknown, up-deads, upon dying, floated up into the sky, up and up and up until lost from sight, never to be seen again, decomposed or otherwise. Those that died in a structure would hover against the ceiling until rotted.

The old woman tied Burnshire's scroll to the bird's leg, soaked its feathers by pouring from a small bottle of liquid that smelled like an herb garden, and took it over to the fire where birch logs lay flaming across firedogs with moth-shaped finials atop their vertical bars.

Widow Ducksbother released the bird into the fire and it rose up the chimney, up and up and up, a burning ball. She called out, "Speak, fire, speak!"

The others all leaned forward to watch the flames, Burnshire most eagerly. He wasn't sure if he could see a face in the fire or not, but he clearly heard a voice, a voice like no voice, a fire-voice born of heat and magic and the ashes of his scroll, which the hungry flames ate.

"*There is no way known,*" the fire hissed, flaring, "*to return a man to his size once the shrink has come upon him.*"

The fire reverted to its usual sounds, the crackling that came less often, less startlingly, than the pops of burning softwood. Burnshire slumped in his seat, morose eyes locked on the flames, waiting for something else, but nothing else came.

"I am little surprised," the widow said. "Were there a cure for *the shrink* there would be none of us hereabouts."

Burnshire could find no words and hardly noticed as the old woman gathered her things, and, accompanied by her granddaughter, hobbled off into the dusk, her purse heavier for the coins that Daisy provided. Daisy had not told Mill that there would be a fee.

The man's brooding was interrupted by the sound of a woman's scream. It came from above. Quicker than the brothers, Burnshire was up off his seat and half up the stairs before they even reached the buttery next to the stairwell. They were still thumping from behind when he entered a bedchamber he had never visited and saw a woman he had never seen.

Laurel was standing by the window in her long sleeping gown, which was marked with blood. She was gripping one red hand with the other, and she was crying. She looked surprised to see the stranger coming at her, but realized quickly who he must be.

"Dear me," Burnshire said, "you are injured."

The young woman looked a tired version of Daisy, the hair not as richly red, the eyes not so verdant in their green. She smiled a small embarrassed smile.

"The window spike," Laurel said, gesturing with a little movement of her head.

"Here, allow me." Burnshire carefully pulled the girl's well hand from the injured and spied the neat circular puncture. He clamped his own hand over it, his palm a bandage, her warm blood against him.

The brothers came puffing into the room and stopped. Daisy was just steps behind.

"Laurel, dear, what have you done?" Daisy asked.

"That terrible cat from over the hill was up the tree again after my gorse-wings. I made to frighten it off and in my haste stuck my palm upon the point."

The culprit was a short iron spike jutting up from the outer window sill. This was where an apple (with a carved skull face) would be stuck to ward off the dangers of Ghost Hasten, the annual late-autumn night when the angry dead were free to roam.

Daisy went to the window and looked up into the branches of the nearest tree. "Did the bird not escape?"

Laurel's eyes welled and she shook her head. "Poor, poor little fellow, didn't he cry out so, and the female left now alone. They mate for life."

Burnshire turned to the brothers. "It's not so very bad. I've seen the worst of wounds in battle and this is but a little thing. More blood than damage."

"They mate for life," Laurel repeated and she looked at the hand of the navy man that was clamped around her own. The navy man with the magnificent nose and the wild curtains of hair and the most soulful eyes she had ever seen. It occurred to her then that she would simply sketch a new mate for the widowed gorse-wing, even if doing so would drain her health further.

The Terrible Snake

A week had passed and still fragments of the *Bold Osprey* were washing up on Small Island. The figurehead, coiled in slick ribbons of seaweed, had been found at an inlet over in Toadbatter, and the beach where Mill Burnshire and Daisy Milkbloom took their stroll offered sad, soggy treasures as well, evidence of lives that had once been. A man's shoe, a partly full bottle of brandywine, the rudder from one of the ship's boats. But there were pretty finds too, amongst the sad, such as polished stones of speckled gray, or off-white. Others were as black and round as a horse's eye.

Daisy was a fetching thing, even in her unfussy gown and bonnet, perhaps more so for the unfussy garments. There was nothing about her that was pretentious, nothing gloating nor grating. She was as peaceful and pleasant as the wildflowers along the path to the shore.

They paused. Burnshire knelt down beside a piece of wood and stared at it for a long moment. He reached and gently touched it. Daisy said nothing, and waited until some short time later to speak.

"I like to think in time's passing you shall find comfort here, and take pleasure in so being, as many in your circumstance have before you. In time they blend amongst the rest."

Burnshire, in that moment, denied the astonishing adaptability of the human animal. He simply could not think it, though he said, *perhaps*, out of kindness, so not to seem contrary.

The sand began to give way to larger stones, then ledges that stumbled up out of the sea. Farther along the shoreline there were high cliffs with precarious trees mocking gravity and sea-moths flashing like a cluster of small moons. Burnshire and Daisy climbed onto a grassy rise. It afforded a better view of the expansive Gantic and something floating upon it.

Daisy grabbed Burnshire's arm. "Mill!"

She felt his arm tense. He saw it too.

A three-masted ship hovered off shore, a Vers-eh-sen speeder, which was more or less a frigate. In all probability this was the ship that had fired upon the *Bold Osprey*.

Laurel heard the chatter of two gorse-wings when she came to after fainting. It was dark in her room, the way she liked it, though her sister often warned her that she would harm her eyes sketching in such insufficient light. The last two drawings had exhausted her, the one of the female gorse-wing's new mate and one of herself. It was not the first time that she had drawn herself healthy, hoping the magic in her art would actually dispel her illness, but this time, like the last, she only felt worse and actually passed out once it was completed. Her heart made worrying motions inside her.

The shore path meandered through shaded hollows in which trees had a touch of autumn color; it divided sunny open spaces of high weed-flowers where day-moths were on the breeze. Burnshire led the way, eager to get back to the village to alert the island militia, to tell the Milkbloom brothers about the ship in the harbor, to get word to Sheriff Kibbinghen, for what it was worth.

"Why do they come?" Daisy asked, breathing hard as she tried to keep up with the navy man.

Burnshire looked back over his shoulder. "I likewise wonder. Have they been before?"

"Yes, for fresh water only, when the stock on one of their brigs was lacking. Perhaps they find themselves in just such a way. "

"Let us hope."

The path climbed higher away from the shore, the edges defined by bracken and thorny tendrils that were dragged down by the weight of their own dark berries. A lesser path, more employed by hare and deer than humans, branched off to one side into a tunnel of leaf and shadow. A spilled basket of blackberries lay at the mouth.

Burnshire observed bent plants and noticed that the earth at the edge of the shore path (where it branched onto the thin, less-worn deer trail) was disturbed. He turned to Daisy, his face tense.

"Where goes this track?"

"A short way to the water—a small cove."

"A cove agreeable to a boat's landing? Sandy, flat?"

Daisy nodded.

The man pointed to the woodsy depths on the opposite side of the shore path. He said, "Haste! Secrete yourself in the greenery," and moved carefully through the snaring brambles, into the cool rustling shadows of the deer path.

Burnshire caught bright blue glimpses of the sea the nearer he got to it. Flashes between the smothering growth. Gulls sounded and smaller birds with more delicate voices, disturbed by his trespass, shrilled and fluttered. The little trail tilted seaward and the foliage thinned at either side and he saw the cove, a treed hollow hugging quiet water. A ship's boat had been pulled up just beyond the waterline and two Verseh-senian men in black uniform jackets, with muskets slung over their shoulders, were pulling a local girl toward the boat where a third man waited. Burnshire's heart startled like the birds in the wood.

The girl's wrists were tied behind her back and she struggled against her captors until one of them, the one who had stayed with the boat, pointed a pistol in her face and clicked back the swan-neck cock. The captive quieted at that, but she had an awkward time getting into the boat, her skirts being long and she being without the use of hands to steady herself with. The two musketeers, each with unruly dark hair sprouting from under tricornes, chuckled huskily. The Small Island girl, who could not have been more than twelve or thirteen, looked like a much smaller child next to them.

Burnshire ducked behind bushes, his chest full of mad birds, his lungs in a vise. He noticed three things. The first was that the man with the pistol (who had apparently remained with the boat while the other two captured the island woman) wore the uniform embellishments of a lieutenant. The next thing he noticed was that the captured girl was Pansy, the granddaughter of Widow Ducksbother. The third thing was another spilled basket of bramble berries, half-hidden in ferns.

What to do, the unarmed man thought, facing three armed seamen of the enemy kingdom. Should he run and summon help? Should he make an attempt to rescue the young Ducksbother?

His first instinct was to arm himself, so, in a crouch, he turned to look for a sturdy branch, but there were only soggy crumbling lengths of old birch visible in the wild growth. He took a few steps, his back to the cove, wading into yellowing ferns as high as his chin. He did not notice Widow Ducksbother—sprawled bloody in the dense ferns—until his foot came down on her slack face, the lilac eye unblinking. Burnshire lost his balance, and with an involuntary cry fell onto his back, swallowed by the ferns.

Cringing, the man rolled over onto hands and knees and peeked toward the cove. He heard men's voices speaking in the guttural Vers-eh-senian language. Then he heard someone crunching toward the path, boots on sea pebbles, then heavy on the earth of the trail. The coxswain could almost feel the ground shake with each step the enemy took, as if a giant were coming.

Still on all fours, Burnshire backed away from the edge of the path and his hand fell on something smooth and hard. It was the neck of Widow Ducksbother's walking staff, the head of which was carved in the likeness of a seahorse.

With the muzzle of a musket leading the way, the large Vers-eh-senian man muttered to himself.

"Birds only," he surmised in his native tongue.

The large man saw no source of the cry that had been heard and decided to turn back once he reached the wider shore path. He started past the tall banking of ferns where the old woman had fallen when he shot her. A smooth length of polished wood poked out of the plants, across the track, catching his shin and he went down on his chest with a thump and a grunt.

Burnshire sprang out of the ferns and swung the staff with both hands, striking the man on the back of the head before he could raise himself. The musketeer grunted again, and once more when the third blow cracked, but only shuddered when a fourth, fifth and sixth blow came down on the back of his skull. There was no need for a seventh.

"Where is that fool?" the Vers-eh-senian lieutenant asked, standing in the shallow water by the boat, a hand on his hip. He started to say something else, but a musket ball struck him in the midsection and he winced, toppling into the calm water. The sound of the shot bounced around the cove and a puff of smoke showed up on the deer path.

The surviving musketeer rushed around the boat and struggled to lift the officer out of the water, affording Pansy Ducksbother the opportunity to throw herself out onto the gray sand and run off into the surrounding woods.

Burnshire had decided not let himself be seen, hoping that the men from Vers-eh-sen would think there was more than one armed man about. Having taken ball, patch and powder from the dead man, Burnshire quickly reloaded the fellow's musket and fired again, hitting the bow of the boat. He squeezed off a shot from the man's pistol seconds later, again to give the impression that multiple islanders were aiming down at the cove.

The musketeer managed to get his lieutenant into the boat, which he then bravely shoved into the water. He dove into it as another musket blast sounded and shot splashed in the water. The man ducked as low as he could and desperately worked the oars.

Burnshire fired several more times until the boat was out of range, safe in the shadow of its mother ship, the ominous Vers-eh-senian speeder.

Everyone, including the failing Laurel, was gathered in the hall of the Milkbloom cottage. They were all watching the fire—the glum-faced uncles, the twin sisters blinking big, nervous eyes, Mill Burnshire, his gaze inscrutable under heavy lids that made him look sleepy and wise. Even the cat, Stump, watched the flames twisting about in the spacious firebox which, to generations, had stood for comfort and home.

No one was talking, though there had been animated dialogue earlier. Burnshire had told of rescuing Pansy Ducksbother, and of the poor old widow's fate. He told of shooting an enemy lieutenant, who may or may not have died. He told of killing a man.

They now had learned why the speeder had anchored off shore, for Pansy, who knew something of the Vers-eh-sen language, had listened to bits of conversation between her captors. It seems the privilege girl on their ship—a woman employed to entertain the amorous men—had died some months before, so they were looking to find a temporary replacement. Very temporary, for Pansy would have died if kept off the island a second longer than thirteen hours. Apparently the ship's captain was eager to have a try with one of the little Small Island women.

Burnshire smiled nervously when he noticed that the Milkbloom sisters, who sat side by side on a high-backed wooden settle, were both staring at him admiringly, perhaps having tired of watching the flames.

"How very brave you are, Mister Burnshire," Laurel said, her smile dimming the shadows that sought to overtake her.

The man blushed. "You are kind to say, Miss Laurel."

Daisy nodded emphatically. "Yes, ever so brave, *Mill.*"

Burnshire sensed a bit of sisterly competition. Both red-haired women were sweet, and not a little lovely, even the sickly Laurel. While the attention made him somewhat uncomfortable, his opinion of himself catapulted to new heights.

Everyone flinched when a hard knocking came at the door. Burnshire bolted up, grabbing the oversized pistol taken from the man he had killed. He reached the door before the brothers did and stood to one side, his weapon cocked and ready. Hobgrey opened it.

"Good evening," Sheriff Kibbinghen said, his dark clothing and the dark night making a disembodied thing of his face.

"I thought to show you this," the Sheriff said, addressing the coxswain. Kibbinghen produced a small scrolled paper from a pocket of his greatcoat.

They had returned to the fireplace in the low-ceilinged dimness of the hall, the lot of them squeezed around it, even several members of the island militia, two of which were hardly more than boys. The other two, wrinkled gents, might have been better off carrying canes rather than the sizeable off-island muskets that barely fit under the low beams.

A sizeable messenger moth had carried the scroll to a farmer's cottage and the farmer had taken it to the sheriff. Burnshire read the note, which, written in the Fellengrey language, said:

You shall surrender the party or parties responsible for wounding our officer or we shall destroy every village on your island. Please to comply by first light or we commence fire.
                                                Captain Neh-bo-twa of The Terrible Snake

Burnshire grew very pale and slumped in his seat. "*The Terrible Snake*," he muttered.

Kibbinghen gave an impression of courage and determination. "I have made to alert militia in Mullbatten and Whitgallow. Others are off about to notify the rest."

Burnshire's thoughts spun. The animal impulse to run from danger sprang up inside him, quick in his pulse. But, this urge collided with his principled self. There was only one thing to do.

Staring at the flames, he spoke slowly and softly, "Come morning they shall pummel the villages with artillery. That done, they will send men in boats, well-armed, well-trained men. They will make to every village and kill all who are found."

Everyone stared at the man with their orange fireplace eyes.

Burnshire straightened. "I must go to them and surrender."

Kibbinghen stood up. "I hardly think so!"

Twilbin, the more vocal of the Milkbloom brothers, launched up from his chair, protesting, "You shall do no such thing!"

Hobgrey flew to his feet, echoing, "You shall do no such thing!"

Kibbinghen, charged with danger, said, "We shall fight them, am I not right, boys?"

The motley militiamen cheered affirmatively, shaking their big awkward muskets.

Burnshire sighed. "Either *I* die or *we* all die," he said.

One of the old wrinkled fellows called out, "Fight, fight..."

His compatriots took up the chant, "Fight, fight..."

The Milkbloom brothers bellowed along, and the dainty sisters on the settle joined in as well, shaking their little white fists. Even the cat, Stump, had a certain defiant look in his eye.

"Fight, fight, fight, fight..."

Burnshire hung his head and wagged it.

Small Island looked a great mound of green floating there at the rear of the horseshoe that was the Drowned Horse Islands. It was sunrise. A coppery-pink came up from the east and skimmed across the morning sea before falling on the baroque cover of trees, which, but for the intermittent thatch of village homes, seemed to smother the land mass.

The six villages on Small Island, each comprised of thirty or so homes, provided a collective militia force of seventy-two fighters, less than the number of men on the *Terrible Snake*. There had not been much time to organize a defense, but the bulk of the volunteers were positioned at strategic heights around inlets where the enemy might be likely to come ashore. Some were stationed in hiding along the few major roads, ready to ambush. An additional number of able men and boys (not of the militia proper) were also poised to fight, scattered here and there and armed mostly with axes and pitchforks and other assorted tools rather than muskets, which were not terribly common on the island, there being no local gunsmith. Muskets were a costly imported commodity.

The latest addition to the island populace, a coxswain named Mill Burnshire, had advised that villagers abandon their homes and seek safety in the most secluded, inaccessible parts of the island, for they were sure to be found if they remained in their towns. Some took his advice, but others stubbornly remained behind, refusing to leave their dwellings, things, pets and livestock.

First light fell on the window in Laurel Milkbloom's bedchamber. It glared on the glass making it hard to see the bay beyond and the dark ship anchored there, its portside facing land, the fourteen portside cannons staring.

A sleepless Mill Burnshire accompanied Daisy up into the simple little room where a young woman was propped up in bed. Too sickly to flee with those who saw the value in Burnshire's warning, she remained; Daisy, of course remained with her. Laurel had no appetite for the tray of food that her sister brought and her hand shook when she lifted a cup of tea.

"You must eat something, dear," Daisy said.

"I cannot," Laurel said, too weak to summon a reassuring smile. Her condition continued to worsen. She heard footsteps heavier than Daisy's and turned to the window where she noticed a figure silhouetted against the sunny panes.

"Would that be you, Mister Burnshire? My eyes work little…"

Burnshire, with a terribly intense look on his face as he gazed out at the ship, turned, his expression softening. "Why, yes, Miss Laurel, it is I."

The woman reached out a pale hand and Burnshire took it. Feeble as she was, Laurel managed to squeeze his fingers.

"I wish you all good luck against the Vers-eh-senians," she said.

"You are quite kind. Thank you," Burnshire said.

Laurel released his hand and gazed up, her eyes still pretty even as she wasted. Burnshire smiled gently at her, then turned back to the window, opening it so as to have a better look, for the glare of sunlight on glass practically obscured the distance. A cool breeze flew in so suddenly that a piece of paper blew out from under the bed and hissed over the wide uneven floorboards. Daisy stooped to pick it up.

Burnshire studied the scene before him, the enemy vessel waiting there on a blush-colored sea, the sea beyond the bay as big as anything could be. He then closed the window and turned to go back downstairs to join the Milkbloom brothers and the sheriff and a group of militia men who were waiting to head closer to the shore. He gave Laurel a long look before stepping out and closing the door.

Daisy looked up from the drawing of a rump whale. "Laurel, dear…*you brought the whale?*"

Laurel's eyes filled up and she leaned her head into the palms of her hands. "I meant not a harm, but desired only to observe it, whales—rump whales most certainly—being so terribly rare in our waters. But what a horror I have done! All those poor men of the *Bold Osprey*…dead for the sake of my whim. My wellness fails as much for my guilt as from the strange disease of the bee sting."

Daisy crumpled the picture in her hands and put it down on the candle stand, though a breeze nudged and it fell back onto the floor. "You mustn't condemn yourself, Laurel, for as you say, you willed no ill upon that ship. It might well have been hit by lightning."

Laurel smiled finally, but it was a bitter smile and the effort of it released the tears that had waited in her eyes. "Yes, lightning born of *my* doing."

It was not lightning that stuck the house just then—blasting through the hall spraying a dusty cloud of wood and plaster—but a nine-pound ball of metal fired from a ship that sat anchored nearly a mile off.

The *Terrible Snake* released a broadside, smoke from the cannons a deceiving rosy color in the daybreak light. Shot howled through the air, punching through tree bough and leaf, flying toward the white village homes perched some short distance above the bay. They hit with the most horrible crashing sounds, the neat sides of cottages broken like toys under angry fists, windows reduced to spitting clouds of glass, the smallest fragments like sparks in the pretty pink sunlight.

On the path to the shore, Burnshire, the Milkbloom brothers and the rest crouched and cringed. They could all but feel the rush of wind the projectiles traced through the air as they passed. The men looked at each other with big eyes. Burnshire stood up before the rest and, armed with the front-heavy pistol he had taken from the dead Vers-eh-senian, charged forward.

Daisy peeked out the upstairs window. She could see the speeder there in the bay, quiet for the moment as cannon crews reloaded for another barrage. She looked over her shoulder.

"Laurel, we must make to the cellar whilst the house stands yet."

Laurel wagged her head.

"Laurel, we *must*!"

"*You* must, Daisy, and be quick about it. Worry not for me."

Daisy wheeled away from the window. "I'll not leave you."

"Please go, Daisy. I am beyond reclamation, but you…"

The thump of nine-pounders came over the bay and Daisy turned to the window, saw the billowing from the blasts.

"They fire!"

Up amidst rocky ledge and spruce, a group of militiamen stood and fired their muskets down at the *Terrible Snake*. One fellow, their officer, sprang up and shouted at them.

"Cease, you fools, cease to fire!"

The men, their weapons spent, knelt back down and began to reload. The officer scolded them, "We are beyond range, you farts! We can afford not to waste powder and shot. Not only that, but you betray our position."

The Vers-eh-sen ship floated quietly for several moments and when the next volley boomed, a ball found the militiamen there on the cliff. Two of the brave souls broke like spoiled fruit, without screams.

Burnshire thumped down the path to the sea and ducked to one side, where vegetation offered cover. Hobgrey and Twilbin were just behind him, the sheriff puffing to keep up. They saw flame and smoke flush from the side of the ship, evenly above the waterline, and heard the balls as they whipped through the air.

Burnshire and the brothers looked back toward the village and watched helplessly as one of the houses lost its chimney, as a barn had a crater blown open in one side, and as the Milkbloom cottage's front door was smashed to pieces.

"No!" they all cried at once.

The house shook when the batten door was knocked apart. The sisters gasped. Daisy threw herself on the bed and wrapped her arms around her sister.

"We're to die!" Daisy cried.

After what seemed a very short time another series of thumps came from the bay. The tree outside shook, spitting frightened gorse-wings, and one of the walls of the bedchamber exploded inward, a hail of plaster and wood hidden in a cloud of dust. The women screamed.

The quiet between cannon shots came on and Daisy lifted her head to see the damage. The ball had come in one side of the room and punched through the other. Cool air blew through the openings, but in between it caught the sketch that Daisy had crumpled and blew it. The ball of paper tumbled, rasping across the debris-strewn floor.

Daisy rose from the bed, grabbed a sketch book off a candle stand and took her sister by the shoulder.

She said, "The whale, Laurel. Draw the whale!"

Laurel looked up with faded eyes and nodded. It made no matter to her that another drawing might squeeze out what little life was left in her. She hunched over the paper and went to work, quickly rendering a great black water beast with a cleave mark dividing its rounded head. She drew a three-masted ship in the behemoth's great mouth.

Daisy turned to the window, saw the ship with its cannons poking out through ports, pointing her way. A divided dome of slippery black breeched the ocean surface and coursed toward the vessel.

Hobgrey, the more quiet of the Milkbloom brothers, knowing that the *Terrible Snake* was about to fire once again, knowing that the cottage sheltering his nieces had been targeted, leaped out from the cover of bushes and ran onto the open sand of the cove where Burnshire had previously battled the Vers-eh-senians. The man fired his musket into the air and waved his arms, shouting, "Here! Here!"

"No!" Burnshire called.

The cannons spewed light and smoke and deadly spheres that flew faster than the noise of discharge could carry. Burnshire sprang from his hiding place and threw himself at Hobgrey, tackling the man around the waist. Both went down in the sand and a cannonball flew over their heads.

Twilbin, the more loquacious of the twin Milkblooms, popped up out of ferns and pointed. "Look there!" he cried.

The *Terrible Snake* was a child's toy the way it broke, an enormous black fist punching up through the center of it from below. Water flew skyward in a great column of displacement, the masts cast free, boards of all sizes flying in the air like gulls in coffins.

The witnesses, both the men on the sand and Daisy up in a window, watched as the halved wreckage splashed back down in the water and was set upon by the rump whale. They were not able to hear the cries of the men that were tossed in the air when the whale struck, nor as men thrashed in the cold water while the whale demolished the separated sections of the ship, crunching and crushing with teeth bigger than what gods should allow.

Twin Frowns

Repairs to the cottage had taken weeks. To celebrate the completion of their work, the Milkbloom brothers and their boarder, Burnshire, sat about the fire well into the frosty hours, singing bawdy songs and drinking dark squall. Was it any surprise that the three, crowded into a single bed and snoring like cattle, slept so late into the morning?

Burnshire was awakened by the sound of complaints.

"Here, now, Burnshire, must you take the whole farting bed?" Hobgrey growled, elbowing.

"Yes," Twilbin started, "you're…"

The fisherman stuck his head up and looked at the fellow in the middle, whose long legs had pushed the covers down, whose clothing, being too small for his body, had torn at the seams and only partly covered him.

Twilbin said, "You be large once more!"

Burnshire sat up and gave himself a look. "I'm grown! I have returned to natural size!"

The twins jumped up from the bed while Burnshire sat there blinking.

Hobgrey looked to his brother and spoke excitedly, "We must be quick and see him aboard the *Twin Frowns* and off land before he again shrinks!"

"Yes," Twilbin said, ready to sacrifice the craft of his livelihood for the sake of their friend, "To the *Twin Frowns*!"

Burnshire, lacking any clothing that would fit, wrapped himself in bedcovers and followed the brothers out into the hall where Daisy was preparing breakfast. He banged his head on a beam, which before he had no need to duck under.

"Owww!"

Daisy's face was not so happy when she saw the enlarged version of Burnshire. She stood as if frozen, befuddled, not even thinking *how* he had come to return to his proper size. Her heart felt like a small gray bird with tightly folded wings.

"You leave then?" she asked.

Burnshire was grinning madly, wild with enthusiasm. "Yes! Yes! They've given to me the *Twin Frowns*. I must away, but oh, thank you for your many kindnesses, dear Daisy! I shall write letters, and send coin of thanks, and oh, I must really be off!"

The door slammed and that was that. Mill Burnshire and the brothers were off for the shore and Daisy stood there half-hearing the water boiling over the fire, thinking how she was doomed to local suitors—grizzled fishermen with scratchy whiskers and hands rough as rope, and hearts small as fleas.

Burnshire stood up in the boat once he had rowed some small distance off Small Island. He waved his arms at the brothers, calling, "Farewell, fine fellows! I shall fondly miss you!"

The brothers waved back and Burnshire realized that he had never seen them smiling before.

"Be well, Coxswain Burnshire," they called.

"I shall be," he replied, and then, more softly and to himself, he said, "I shall be."

Daisy moved numbly about the hall, her body going about its duties while her mind was off in some far sad fog. She put tea and humble breakfast on a pewter tray and carefully carried it up the tight staircase that was close to the buttery. She could hear gorse-wings singing off somewhere, a lovely song to the sunny autumn air.

She balanced the tray with one hand and opened the chamber door with the other. The room was bright for once, the curtains pulled open so that Laurel could see the bay. She was facing that way—though her eyes were closed—propped up in bed with a sketch pad in her lap. Daisy glanced at the water, at the *Twin Frowns* heading out between the arms of the island horseshoe, carrying Burnshire away.

"Do you care to eat?" Daisy asked dully, carefully laying the tray across her sister's lap.

Laurel said nothing. Daisy took her hand, which was cold.

"*Laurel?*"

Daisy sat gently on the edge of the bed and lifted Laurel's slack arm, touching her sister's hand to her cheek. Warm tears fell against the cold fingers.

"Dear, dear Laurel."

After sitting that way for some time, Daisy's eyes fell on the killing sketch, the artwork that had drained the last of Laurel away. It was a fine bit of work depicting Laurel standing side by side with Mill Burnshire. They were holding hands, but she looked like a child next to the coxswain, who was the size of an off-islander.

Privet

1

Fields

A sea-moth landed on the roof of the farmhouse the day that Hale Privet was born. This, according to the old folk, was a sign that the babe was destined for adventures at sea, but that seemed unlikely, seeing as the birthplace was far from the nearest shore. It was all the more improbable when one considered that there were no sailors in the Privet line; they had been planters and herdsmen, so far as living memory knew, and if there had ever been a briny misfit in their ranks, he was long forgotten. No, the boy was born into a landscape of orchards and sheep-meadows, where the only rippling ocean was comprised of barely and rye.

The elder Privet, Burren, who witnessed the silvery creature skimming over the thatch and lighting on the chimney of his round stone cottage, cursed and threw rocks. The moth lifted lazily into the air on wings the size of dining plates and floated off for the west. The man was not happy with the thought of his son going off to sea, for much as he cherished his four daughters, Burren had long wanted a male child. Every planter could use a good son or two to help with the keeping of a farm.

The boy knew little of the Gantic Ocean, growing up inland at the rural village of East Whittle. His father was moored to the seasons and happy for the generational roots that connected him to the earth. The lessons Burren bestowed upon his son were practical, and mostly had to do with farming, but for the occasional ethical observation, such as, *never kill a thing but for to eat it, or if it means to do you a harm.* Hale's mother, Fern, like her husband, was not a dreamer, but she provided love enough, and told Hale stories about the history of the country, tales of armies and kings and mighty navy ships that had made the nation great. These tellings nailed the rapt young Privet to his stool by the fire, from whence he stared up at the woman with large brown eyes. Later, when he retired to bed in the little attic

45

chamber, he'd listen to the wind in the corn, imagining it was the sound of a sea. In summer he pretended that the sound of thunder was the din of cannons from clashing warships.

It was late autumn, 1740, and the leaves were gone from their trees. Hale, who had recently turned ten, was lugging armloads of wood into the house, where both sets of twin sisters were about their own chores. Father had set a ladder against the side of the house and was up the conical roof, hanging a wreath of brittlethorn on the front of the chimney, as he did every year at this time.

This was Ghost Hasten, the most dreaded day of the year, when the souls of the angry dead were free to dash across the earth and wreak havoc on the living. Preparations—like hanging wreaths of brittlethorn to discourage chimney visitations—had been going on in the village for days. Coveted silver nails, which, generally speaking, were the most expensive articles that local planters were apt to own (and kept for this express purpose) were scattered about the front door stoop. It was a well-known fact that cruel ghosts hated silver. A rusty iron spike poked up from the outer sill of every window and upon these had been impaled apples, crudely carved with the features of a skull.

Finished with his work on the roof, Burren moved down the steep thatch to where the ladder had been. *Had* been. Hale was standing below, grinning up with the ladder resting on the ground beside him. At times the boy was overcome by an irresistible mischief.

Burren glared down. Not one for striking children, he periodically resorted to threats, "You'll have that ladder up swift enough, young sir, or you'll find yerself on a ship for the Colonies!"

Hale stood the ladder back up and, after his father climbed down, was ordered to return the thing to the barn. The boy was dragging it behind himself as if pulling a plow, when he noticed a horse and cart rattling along the road. Burren noticed too, and stood watching as the vehicle came near.

"Hallo!" the lone occupant called.

The cart was a sad, worn thing, like the beast pulling it, and a simple wooden coffin was roped to its scuffed wooden bed. The stranger reined his horse, climbed down and bowed. While tall and sturdily built, he was a shabby figure with wild graying hair and a wild graying beard and a face that weather had not been kind to. He might have been handsome without all that pewter shrubbery, for the features were good, the eyes raptor-keen and dark as treacle. A drab brown cloak hung from his shoulders, draping down to obscure the rest of his dusty garments.

Burren gave the vagabond a cautious nod.

"Good man," the visitor said, his voice full of rich tones, "the most terrible night is near upon us and here I, a creature lacking shelter or coin, stand at the mercy of your good will."

Burren knew nothing of this man, but with dusk fast approaching, and a storm of ghosts pending, he could hardly turn a fellow away.

"You may shelter here," the planter said, "but no weapon might pass through the door."

"I've none, kind host, and ne'er the cause for the like. See this to be true."

The man opened his cloak to reveal the long rust-colored coat beneath, and the vest and breeches under that. Burren saw no suspicious bulges. The man's shoes were too short at the ankle to conceal a boot-blade.

Burren nodded. "I take you on your word, Mister…"

"Noll Slate would be my name." The man said with a smile and a charming squint of the eye. He bowed again—his arms out like wings—a more graceful bow than one would expect from a raggedy man. He thanked Burren profusely.

Hale stood silently by his father's side, staring at the stranger's grim cargo. Slate noticed this and explained, "My brother, poor soul. We been north at Ficklebridge, working the saw-mills. There was an accident…"

Slate gazed off with a mournful look, rather than indulge tragic details.

"Sorry, sir," the boy said. "Where do you take him?"

Slate sighed and went on to explain that he was far from any kin, without permanent lodgings, and no different from other itinerant workers common to these parts in the days of harvest. He and his brother had been traveling about for the last three years, working where there was work to be had, sleeping where fate and generosity allowed. As to where to set his brother to rest…he was seeking just the right spot, but as yet had not found it.

The gray sky was deepening and valuable time had passed. Burren still needed to safeguard the dovecote and chicken coop before the ghosts arrived. He instructed Hale to see that the guest's horse and the coffin were put in the barn. Unfortunately there would not be room for the traveler's cart.

The planter turned and surveyed his cottage, a two-story round construction of stone with an enclosed wooden entryway (known locally as a "throat") poking out from the front. He was pleased with the precautionary steps he had taken: the wreath, the apples, the silver nails.

Hale unhooked Noll Slate's horse and led it into the barn. This gave the man time to slip a key from his coat and lock the compartment under the hinged seat of his cart, securing the charged dueling pistols inside. By the time the boy came back out, Slate was in the rear of the cart, kneeling by the simple pine coffin.

"Looks to rain," Slate noted.

"It always rains at Ghost Hasten," Hale said.

The Privet family and their company sat in relative darkness, close by the parlor fire as night raged round the house. Five owl-eyed children huddled together on the floor-cloth at the feet of their father, while the pleasingly round Mrs. Privet, cocooned in a shawl and fortified with a bowl of warm slush-apples, sat opposite. Slate had been given the best slat-back chair, as custom dictated, and sat stroking the Privets' white cat, Milk, who had curled up on his lap. The man seemed oblivious to the storm.

"Worst we've had in years," the father observed with his usual restraint.

Indeed. The rain and wind were full of terrible cries, a cacophonous intermingling of voices that whipped at the windows as if natural emanations of the gale.

A woman was shrieking outside the buttery window and a man's voice, which sounded like something one would hear underwater, called at the front door—*come out, come dance with me.* Most of the spirits simply flew past, their words indecipherable, their fingertips light as rain as they glanced across the windows.

A good fire blazed, and the planter was thankful for his supply of oak and ash and beech. Fern Privet rose; shadows from the lacy rim of her bonnet made her face look more wrinkled than was the case. She poured Noll Slate more tea. Hale left his place by the hearth to fetch logs from the woodbox in the kitchen. This was one of his many duties. The house was dark but for the light from the blaze in the parlor, and that from the small fire left burning in the kitchen.

This latter room, with its sooty hearth and hanging arsenal of cooking implements, possessed a low ceiling of great exposed beams and had two straight walls adjoining a longer curved wall that conformed to the outer shape of the stone structure. The woodwork, even that of the plain batten shutter that the boy now found himself drawn to, was unpainted.

Hale listened at the closed window, hearing strange moans and whispers passing by. How could he resist taking a peek, curious cat that he was? Hale glanced over his shoulder to make certain he was alone, then quietly swung the window cover open.

It was dark out to be sure, but there was, at the same time, a peculiar luminosity that wasn't present other nights of the year—something other than moonlight. Trees were dancing, leaves were flying and figures—more rain than flesh—blurred by in tattered shrouds, trailing misty hair. One face glared in as it passed, its lower features obscured in a flutter of loose bandages.

Screams came from the parlor.

Hale slammed the shutter back in place and dashed into the other room to find his four sisters, his father and mother standing away from the hearth. Noll Slate remained seated, unruffled.

"Something's fallen down the chimney," one of the older twins reported, having spotted Hale and the quizzical look on his face.

"Made a dreadful noise," that twin's replica added.

"Gave me an awful start!" Mrs. Privet said, holding a hand to her bosom.

Burren Privet took up his tongs and fished the object out of the flames.

"A dagger!" Hale noted with interest.

"So it is," the father said. Still using the tongs, he held it close to his face for a better look. He blew ashes from it and squinted. "A military blade, I should think—finer than what one would hope to find 'bout these parts. Oh, yes, have a look there-—it would be that of a navy man, to be sure."

It was a handsome weapon with a twelve-inch blade, an ivory grip, and a gold lion head pommel. The grip bore an elegantly incised crown on one side and an anchor on the other.

One of the younger twin sisters hurried to Hale's side and whispered, "A terrifying man's voice called down the flue just afore the blade dropped."

"What did it say?"

"Only a name. Rye Blackbird."

"*Rye Blackbird…*" the boy repeated.

The children's father was still studying the dagger.

"There looks to be an inscription on the blade. Have a look, will you, my dear?"

Burren had never learned to read well, so he turned to his wife.

The woman adjusted her spectacles, leaned close, and narrowed her eyes.

"Captain M.R. Wibbingshire," the woman read.

The visitor, Noll Slate, looked up suddenly. For a moment his features suggested alarm, but he shortly got back to gazing into the flame, stroking the purring white cat, which was not at all alarmed by the activity.

Hale lit up. "Captain Wibbingshire!"

Burren turned to his son, bemused. "You know of him?"

Hale's mind was a library of all that he had heard as concerns the sea and its adventurers. "Yes, Father, it was he and his coxswain was killed and cast overboard from the mutinied *Lion Squall* not three weeks past. It was a Lieutenant Blackbird, they say, who done it."

"Yes, yes," Fern said, "I heard tell of such. A bit of treasure went missing. A terrible thing."

Burren was happy for the effectiveness of his ghost deterring precautions. The dagger had made it into the cottage, but the brittlethorn wreath on the chimney had kept whatever brought the weapon at bay.

Nothing so dramatic as a dead man's knife dropping into the firebox happened beyond that point. The rain and ghosts continued to sound at the windows and eerie bluish light fell over the land making wild skeletons of the trees. Hale slept little, lying alone in the dark loft, listening to the moaning night, thinking about that face in the window, and the other specters he'd seen sailing through the storm. He tried to fill his mind with other, more appealing things, imagining a body of water bigger than the rolling countryside where he seemed doomed to spend his days.

Not all the homes in the village fared as well as Burren Privet's. The ghosts knocked down fences, broke windows and even killed some livestock. Old Widow Fenstick made the mistake of answering her door in the middle of the night and received a terrible bite on the nose from something with a face like a moldering turnip. Still, things were back to normal in a matter of days.

With Ghost Hasten behind them, the locals turned their attention to winter. Wheat and rye and oats were in need of threshing. Women were busy salting meat, and girls were making charms for warding off fever and cough. The seasons exerted more power than the Crown in these parts, and a certain quiet—like the pause between heartbeats—held sway over the villages dotting the windy lowlands of the Broadfinch Vale. It was a precarious pause between autumn and winter. For the moment all seemed well beneath good thatch, from fermenting cider kegs singing in cellars to house cats dozing near capacious kitchen fireplaces.

Something good had come of Ghost Hasten. Burren and the vistor Noll Slate had been afforded the occasion to chat. Sitting by the logs, once the other members of the Privet household had gone off to bed, they made an arrangement. Slate wondered, perhaps, if he might stay on for a number of weeks, helping with winter preparations in exchange for food and shelter. The planter was, in fact, wanting for a hired man, but the last three years had been hard on the purse, his fields suffering drought and storm and a killing spell since referred to as "The Small Winter." So, while there was need, there simply wasn't money to spare for help. Slate's offer, which required no monetary compensation, was persuasive.

And so it went. By day Noll Slate labored around the farm, threshing, mending fences, feeding livestock, and by night he brought song and fancy to the fireside. He told the young Privet flock about a sheep (its five heads facing out like the spikes of a star) that did nothing but eat, and a ship, with a figurehead at either end, that could not decide which way to go, and a woman who ate a chrysalis and gave birth to a thousand moths. Burren had little interest in whimsical fictions, though his wife was entirely charmed by the evening entertainments. Slate, in a very little time, had become one of the family.

"Tell again of the ship, Mister Slate," Hale would plead.

"Tell about the sheep!" a sister would cry.

Slate was a courteous border and never once complained about sleeping on the hard little bed, which at night was set up in the kitchen. He was a curiosity in ways, though, for handy as he was at carpentry and practical matters, he could, without hesitation, recite the works of the great poets Dilton and Nettles. Burren Privet found himself unexpectedly sad to see how very fond Hale had become of the man. Father and son had never been terribly close; he'd never had enough time or imagination to share with a boy. Boys and men were meant to work.

"I have come to think upon this place as something of a home," Slate said importantly, gazing upon the rolling hills and wholesome meadows of the Broadfinch Vale. "And no better place have I found for to lay my dear brother to rest."

To the north lay sullen moors, separated from the fertile terrain by a great ridge of partly submerged stone that may have been the awkwardly interred remains of some impossible gargantuan. It was not, after all, uncommon for ploughs to unearth petrified bones in these parts. Noll stood commandingly upon an outcrop of rock, his long ruddy coat snapping and flailing in the cold wind.

Hale helped him pick the exact spot, there in a corner of open Privet land, up a gentle knoll with a wide pastoral view. The burial was without fuss or audible prayer and the dirt drummed on the coffin as clouds—their bellies full of snow—came lumbering out of the west.

Bramble-thorned and gold-winged autumn had succumbed to frost some weeks back, and snow had come in the night, the first snow of the season. Little more than a dusting, it did little to obscure the tired browns and flaxen hues predominant to the eye. Mrs. Privet sent her oldest daughters, Alba and Betony, to choose some birds for the three-dove pies she was planning to make. The girls, both thirteen, had wrapped shawls about their shoulders, rather than bother with winter cloaks, but found themselves half-running to the dovecote for the day was cold.

They had just made the scuffed batten door of the little building when a trio of bold horses came thumping on the road that passed close by the Privet house. Three young men, each with a wide-brimmed black hat and a warm cape over a dark coat, sat high in their saddles. The travelers spied the girls and the lead, a handsome specimen with a thin mustache and long golden hair, swept his hat off and bowed.

"Hallo, my young lovelies!"

Alba turned and smiled toward the strangers, but Betony, who had opened the door of the dovecote, grabbed her twin's arm and pulled her through the threshold.

"Have not these men passed this way before?" Betony hissed. "And has not Mother spoken ill of them?"

Alba peeked out the doorway, grinning. "Oh, but he's a pretty one! And see how fine is his dress."

The pretty one dismounted and swaggered over, holding his hat over his heart. He, like his rather brutish-looking companions, wore a sword at the hip, though he was dressed more handsomely, his open cloak and coat revealing a honey-colored waistcoat decked with fine embroidered patterns of ivy vines and moths. His cravat was frilly, and the buckles of his shoes shined as only silver can.

"My, my," the man said, leaning in the doorframe, "I'd not hoped to see pretty flowers in the midst of so bleak a season."

Alba blushed and giggled.

"What would be your names?" the man asked, smirking.

"Alba," Alba said.

Betony said nothing.

The traveler stepped into the small building and Alba felt herself being tugged backward by the twin behind her. At this shortened distance the girls could see a birthmark in the shape of a pear—a russet thing small enough to fit in the cap of an acorn—positioned near the outer corner of his right eye.

"*Alba*," the man cooed, "a lovely name!" He came forward until the sisters had no place to back up to. Agitated birds sounded at either side. With a studied slowness the stranger removed one of his gloves and held it by one finger, the way one would hold a dead mouse by the tale. He placed the bare hand against Alba's cheek and brought his face close. "My, my, you are a fetching little blossom. Let's have a kiss, eh, my sweet?"

Hale and Noll Slate were in the kitchen depositing armloads of birch into the woodbox when they heard a scream. Both rushed to a window and saw three horses by the road—two occupied, one not. Slate grabbed a copper sauce pan which had a black iron handle nearly the length of a man's arm, and headed swiftly out the side door. Hale was quick on his heels.

The two roughs sitting on their mounts watched with interest as a man with wild gray hair and a wild gray beard, dressed in a shabby rust-colored coat, appeared. A girl's scream directed Slate to the dovecote. He made the door in a flash and threw it wide.

Alba was crying, her garments in immodest disarray and Betony was sitting on her rump, bleeding from the nose. A handsomely dressed young man with a spill of golden hair whirled to meet the intrusion.

Noll Slate barked, "*Swine!*"

Hale arrived in time to see the mounted men give one another a look and swing down from their steeds.

"Mister Slate!" the boy warned.

Despite the cramped confines of the dovecote, the fancy stranger managed to draw his sword, a double-edged straight blade measuring thirty or more inches. He pointed it at Slate, who stepped back, allowing the man to come out into the muted daylight.

"No harm, done," the blond fellow chirped, smiling.

"Defend," Slate snarled, his dark eyes flaring with an intensity that Hale had never seen in them before.

Something else Hale had never seen was the pose his friend now took on—the sauce pan held out straight, his right leg leading and partly bent, his spine rigid, free hand at the hip.

The scoundrel also assumed a duelist's posture and laughed. "What? Are you to *cook* for me?"

Hale marveled at the grace—nothing short of beauty—with which Noll Slate now moved. He swept forward like a rust-colored bird, the copper pan a blur as it swatted away the blond man's sword and then found his snide face. A terrible clang muffled the man's cry and was still ringing in the air when he thumped bloody into the snow.

Slate spun to meet the other two, who, having drawn their weapons, came up fast from behind. With a dancer's precision and a deer's darting speed, he lunged and dodged and disarmed the opponents. One lay on his back stunned and gagging on his own teeth, while the third ran for his horse, clutching broken fingers with his good hand.

Alba and Betony had made their way into the house, and by the time Burren Privet came outside with his hunting musket readied, Slate was standing triumphant above the wounded, instructing them to mount and leave and never come back.

"...Or else you'll get better than you've known this day."

It snowed again that afternoon and a wintry quiet fell over the landscape. It was a quiet that seemed to come from everywhere, from the muffled horizon and the chill air, from the sedgy north, from the Privets' shorn cornfields. These expanses were a muted color that was not quite tan and not quite gold, a color imbued with memories of summer green and the rush of harvest. The snow flitted and settled amidst the stubble of the fields, between the truncated stalks, lending strange texture, and here and there crows swept down to pace and peck.

It was cozy in the kitchen of the Privet cottage and the matriarch's three-dove pies proved hearty enough to satisfy every belly in the building. Afterward, there were apples roasted over the fire, and a punch made of wine and lively spices that had crossed the sea from far mysterious lands.

Toward evening's end Hale joined Noll Slate in going out to fetch more wood from the shed.

"Mister Slate, sir?" Hale said.

"Yes, my buck?" The man's voice was as dark and rich as a glass of squall.

Hale looked up at the man. "How is it you came to fight as you did, as a master swordsman might?"

Slate paused outside the side door of the cottage and smiled warmly at the boy. "Oh, I've been witness to some few duels in my time, is all, and thus took note of the fighting styles of the participants."

Hale shifted the load of oak splits in his arms and, after thinking a moment, asked, "Could you not teach me to fight as such?"

"I shall think on it," Slate said. Then, inhaling the nippy air, he remarked, "A lovely night, is it not, my buck?"

"Yes, Mister Slate." Hale tipped his head back, closing his eyes, allowing snowflakes to kiss him—the cold lips of a hundred tiny ghosts.

Weeks passed and Noll Slate found himself residing with the Privet family for longer than he had planned. But there was still so much to be done before the heavy snows of the season arrived, more than Burren and his boy could handle on their own. The winds of Ghost Hasten had done more damage to the fences defining the planter's land than was initially thought, snapping rails, uprooting posts and even knocking down sections of fieldstone border. In one spot the spirits had taken stones from a wall and arranged them to suggest a crude skull measuring some twenty feet at its widest point. It had the look of a line drawing done by a small child. There remained a need for Slate's carpentry skills, for the barn, the chicken coop and "the necessary" were all in want of repair. How could he, in good conscience, up and leave such a burden on those who had shown him so much kindness? While the road was calling to him, Slate ignored its voice.

Willow switches made for fine practice swords, and when time allowed or when the planter Burren was not around, Noll Slate and his student were in the barn dueling. Their shadows were wild upon the walls, restlessly painted by the solitary lantern which did its best to counter the bleakness of the dimming day. The confines smelled of hay and lanolin, and dung from the two milk cows, who, like the sheep and horses, had become more or less accustomed to the human activity.

Hale marveled at the elegance and agility of his instructor, how Slate could move with such speed that at times it seemed whole portions of his body became invisible to the eye. His willow stick—still green where smaller branches had been cut off—sliced through the air, no more than a whisper and a blur.

By the evening of his final lesson, Hale had progressed nicely. He was quick enough and proved more than proficient in terms of technique. A hearty Slate remarked, "Woe to the villain who is fool enough to cross the swordsman Hale Privet!"

The boy beamed, of course.

At night, up in the garret of the cottage, Hale lay in the dark, prefacing his dreams by swatting away imaginary opponents with an imaginary blade as pale and cold as moonlight.

Morning came to wide reposing pastureland (now lonely for sheep) and the quiet round hills shading the River Hawnts. It had snowed in the night and the accumulation lent contrast to those bare trees which stood in view, and made a strange clean hat of the Privet cottage's conical thatch.

Even at this early hour there was activity on the farm. Hale was fetching wood for the fireplaces, the older twin sisters were in the barn milking, and Mrs. Privet, along with her younger daughters, hunched over the sooty hearth fixing breakfast. Burren and Noll Slate sat at the big kitchen work table over tea, discussing what tasks to take on.

Something caught Fern's eye. She moved quickly for her size, whipping toward the window with such speed that her apron flapped like a flag in a wind. "Oh, my!"

A horse and rider stood directly outside in the modest light, the rider aiming a long black musket at the building.

Hale dropped a log on his way out of the woodshed and bent to retrieve it. When he stood he found himself nose-to-snout with a towering horse, a *snow*, well-muscled and white as the groundcover, but for the faint gray marking like a fiddle on the beast's forehead. A man in a black cloak and a tight black helmet was pointing a long black gun.

Looking beyond, the boy saw another rider, and another and another. They had surrounded the house. Hale ran for the front door.

Back in the kitchen, Burren was now peering out, pushing his wife away from the window. "Black Guns," he noted.

Black Guns, rarely seen in these parts, were keepers of the law, agents of the Crown, and named for their uniforms and the shiny black wood of their muskets, which were fashioned from desirable hardwood harvested in the Colonies.

Slate flew up from the table, ducked into the buttery, and disappeared through the little doorway under the staircase. He was gone only a moment, and when he returned from the cellar he was holding a long heavy flintlock pistol in each hand. Unbeknownst to his hosts, he had taken them from the compartment under his wagon's seat and hidden them within closer reach, in case the men he had pummeled with the cooking pan had mind to come back seeking revenge. All the eyes in the room grew big when they saw him.

"Stay from the windows!" Slate ordered, his eyes dark and intense, his voice a bear's.

The next voice came from outside.

"Rye Blackbird," a man called, "we have surrounded the house. Make yourself known or we shall open fire."

"*Rye Blackbird,*" Hale muttered. It was the mutineer's name spoken down the chimney the night of Ghost Hasten, just before the dagger of that murdered captain dropped into the firebox.

The Privet's boarder, with his wild gray hair and wild gray beard, pressed his back to the wall and peeked around the window frame. He had clicked back the cocks of his dueling pistols and held the weapons pointing at the rafters, the handles on level with his chest. The sturdy stone cottage would have well withstood a battle, but he wasn't about to risk his friends' lives. Besides, outnumbered as he was, the Black Guns would breach the building eventually, after his bullets ran out.

"*Mister Slate,*" Hale said, his voice quavering, his large brown eyes full of tears.

"I am sorry, dear Privets," the man said, "but I am who they say. The wandering, raggedy Noll Slate has been a deception. I am Lieutenant Rye Blackbird of the Lion Squall."

"My good stars!" Burren breathed, his missus looking like she might faint. "The mutiny…the murder of the captain and his man…would it be true?"

The voice from outside roared again, "Blackbird! Come, or we shall commence to fire!"

"Yes," Blackbird replied, "Sadly true. But find no tears for Captain Wibbingshire and the coxswain, for they were not so lily white. The captain was more a scoundrel than might be told, and designed, with the coxswain and some few others, to take for themselves our cargo of treasure, leaving those resistant to the waves."

"You *killed* them…" the planter's wife was incredulous.

"There was to be blood in the water one way or another; better theirs than mine. Following the terrible deed, I and my men left off the ship at Dillmitten Cove and went our separate ways, all with a share of the fortune. I thought it best to make the field-country where one would hardly think to seek for a renegade shipman, most especially if that man were in the guise of a humble traveling hired man."

Burren spoke, "But why come here when your riches might have transported you to quarters of the highest, or great distance?"

"Ahh, a curse falls on money taken with blood, and one must wait the new moon for the magic stain to pass. Thus, I could spend not a coin of it. But, on my word, it has been my intent from the start to leave you a sum at my parting, more than you could reap from a thousand harvests."

Burren nodded. "But the new moon has come and passed and yet you stay on."

Blackbird smiled sadly. "Yes, stayed for the fine companionship that has been my joy to know."

A voice called from outside, "I shall count twelve, Blackbird, and then we fire!"

Blackbird lowered his pistols so that they pointed at the floor and held them out to Burren. "They are yours, fine fellow, as is the body of my brother..."

They could hear the loud counting outside. Blackbird took his rust-red coat and tatty cloak from their hooks and put them on before heading for the side door.

"My thanks for all that you've done."

"Mister—" Hale took a step after the man.

Blackbird smiled over his shoulder. "Farewell, my buck."

It was brisk outside, the sky all gargantuan splotches of gray and white. The cloaks and dark uniforms of the Black Guns showed starkly against the snowy countryside. A tall, straight figure marched out from the house into the chill and stopped. He bowed—his arms out like wings—the sort of graceful bow one would expect from a naval officer.

"I am Lieutenant Blackbird," he announced.

Black Guns on foot closed on the man, searching and manacling him. A stocky middle-aged man with spectacles and wavy reddish hair poking from the sides of his hat approached. He was Henwhistle, the High Sheriff of the county, handsomely attired in black and wearing a fine cocked hat. He blinked watery little eyes against the sharp air, cleared his throat and proceeded to read the arrest papers to the captive.

Joining the sheriff was a well-dressed young fellow with long blond hair, a bruised, bent nose and a small birthmark shaped like a pear by his right eye. He sauntered up to Blackbird and said, "He's the one, all right, Sheriff. Didn't I know a shabby man would not have fought as he did."

Blackbird regarded his past opponent impassively.

Burren Privet had come outside and conversed with Henwhistle, who readily took it that the planter was wholly unaware of the true identity of the man whom he'd been harboring. Then, the officer apologetically let it be known that the buildings on the property were to be searched for the treasure that was stolen from the *Lion Squall.*

A stream of men surged into the cottage while others turned to the dovecote, the barn and the coop. They searched thoroughly, but the treasure was not to be found. The children were kept in the kitchen by their mother, the lot of them trembling. Hale stared out glumly and once Alba looked out and that golden-haired man, who had cornered her in the dovecote, noticed her and winked. The girl recoiled, horrified.

The lawmen were set to go, their prisoner now seated on a horse, his arms behind him, linked to the saddle by chains. The sheriff paid a small sum to Burren to compensate for the damage done to the cottage during the rummaging of his men. Floorboards had been torn up and some walls opened, and the fermenting kegs of cider in the cellar had all been smashed.

A hasty parade set off on the snowy road, leaving the cottage behind. Hale had rushed out to watch them and did not return to the house until well after the last of the graceful white *snows* was gone from view.

The party of riders was headed for Stubswick, where the offices of the sheriff, and the county's best jail, resided. Passing under the arms of a great twisted oak, the pretty blond man, whose nose was not so pretty anymore, fell back from where he'd been riding with the sheriff at the front and came alongside Lt. Blackbird. He leaned over to the captive and whispered, "You're to hang, you *swine.*"

A few weeks passed before Burren decided that it was safe to exhume the coffin. He and Hale rode out to the knoll with its view of wintered moorland to the north and smooth cornfields sleeping under white. They dug through snow and a modest layer of frost-hardened earth to find the soft dirt and simple pine box below. The top creaked when they pried it open.

The contents were wrapped snugly in bedding, which explained why Hale did not hear metal objects sliding around in the container those times when he helped to move it. The two Privets hovered for a moment before unwrapping, and, after they did, the father climbed up out of the grave and sat numbly on the ground. He had never seen, nor even dreamed of so much gold as was bundled in that casket.

Hale's awe had little to do with the money. He had uncovered Lt. Blackbird's silvery metal chest plate, and his silvery metal helmet (like a bowl with lamb chop sideburns) and the black boots and breeches, and dark green double-breasted coat of a naval officer. There was a black tricorne as well, and something else coiled in a length of cloth…

"His sword!"

Hale lifted it reverently and carefully drew the blade from its scabbard. Even under cloud cover the sharp edges gleamed, shimmered as if the very metal were infused with a restless light. It was handsome with its straight thirty-inch blade of double-edged steel. The grip was smooth dark blackbirch wood from the Colonies, with a knuckle bow curving from the shaft to the pommel, which in this case was a silver lion's head. Hale held the blade up, dowsing moisture from the clouds.

Burren looked down at his son, at the look in the boy's eye, and then looked away, out at the fields that Hale would one day leave behind.

Much as Hale wanted to keep the helmet and chest plate and the sword, his father would not have it. One never knew when the Black Guns would be back to snoop around for the treasure, whether on official orders or for personal gain. Evidence so strong as a naval officer's property would prove that they knew where the riches were hidden. Careful man that he was, Burren exerted restraint over himself as well, only taking a moderate amount, initially, and not spending it indulgently, which would only have garnered suspicion.

Hale waited until spring's thaw before sneaking back to the grave and disinterring the sword. He kept it hidden in the barn for the next eight years, and when time and privacy allowed, practiced the skills that Rye Blackbird had taught him—the art-like killing dance of a swordsman—all the while relishing the weight and gracefulness of the sword. He imagined himself a brave naval man fending off foes of the Crown.

The last time Hale saw his family all together was the day the Privets rode into Oxmarrow, where the stagecoach regularly stopped at Fimble's Tavern. It was a fine spring morning and the trees were flowering. His mother and sisters, who were all crowded into the new wagon Burren had purchased, were wearing their finest skirts and hats. Eighteen-year-old Hale sat up front with his father, his belly full of moths.

Not much was said while the clan awaited the arrival of the coach, and the only other traveler waiting outside the wide round tavern was an old woman with a sickly-looking cat in her arms and a sad rumpled sack at her feet.

The coach came jangling along after a time and Hale was smothered in teary hugs and kisses. His father stood to one side, apart from the rest, looking off, looking smaller and older than Hale had ever noticed him to be. It was not until Hale was moving toward the coach's metal stairs, carrying his sheathed sword and meager baggage, that the man stepped forward and embraced his son.

"I shall be proud of you, my dear boy," Burren said.

Hale wanted to say much more than the *goodbye, Father* that he managed to choke out. He wanted to say how proud he was of the fine planter that his father was, and for the strength and integrity the man possessed, and he wanted to tell his father that he loved him.

The coach, with its team of four, jerked forward and went on its way. Hale watched out the rear window until the two sets of twin sisters, his mother and his father shrank to the size of little waving dolls and were gone.

A mile or so into his journey, Hale introduced himself to the other passenger, a Mrs. Kinner. "I'm to join up the navy," he said, having recovered enough to feel some enthusiasm.

"Ohhh, how lovely," the woman cooed. "My Uncle Malt was quartermaster on the *Fighting Swallow.* Long before you were born, yes, long before. Poor man...lost at sea, out on the Kellingrey Shoals. A dreadful thing."

The woman's cat wheezed like a breeze in reeds.

Hale's smile faded. "How very sad," he muttered.

The woman touched his hand. "Not to worry, dear, *you'll* be just fine."

There was just the road now, with wide fields sprawling on either side, and distant figures—men who were married to the fields—out with their horses and oxen and plows.

Several days later Hale reached the ocean. He smelled it before he saw it, and his first glimpses were brief, just hints showing between buildings and clusters of trees. When at last he stood before its stunning breadth, his mind spun inside, a dizzy combination of sensations flooding him. There was fear, and an urge to be home surrounded by sisters, near the fireplace of the Privet cottage, and, perhaps stronger than the rest, the urge to be out on a ship riding the cold sea's waves.

"*The Gantic,*" Hale whispered to himself.

A pewter-colored sea-moth bobbed above the rocky shore, by a great blanket of shifting gray water that looked to cover half the world.

2

The Fort

Smack in the chill waters of the Gantic Ocean, not far off the coast of the continent proper, sat two large kidney-shaped islands, the twin halves comprising the kingdom of Fellengrey. The space between these green landmasses (a thin, fairly straight vertical representation on a map) was the tidal strait known as the Tween. Along the Tween, at irregular, if strategic, intervals stood forts of varied size and age. Some were renovated castles. One of these, on the western kidney, West Fellengrey, was Fort Haddox, where Seamen Privet began his life in the Royal Navy.

It was required of every starter to spend his first year at one of the forts, which, depending on the location of the complex, was overseen by either the navy or the land-based army. Haddox was the third fort down from the top of the left island, facing the Tween. Bloodingsham, the topmost stronghold of West Fellengrey, was in the navy's hands, while the next below that, Splitbriar, was the army's charge. Haddox, as one has already deduced, was a naval outpost, complete with vessels of various size and fighting strength.

Haddox, truth be told, lacked the prestige and crucial placement of Bloodingsham, and with a more significant fort fifty miles to the south guarding the Tween from the eastern side of the kingdom, was considered a minor site. The commandants were not seen as topnotch by those who mattered, and the fighting force was a mere one hundred men.

But today, the fighting force was *fighting*.

Shots rang out from the ramparts, while cannons poking from crenellated stone heights, and peeking from the gray walls fronting the Tween, were booming their smoky thunder. Plumes leapt from the water where the heavy balls landed and spray danced up denoting the inaccurate strikes from muskets. The object of all this attention was a small single-mast vessel, dreadfully outmatched. But it had invited the fight.

The ranking system at the fort reflected that which one would find on a ship, and so it was a captain who shouted commands to his men. Rusty at war, nearsighted, and retired from riding the waves, this officer was Post Captain Finchberry of the shrubby beard and hardly haired peak. Finchberry was breathless from dashing up stone steps to one of the high walls, and stopped to scoop up his bicorne, tugging it back over his pate so that it was somewhere between straight and sideways on his head. He gestured with his short-sword as he called instruction and insult to the nearest cannon team.

"Have you no eyes?" he was bellowing. "Hit the blasted thing!"

It was only now, squinting through his spyglass, that Finchberry got a good look at the opponent. The vessel was a simple single-mast thing, perhaps a ship's boat requiring the sparest of crews. It did not appear to be armed, beyond the weapons of those persons onboard, and its sides were baroquely weighted with barnacles like calcified fish eyes.

A loud bang and cries of pain came from below, within the walls of the fort. The captain looked down at one of his officers and snapped, "Who is hit?"

The man shouted back, "Pickersmythe, sir. He's shot his own foot."

Below the raised cannons of Haddox's business wall were three grassy ramparts, the remaining defenses of an ancient castle whose wooden structures were long ago devoured by time. A handful of men with muskets had made their way over one of the encircling hills and ducked down behind the next. At their lead was a young Seamen Privet, handsome in his sage-green uniform coat and white breeches, a tight, lightweight gray chest plate showing underneath in place of a waistcoat. He wore a slate-colored bowl of a helmet, its cheek-plates like lamb chop sideburns.

He scrabbled up the steep bank, made the top, sighted down the musket barrel and fired. A fist of smoke punched the air. His mates followed, two pausing to squeeze off shots before jogging down into the furrow between the second and final earthwork.

"One more to climb, fellows," Privet panted. He knelt, primed his pan and rammed a ball down the throat of the musket. Clinging to the lovely reddish wood of the weapon, Privet started up the next slope, hearing shots bark from the enemy craft.

They made the top, and there was the Tween, and the distant landmass of East Fellengrey, and the docks with their circular stone guardhouse at the shore end, and moored vessels belonging to the fort. And the enemy boat.

The rampart shook, a poorly aimed cannonball from the fort thumping into the earth some yards away.

"*Who do they shoot at?*" one of the footmen was bewildered.

Puffs of smoke obscured the hunched and scurrying figures on the boat's starboard side and Privet heard something whiz past in the air. He lingered at the crest of the parapet long enough to fire, then started down, in the open, those behind him pausing at prearranged intervals to shoot, until the last ball was discharged from its barrel and all had made it to the outside of the ramparts intact.

The captain, displeased, observed through his glass. "Whatever is that Privet about? This be no way to fight! There is no sense of order! They ought form line and hold position, not run about like a pack of farting monkeys!"

"I believe he's leading a charge," one of the cannon team droned.

With the earthworks behind them, Privet and his companions, too far from the round guardhouse to benefit from its cover, were forced to duck behind rocks along the jumbled shoreline. Privet and his friend, the tall, wiry Willows, found a rise of granite big enough to block the both of them. From here they could see poor Smudge, lying on the dock, dead perhaps. He had been on duty in the guardhouse when he noticed the boat quietly making its way south on the Tween, had called to it without response and then, raising his voice and pistol, and ringing a bell on the side of the structure, had demanded that the vessel stop. That was when someone onboard shot him.

"If only I were closer," Privet said, peeking up over the jagged stone.

"There's no getting closer, Privet, not without making a target of yourself."

"Right." Privet thought for a moment, then he called to those men off to his right, and then to those scattered left, saying, "On my word," and he pointed forward. He received nods back from all but one, who, like himself, and most of the others, had never seen combat.

Once the muskets were charged, Privet, his hand trembling, snapped back the cocking mechanism of his gun, and got up off the cool damp pebbles that had darkened his knees. He was about to give the order to charge when a cannon blast, the first to actually find the boat, tore into it—a cruel, concentrated little storm. Up at the fort, Capt. Finchberry had called for the use of grape shot, with its numerous projectiles (more commonly reserved for close combat at sea), thus the hail of iron balls—a lethal swarm—which pierced both men and wood, and tore holes through the sails. Figures screamed and dropped. Other cannons roared, coughed light and smoke, and well-placed strikes by round shot hit low on the boat's mast and sent it toppling, ropes snapping, the canvas flailing its way to the water.

Then there was silence and that sad vessel just bobbing there, its largest sail drooping in the water like the wing of a drowned bird. The looming gray of the fort was softened behind smoke, waves of soft white floating down, dissipating over the ramparts, fading off before reaching the rim of the water. Privet and the other low-rank navy men rose slowly from behind their rocks and gingerly started forward.

"We board her," Willows said, moving ahead of the rest.

Privet fell back a few steps, the sensations that had been like heat and light in his head—the urgent racing and an animalistic instinct to defend—only now coalescing into fear. He had been to battle.

He caught up with Willows, ahead of some of the others, and kept his musket trained on the crippled boat, only half-looking where he was walking. They made the nearest of the long docks, dark water kissing its posts, and thumped toward the fallen figure at the other end. The quantity of blood on the planks told them all about Smudge. A brief, icy dizziness came over Privet at this, his first view of a violent death.

Three small rowboats were unhitched from the dock, and manned by teams of three, each with a rower and two men at the bow, their "longs" trained the whole while as the craft edged out into the dark water. They encircled the larger boat, as best as three of anything can encircle, and gradually made their way closer.

Privet was in the middle boat, squinting down the long barrel of his weapon. The enemy was listing portside, the sails from the toppled mast undulating on waves that made the vessel rock as if a drunken thing. Loose ropes trailed chaotically and the clothing on the bodies that were visible fluttered as a breeze swept up. Each of these motions caused Privet's heart to quicken, his finger to tense at the trigger.

The boat carrying Willows came alongside the cripple and the lanky man scrabbled aboard. His musket was passed up to him from the row boat. Privet was next to board, the damp, tilted deck slippery under high black boots.

Up close, the boat was an unremarkable thing at best. Not the healthiest specimen for sea-travel even before being blasted with cannon fire. There were six crewmen, apparently, each in the sad, dropped-looking positioning of the brutally dispatched. The blood, heeding to gravity, all ran portside. They were each dressed simply, practically, for sea-work. Three were lying close to fallen muskets and the contents of a spilled cartridge case had rolled and collected at the low side of the deck. The hull, pocked where grape shot had hit, was taking water and made the idiosyncratic creaks and gurgles of a sinking vessel.

Willows and Privet made their way to the aft, which had been modified to provide a small raised cabin. The door was ajar and a curious blue luminosity showed from inside. They looked at each other with raised brows, then nodded and went in, a boot knocking the door wide, two barrels thrusting.

"Heavens!" Willows gasped.

The ghostly light emanated from a large glass jar that encased the head of a figure who, with legs out straight on a cot, was slumped against the cabin wall. The body was dressed in a gray greatcoat, gray waistcoat and gray breeches, and wore nice shoes that looked like they hardly saw use.

"Is it dead?" Privet asked.

Willows leaned closer to gaze in at the face, which was that of a clean-shaven man in his thirties, vague in a dusty mist of webs, complete with dried dead spiders. The half-closed eyes fluttered.

Willows pulled back sharply. "Alive."

This was not the only living inhabitant of the boat, for it turns out that one of the bloody musketeers still had some breath in him. The wounded fellow, and the man wearing the jar, were removed to land along with three small casks—too heavy to be containing liquid. These latter proved to be filled with coins, golden hundred-moth pieces and silver fifty-moths.

Lieutenant Brittles, a younger, more reserved officer than Capt. Finchberry, oversaw the demolition of the damaged craft, once all the dead were taken off. Meager provisions, muskets and several trunks were salvaged as well. Finchberry didn't want the wreck cluttering up the Tween, and felt it best to blow the thing up, to break it into smaller parts, more apt to float away.

The sound of the explosion was better than that which the cannons had made and caused an older woman, Lady Swellbrook, high in her turret confinement at the fort, to gaze out a window at the wreckage. Small pieces of the boat flew in the air, a mockery of birds, while larger portions rolled over, slurping away into dark, salty water.

Privet felt he was marching the steps of a hanging scaffold as he made his way up through the back tower to Capt. Finchberry's office. He'd replaced his helmet with a tricorne, the band around its rim the same dull green of his coat. He knocked.

"Enter."

Privet, a rather handsome specimen with warm brown eyes, his auburn hair swept back across the ears and terminating in a tight ball-like tail, walked in, stood straight as a candle, saluted. Finchberry was behind his desk, like a robin the way his red waistcoat rounded over his belly. Puffy white sleeves hid puffy white arms and the folds of his neck overlapped his moth-wing cravat (a favorite of officers).

The office was finer than most other rooms there at Fort Haddox, its curved stone walls plastered over; the wainscot that conformed to the curvature was painted a stately grayish-blue. A handsome miniature of the ship Finchberry had once commanded was anchored to his desktop beside a plain pewter inkwell.

Lt. Brittles was standing back-to, hands folded at the spine, gazing out the small panes of a window at the wide green land to the west. He turned and gave an acknowledging nod. The captain made a little gesture and Brittles went stiffly out, Privet stepping aside to let him pass. He was alone with the fort's commandant.

"Aren't we the daring lad?" Finchberry said, his small, sarcastic smile unappealing.

"Sir?"

"You may well know, Privet, that unauthorized heroics might hasten you to the grave."

"You'll pardon my saying, sir, but heroics were not my intent."

Finchberry lit his pipe. Privet recognized the scent—both earthy and sweet—the powdered wings of speckled brush moth. His uncle had smoked it. Not a gentlemen's choice of "puff."

"Hm. Perhaps it is merely that, in my age, memory falters, for I've no recollection of ordering a charge."

Privet said, "You did not, sir."

"No, I didn't, did I?"

Finchberry had the habit of running the fingers of one hand over the bare part of his head while fondling his beard with the other. He did this now.

Privet did not wish to appear defiant, but he felt compelled to explain. "Sir, if I may... My, ahh, actions might best be likened to those of a beast which, finding itself attacked, springs to defend in the heat of instinct. It was, by no means, a mindful insubordination."

"Seaman Privet, we do not respond *in heat*. Your recklessness might have seen you and others of my charge deceased. In future we shall await orders, regardless of situation, and harken always to your training, *not* instinct."

"As you wish, sir. I am sorry, sir."

Finchberry sat back, hissed smoke and crossed his meaty hands on his desk. "Right. Now, on to a related matter."

Privet had wondered if there were some form of punishment in the wings.

"I have a particular position in mind for you, something that should afford you time for reflection."

Lt. Brittles was waiting out in the tight foyer when Privet was released from his meeting with the captain. Sharp in his dark green officer's coat, Brittles slapped Privet on the arm and smiled. He was a fellow in his early thirties, clean-shaved, with a continuous squint and lean, angular features.

"Your courage is not without notice, Privet. Perhaps applause might better have been in order, rather than a spanking, so to speak."

The praise was entirely unexpected, and it put a smile on Privet's sad face. "You're quite kind to say, sir."

"Not jolly about your new orders, eh? Mind, it might yet have been worse—least he left you *privileges*."

Brittles referred to the two "privilege girls" in their little quarters just south of the kitchen. Each man stationed at the fort was allowed so much time a month in the company of these women. Extra time could be had, but at a cost to the indulger's purse.

Privet grinned and nodded. "I suppose I should be thankful. Tell, sir, is there more to be known of the captives?"

The lieutenant's face grew serious. "A mystery," he said.

Fort Haddox, a great rectangle, stood in angular contrast to the roundedness of the primitive earthworks that enclosed it. Two tall stone towers comprised the far corners of the facade, facing the Tween. Cannons—ranging from 18- to 42-pounders—were placed atop these, and along the walk, peering through its crenellations. More than merely a wall, the front of the fort was thick enough to accommodate two interior compartments, cannon decks, so to speak, one midway up, one on ground level. Wooden shutters presently blinded the windows that had boomed earlier that day.

Within the granite walls stood a complex of buildings: a guardhouse, a well house, armory, stable, livestock barn, magazine and fuel shed. These, unlike homes of that period, were rectangular in shape, including the kitchen, barracks and even the little wooden privilege house. The soldiers' barracks, tucked in the north-west corner, occupied a large two-story brick structure with twin chimneys and a steeply pitched roof of fern-stone shingles. The interior consisted of a center staircase bordered by four rooms, two up, two down, each shared by twenty men. The garret could hold twenty more.

Privet, up in the garret, sat on the edge of his bunk, hunched over his portable writing desk, goose-quill in hand, penning a letter by the light from his iron candle stand. The fort provided a limited number of candles per man per month; extras had to be purchased. Candles, along with the nice wooden writing set—with a lid that could lock—were the only luxuries he had allowed himself.

"Penning a love letter to your new charmer, are we Privet?" one of the young man's mates called from a neighboring cot.

Word of Privet's new assignment had traveled quickly in this small community. The others all knew that he had been dealt the dreaded task of guarding Lady Swellbrook.

Privet ignored the taunt and continued with his business. He was writing home to tell of the day's adventures, about the battle against, and defeat of, the enigmatic boat, and the discovery of the strange man with his head in a glowing jar of webs. He told how one of the crew members from the vessel had sustained a wound, but was yet alive, comatose in the infirmary.

Brief mention was made of the fact that one of the seamen at the fort had died, but he spared his family the bloody particulars, and shared nothing about how troubling it was to see. He imagined he would revisit poor Seaman Smudge, dead on the dock, and possibly the perforated corpses found on the deck of the ruined vessel, in his dreams. He might even dream of that eerie blue face in its filmy nest of webs.

Privet also wrote about his new duties:

Lady Swellbrook is a shunned and somewhat notorious creature, an incongruous figure in our midst, and her very presence provides fodder for mirth of the cruelest sort among my fellows. She has been here exiled for a crime out of her past, an infidelity of some thirty years past. In recent months her husband happened upon a store of old love letters by which he came to know of her folly. You will remember her as the wife of the Duke of Snoddingshire. She has been stripped of title and inheritance and sentenced to spend out her days at this dreary fort.

Privet looked up at the bare rafters and wide boards that slanted overhead. He could hear rain slapping heavily on the slates of the roof. His candle was beginning to flicker as it burned low and there were no others stashed in his trunk to replace it. He would need to purchase more.

I have seen but little of the woman, truth be told, for she is secluded in her chamber the largest part of the time. Once or twice I have spied her atop the battlements, looking upon the Tween, feeding the spring birds that come for the bread she shares.

"Oh, just write '*with all my love, dearest*,' and have done with it, Privet. Your farting candle's blinding me," that other seamen, Fimble, called. He was a rather loutish looking individual, whose long thin smirk made Privet think of a toad.

Privet gave the fellow an icy look. "I shall finish all the sooner if I am not interrupted."

Sadly, it is my lot to mind the old adulteress's door lest she dash for freedom, and likewise accompany her about the grounds, to prevent her escape. My mind can hardly conjure a more mundane task!

Yours,

Hale

Privet put the letter away for the night. He slid his little desk under his bunk, blew out the candle and climbed under covers. The sound of mock kissing came from somewhere in the dark.

More than the usual number of men were awake into the late hours, added sentries having been pressed to duty on the chance that compatriots of the mystery boat's crew might be on the prowl. But these guards did not entirely account for the increase, for the most important figures at that facility were up and about as well.

The fort healer, Mealton Skiggs, a tall, gaunt, older gent with long silvery hair, was minding the infirmary. Candles in wall sconces offered faint illumination, but the whitewashed brick walls, set off starkly by the sturdy blue color of bare ceiling beams and corner posts, suggested a more substantial brightness.

He had tended the wounded stranger from the cutter as best as his abilities allowed. A musket ball or some cannon shot had cut a nasty groove along the left side of the man's head, quite possibly causing damage to his skull and the organ it encased. A fractional difference in the angle of the projectile would have proved fatal.

The patient remained unconscious, his head oversized for the pale dressing, the bandages treated with a pungent blend of curative herbs. He was an unexceptional specimen otherwise, clean-shaven, no older than thirty.

"Who might you be?" Skiggs whispered, expecting no answer as he bent a skilled ear to listen to the patient's breathing. He pressed an ear to the man's chest to hear his heart, which, like the working of the lungs, was regular.

This was not quite the case with the other prisoner, the one with his head up a jar. Capt. Finchberry had just been by to inquire on the healer's examination of the oddity.

"Well, what of him?" Finchberry asked, his hands on his hips.

"He seems alive." Skiggs said.

Finchberry was huffy, "*Seems?* Well, a thing is either alive or it is not, which would it be, Healer?"

"Alive. If not, perhaps, in the conventional sense of the word."

The inner perimeter of the fortress contained bomb-proof rooms suitable for shelter from bombardment, but generally used for storage. Lt. Brittles and one of his trusted men opened a rusty metal door and entered into one of these chilly stone compartments, ducking out of the rain.

A lantern showed them the casks and trunks that had been taken off the tresspasser prior to its destruction. The confiscated muskets were there as well. The seaman, ready with tools, pried the casks open first. Candle light gleamed on the many coins, both gold and silver. Then he went to work on the trunks. The first contained maps and clothing and a flintlock pistol with silver mounts, which showed pleasingly against the rich hues of the walnut stock. The left side bore a decorative ivory inlay of a leaping dolphin.

The next trunk, smaller than the first, offered up a felted fur tricorne, a beautifully crafted silver inkstand, bayberry candles, three bottles of wine and a pair of pewter candlesticks.

The third trunk proved the most interesting. In addition to a number of mundane items there was a large empty glass jar, snuggly bound in bedding. It was not dissimilar from that covering the head of the nameless fellow taken off the boat. The mouth was wide enough to fit over a person's head, and there was a leather collar with it, like that worn by the captive, a little garment that held the vessel tight to the man's neck.

The lieutenant's companion found a crude glazed bottle of glimmering red and held it up for a better look. The mouth of the thing flared wide, the neck tapering down to a smooth round base.

"What make you of this, Lieutenant?"

Brittles moved closer, squinting more than usual. He noticed the simple, stylized skulls inscribed along the full base of the vessel. "That," he said, "would appear a 'soul snare,' common to the North Islands." Brittles, in his time at sea, had visited those strange destinations during two of the kingdom's ambassadorial missions. "The natives entertain a notion that the souls of the dead might be entrapped, as it were, and preserved beyond the vehicle of flesh."

The man held the bottle away from himself and grimaced.

Lt. Brittles chuckled. "Not to fear—it seems not occupied."

A cork stopper hung by a cord from the bottle's neck.

One other item remained in the trunk. It was an unadorned box of pine, no bigger than a tea caddy, with small holes poked in the top. Soft blue light leaked out when the lid was opened. The box contained spiders, spiders of a type unknown. Oddly glowing blue spiders.

The brig was located under the fort, one of several enclosures accessible through a series of dank tunnels. The air down there held to a certain middling temperature: never hot, regardless of summer, and water never got cold enough to freeze. Four men with "longs" stood outside the one occupied cell with Finchberry and his assistant, Brogley Nyne, who had served with the captain as coxswain. Nyne was a nervous little man and he kept his pockets full of fiddle nuts so as to give his hands and mouth something to do.

The man with his head in a jar of webs was lying on the bunk on the other side of the bars, eyes half-shut, the craggy wall beside him bathed in a sleepy blue light. Webs trembled gently as he exhaled. He had made no sound, nor movement of his own, and seemed no more conscious than his friend in the infirmary.

There was hushed speculation among the observers as to the origin and purpose of those who had attacked the fort. Nyne wondered if perhaps the antagonists belonged to The Pails, a fanatical religious sect devised by Ember Pail in the late 1600s. In accordance with the madman's writings, adherents were required to kill another person annually. But, Capt. Finchberry argued, The Pails were a stealthy lot and hardly prone to firing upon an armed fortress in the bright of day.

"Whatever they may have been about," the captain said, "there is some queer manner of spell at work. Mind this one closely. No telling what it's like to do. Yes, some queer magic engaged here."

This was evident, for the healer, Skiggs, in examining the stranger prior to the man's placement in the brig, noted that a musket wound to the chest would not likely have been survivable. The injury was skinned over, but with a faint layer of dead-looking flesh, not the mark of common healing, which gave the men question as to the actual state of the man. While there was something like a heartbeat to be heard, and a slow, hollow breathing in the lungs, the man's condition was rather mystifying.

There was another wound as well, on the man's abdomen, just under the ribs. A large fissure sewn shut with sturdy twine, still visible along the closure.

"*That* wound," Finchberry muttered, "should surely have caused his death."

Nyne cracked a fiddle nut in his fingers and said, "Perhaps it did."

It was a cool gray morning in the spring of the year and Privet was up on the wall-walk with Lady Swellbrook and her servant Lily, whose face was obscured by a loose gray hood with only a slit for the eyes. This was now the older woman's morning ritual, coming to feed the birds.

Privet spent twelve hours a day monitoring his charge. He was glad only in that he had not been assigned night duty. Another fellow suffered *that,* standing and standing and standing outside the lady's chamber door as the slow hours crept along.

The decorous Lady Swellbrook had chosen to wear mild colors, blues and grays, but for the off-white hat with its flat crown and wide brim. This she wore over a linen day-cap. Her cloak, which largely obscured the flared skirt hips, petticoat, and the trim bodice of her gown, made Privet think of the sober blue of the wainscoting in Capt. Finchberry's office. The young woman also exhibited reserve in her selection of shades, her concealment in concert with the rest of her garb.

Lily, as the story goes, was born with a plain face and sought, through the application of a beauty spell, to make herself lovely. But magic was an unpredictable resource, and the faulty charm had tragic results…now none were allowed to gaze upon her hideous countenance.

Privet, in his sage-colored navy coat, wearing a pistol from a hanger that crossed his chest plate, along with a sword, had mastered the art of standing rigid, facing impassively forward while in fact seeing much more than it appeared. Today was the same; he remained off to the side, angled toward the wide Tween, as inconspicuous as conditions allowed, while the woman delivered bits of bread to the birds that fluttered down to light on the merlons. Lady Swellbrook was graceful for her age, not stooped, nor feeble. There was a straightness in her stance, and about her general air, that spoke of a certain dignity.

"Where is the gorse-wing?" Lady Swellbrook asked of no one in particular. She looked down the walk, away from where the sparrows were feasting. The gorse-wing, sleeker and smaller than the sparrows, had nonetheless flocked with them, in relative harmony, somehow separated from its own kind. She had favored it for being a misfit of sorts, herself a misfit at this place.

"Oh, dear!" There was alarm in the woman's voice, and the uncharacteristic speed of her movements made Privet turn his head fully to watch.

The little gorse-wing was lying on its side as if asleep, the tiny black eye mostly closed, the pretty yellow wing tight against its side. The woman knelt and ever so carefully lifted the dead bird into her hands.

"Poor creature," she whispered.

The woman rose and walked over to Privet, cradling the gorse-wing, her thin hands trembling. He had not stood this close to Lady Swellbrook before, and he thought how pretty she must have been at one time, and even now her creases could not entirely detract from the elegance of her features, or the soulful robin's egg eyes. She hardly conveyed an impression of the betraying harlot that the other enlisted men took her to be. Lady Swellbrook looked as though she might cry.

Retaining her dignified voice, Lady Swellbrook addressed him, "Young man, might we please bring this bird out for to bury?"

Privet looked down at the thing for a long moment, holding his face in a stiff military mask.

Swellbrook asked, "Something lovely deserves rest in a place less dreary than this, don't you think?"

Privet found his voice. "Yes, madam, I suppose it does."

The smell of the Tween was salty in the air, and cool gusts came rippling over the water to where the burial party stood on the ancient ramparts. Early flowers showed against the grassy slopes and colorful day-moths were flitting about, sampling.

Privet stood, arms at his sides, staring ahead while Lily, armed with a spade he had taken from the barn, began digging in the earth. Lady Swellbrook hovered by, holding her dead gorse-wing. Lily was getting her gown dirty, her knees in the damp grass.

Privet felt heat in his face, an increasing measure of shame as he watched the laboring servant from the corner of his eye. At last, with a sigh, he found himself kneeling beside Lily, gently taking the spade away from her. He dug the rest of the hole.

"Thank you," Lily said in her timid voice.

It was Lady Swellbrook who bent down and placed the bird in its grave. She had found a dry dead spider in the barn and now broke this up and sprinkled it over the small corpse, as burial customs dictated. The woman remained hunched for a minute, praying perhaps, and when she got up Privet filled in the hole.

Finished with his task, Privet glanced over at the wharfs where a cutter—a small gaff-sailed sailing vessel—was docking. The plum and gold flag of the kingdom flew from the one-master. *Who would this be?* he wondered. He felt something touch his arm and turned.

Lady Swellbrook took her hand away from the handsome young navy man. "Thank you, Seaman…"

"Privet, madam."

She smiled kindly, her robin's egg eyes creasing, "Thank you, Seaman Privet."

Capt. Finchberry and Lt. Brittles greeted the arrivals at the dock. The first was a dashing young fellow in a scarlet cloak with a lacy neck cloth gushing at his throat. He wore a dark cocked hat with a decorative gold badge, and a lavishly festooned cream-colored waistcoat, its metallic threads depicting a pattern of pinecones and doves.

The man had sardonic good looks: a dark wavy mane, trim mustache and pointy little beard. "Good day, gents!" He bowed.

The other passenger, some few years older than the first, was a plump fellow of a more tempered appearance. Coat, waistcoat and breeches were all the color of bricks. He had a mild, boyish face, if a bit puffy, with spectacles, and light hair drawn to a knot.

This was Neelam Hentwidge, who, in his wide travels as a kingdom document-arian, had found himself in predicaments which required him to put his sword cane to good use. But, for this occasion the blade was dormant within and the accessory appeared harmless enough. He bowed to the officers and commented on the bleakness of the day.

They were soon inside the walls of the fort where they were met by Finchberry's clerk, Brogley Nyne. The stylish one, Heron Swellbrook, walked alongside Finchberry while Lt. Brittles, in a hushed tone, was busy updating the documentarian on the recent dramatic events.

"I trust you're taking all good care of my dear aunt," Heron said good-naturedly.

"Indeed we are, Mister Swellbrook." The captain replied, leading with his belly. "The comfort of Lady Swellbrook weighs chiefly in my mind."

Lying swine, young Swellbrook thought. *He stinks of cheap "puff"—something a planter would smoke.* "Terribly glad to hear it, my dear Captain."

While private sea-coaches were common for travel up and down and across the Tween, where pirate ships very rarely ventured, the charming Heron Swellbrook had heard tell of the naval cutter heading for the fort, transporting Neelam Hentwidge, and, persuasive fellow that he was, managed to arrange for the vessel to stop along its route so that he might go along. Being the nephew of a duke entitled him to such consideration.

Capt. Finchberry's office was in the rear tower, which stood higher than the two at the front of the fort, centrally situated in the long back wall of Fort Haddox. Cannons perched on top of the structure, and a high chimney above those. Lady Swellbrook's chamber occupied the topmost floor.

Privet was escorting the older woman and her attendant back to the tower when they came upon the officers and visitors. Heron, with the best and biggest of smiles, broke from Finchberry and rushed to meet them.

"Auntie! Stars and gods it's lovely to see you!" the man bowed theatrically.

"Nephew." The lady replied dryly, with a stoic curtsy.

Privet, in his inconspicuous way, observed the disdain in Lady Swellbrook's eye.

"I have come to visit," the handsome young man declared.

"How lovely."

Privet stood outside the heavy batten door of Lady Swellbrook's room while she took tea with Heron. The young seaman was still some months away from finishing his year there at the fort and he found himself in sympathy with the woman he was required to watch over. In a sense, they were both prisoners there at the sad gray fort, but at least *he* would have the chance to leave one day.

After a time a huffy Heron Swellbrook wheeled out of the room, slamming the door behind as he muttered, "Stubborn old hag!" and thumped off down the stairs.

Privet, forgetting to knock, opened the door and hastily poked his head into the room. The scorned matriarch was sitting by a little fire, trembling. Lily stood by her, wide skirt eclipsing the better part of the fireplace, a comforting hand on the shaken woman's shoulder.

"Are you well?" Privet asked.

Lady Swellbrook, though visibly shaken, managed a little smile. "Yes, quite well. Thank you, Seaman."

Privet collected himself. "Right. Well, I'll be about my post."

The young man slipped back out and softly closed the door.

After suffering tea and small talk with the fort's captain, Neelam Hentwidge got right to business. It fell upon Lt. Brittles to take the documentarian around the fort so that he might have a view and a sense of what needed to be recorded. The twin Kings, Aven and Alder, who shared the crown of Fellengrey, were sticklers when it came to their empire's history, and so a number of trusted subjects were regularly sent out to take account wherever events of note took place. His purpose on this trip was twofold: he was to write of the internment of Lady Swellbrook, and of the attack by the mysterious boat.

Hentwidge studied the Tween from the wall-walk, listening as Brittles described the battle, then interviewed some of the men involved in the fight. Brittles showed him the cannon that delivered the blast of canister shot that struck the opposing craft. Hentwidge then spoke to Privet's friend Willows about the boarding of the boat and the discoveries made upon it.

Then it was on to the infirmary where Mealton Skiggs was checking the condition of the foot on the seaman who accidentally shot himself the day of the battle. Fortuitous timing, that, for Hentwidge listened quietly to the blundering fellow's testimony.

A pale man of unspectacular features, sporting a puff of bandages about his head, lay on one of the bunks, this being one of the two survivors from the boat. He remained in an unconscious state. When asked about the man's situation, Mealton Skiggs said, "His condition is no better, and if he wakes not soon I fear he may starve."

Hentwidge very much wished the fellow awake so that he might question him about the attack. Why, he wondered, had the small vessel, with only a small crew and meager weaponry, attacked the heavily armed, well-fortified outpost?

Next it was on to the jail in the dim, dank under-chambers of Fort Haddox. Four armed men stood outside the cell. Hentwidge stared through the bars, his arms crossed over his chest. Many mistook his purposeful approach as rudeness, for the documentarian had no time or tolerance for light chat. He was obsessively devoted to his cause.

The man with a bottle over his head lay on the cot, his features vague behind webs, dead spiders like raisins stuck in the webs. Eerie blue light—like that from berries of ghost eye vine—radiated in a nimbus.

The prisoner had not eaten a thing during his stay and no one seemed to know whether he had a need for food or not. They dare not remove the jar from his head, fearful that it might unleash some terrible magic, or plague.

"Does he not speak?" Hentwidge, with keen little eyes peering over his spectacles, tapping his cane impatiently on the floor, asked one of the guards.

"Only in the deep of night, I'm told," the man returned. "A name, spoken in a voice like a hissing sea."

"Which name might that be?"

The man blinked a few times, thinking. "I fail to recall proper, sir. The fellows of night watch might better tell."

Hentwidge nodded. "Very well."

Gifted with a remarkable memory, Hentwidge never had a need to write a thing down. He held it all in mind, including his brief interview with Lady Swellbrook (in which he asked her about her life there at the fort) until later, in his chamber, when he hunched over a table with ink and quill, scrawling into the late hours.

Privet was writing too, penning a letter to his family back in East Whittle. A new candle was glowing in the iron stand by his bunk and he could hear the snoring of other men, their bunks spread equidistantly through the lengthy garret space.

"Yet another proclamation of love for your new charmer, Privet?" the loutish Fimble spoke from the next bed.

Privet regarded the man's wide toad smile impassively and got back to his missive.

Fimble wasn't finished, "Tell, Privy, have you slipped your prong to the old slut yet?"

Privet flew up, his travel desk tipping aside, the ink spilling into the air like a black flag. He lunged, grabbed the edge of Fimble's bed and heaved, flipping it on its side, sending the bigger man hard to the floor. Surprised at his own rage, Privet took a step back, his face red, his fists clenched and trembling.

"Not another vile word from your mouth, Fimble," Privet warned.

Fimble looked up and smirked. "*Well!* As you wish, Privy."

The sparrows were waiting on the fortress wall. Small, brown and white, they fidgeted, watching for the lady that fed them. She came shortly after the sun peeked up from the east, a sack of bread crumbs in hand, accompanied by her hooded attendant, and a seamen with a gray helmet and sage-green coat.

Morning light fell softly on the Tween making the surface copper, restless with breezes. Sea-moths as big around as dining plates caught the light on their pewter wings as they fluttered down to the shoreline to see what the tide had left them.

The early spring night had been chill and there remained a touch of wood smoke on the air from warming fires, this enhanced by billows from the kitchen. Privet, stiff as a statue, with his hands down at his sides, was enjoying the air, and the view of the saltwater channel with the eastern island of Fellengrey far on the opposite side. He glanced over at Lady Swellbrook as she spoke to the birds and sprinkled bits of bread on one of the merlons. Some of the sparrows were practically tame now.

He heard something metal clank against stone and noticed a naval hand grenade, a small cast-iron shell not four inches in diameter, rolling toward the raised blocks that ran along the outer edge of the wall-walk. Fuse spitting, it rolled directly under Lady Swellbrook's wide skirts.

Privet leaped through the air and thudded against the older woman, knocking the wind from her, and together they rolled on the stone floor of the walk. A terrible roar shook the fort and light and smoke and chunks of stone were in the air for what seemed a very long moment. Privet glimpsed Lily tumbling out of the glare, falling face-first beside him, face down, her hood thrown from her head. Pieces of the shattered merlon rained on and around them. A pebble pinged off Privet's helmet.

Ears ringing, coughing, Privet lifted his head. The air was full of smoke and feathers. He rolled Lady Swellbrook over. She looked up at him, dazed and whispered, "Lily…"

Broken sparrows were scattered in the rubble, splashes of blood amidst bread crumbs. One bird, still alive, was on its side, delicate legs kicking spasmodically. Men could be heard running, calling to each other. Privet picked himself up. He was dizzy, unsure if the concussion of the blast or the smoky air was responsible for his blurred vision. He stepped carefully over Lady Swellbrook and knelt next to Lily.

The young woman's day-cap had fallen off along with her hood, and for the first time he saw the warm gold hair at the back of her head. He took her by the shoulders and began to turn her, unafraid of seeing how ugly she was, only worried that the blast had taken her face entirely. What he saw stunned him. Lily, with her summer-green eyes, pale, smooth skin and rosebud mouth was the most beautiful woman he had ever seen.

"Have I died?" Lily asked, befuddled.

"No," Privet said.

"My lady, is she well?"

"I believe she is."

Lily smiled and fainted.

Privet refused the infirmary, Lady Swellbrook as well, though she had received some bruises and scrapes. Lily, who quickly retained her guise, had taken the worst of it, suffering some minor cuts, and tears in her clothing. Still, she opted to be tended by her lady. The aging Swellbrook possessed some measure of healing skill, having helped the local midwife on occasion when a girl, and had learned to fashion a spell in the form of a powder, an art learned from her grandmother. It was a magic she put to use when her own busy mind had no regard for the lateness of the hour. She had never used it on others though, until that day.

Lily had been in such a state, following the explosion, that Lady Swellbrook thought it a mercy to offer rest to the poor creature. She whispered an incantation of strange words as she made up a sleep powder using some herbs Privet had obtained from the kitchen, and then she offered some to the maid.

While the lovely Lily was sleeping quietly in her cramped quarters adjacent to the lady's, Privet asked about the hood and the tale he had heard about Lily's awful disfigurement at the hands of a fouled beauty spell.

"The hood and sad story were of my design, in actual fact," Lady Swellbrook admitted. "Dear little maiden was all nerves at the thought of being amongst a legion of roughs, here at the fort. I thought best to disguise her appeal, that flocks of lusty lads not beleaguer her."

Privet laughed. "You are a clever woman, Lady Swellbrook."

"Thank you, Seaman Privet. And Privet?"

"Madam?"

She reached out and took his hand, gazed at him with her soulful blue eyes. "Thank you for saving my life."

The scene of the bomb blast drew significant attention from the fort's main officers, and the documentarian Hentwidge. Heron Swellbrook was on scene as well, scarlet-cloaked and smirking.

"Do you not suppose," Lt. Brittles asked Hentwidge, "there be some like source behind *this* and the attacking boat?"

Hentwidge, an impatient man who despised being questioned while in the midst of thought, sighed, looked up slowly and said, "It is not unreasonable to speculate as such, I'll grant."

Heron Swellbrook kicked a tiny piece of iron leftover from the grenade's decimated shell between the shattered merlon and the cracked block next to it. The bit of metal dropped down into the grass at the base of the nearest encircling earthwork.

"I'll not rest until the scoundrel responsible for this swings," the nephew of the fort's infamous prisoner declared, flicking his mane, a hand to his breast.

"Whoever might wish your aunt dead, young sir?" Hentwidge asked, peering over his spectacles, poking a dead sparrow with his cane.

"Oh, the world be a restless nest of malevolent creatures, Mister Hentwidge. I've none to offer in particular, but I trust suitable suspects abound."

The inscrutable Hentwidge nodded. He thought a moment and turned to the captain, who, with his bicorne squashed under one arm, was rubbing the bare spot on his head with one hand and pulling at his beard with the other.

"You'll want to increase the lady's guard," Hentwidge noted matter-of-factly. While not a military official, the documentarain was held in the highest regard by Kings Aven and Alder, and could impart orders to the captain if need be.

Finchberry responded, "She refuses the notion and trusts only Seaman Privet, and her night guard, Winpoole."

Lt. Brittles spoke up, "Privet and Winpoole will do well enough. They're good men, the both of 'em."

Hentwidge, who valued Brittles' word over that of the captain, gave a satisfied nod.

Hentwidge bent down close to the rubble and picked up a feather. "*Who*," he asked himself more than the rest, "would benefit from Lady Swellbrook's death?"

Hentwidge and Lt. Brittles went off to interview all those who were on guard duty (or anyone who had been in the general vicinity) at the time of the explosion. So far as it was known, no one had actually seen the culprit who threw the grenade. Finchberry and Heron, meanwhile, walked back to the captain's office.

Privet was at his station outside the notorious Lady Swellbrook's compartment. There was just enough foyer for him to pace back and forth and he glanced repeatedly out the little window until he saw the men approaching. Heat rushed to his face and he thought of the bomb rolling under the old woman's skirt, of the horrible blast, of small birds scattered amidst smoky rubble kicking their last. His hands had not stopped shaking since the explosion, his ears had not stopped ringing. Without a thought of consequence, he found himself rushing down the stairs.

Captain Finchberry was reaching for the door latch when a rather feral-looking Privet flung it open. His eyes dark with anger, the young seamen stepped outside, thrusting a finger at Heron Swellbrook, "You will cause no further harm to Lady Swellbrook," he growled.

The captain and Heron each took a step back. The younger of the two threw his hands in the air. "Harm?"

"*Someone* has made an attempt on her life, and only yesterday, with my very ears, I heard you speak venomously of your aunt. Just this morning her attendant confided in me as regards the particulars of your conversation over tea."

Heron turned a shade of turnip. "I've not the slightest idea what your meaning is!"

It was true that Lily had spoken to Privet about Heron's visit to his aunt's chamber, how his pleasant facade had swiftly left him when he asked her the whereabouts of certain costly pieces of jewelry that could not be located at her husband, the duke's, residence. Not only had Lady Swellbrook been stripped of her inheritance and stolen away from her beloved cats and gardens when she was exiled to Fort Haddox, but her articles of finery were confiscated as well. The most valuable of the bunch had gone missing.

Shortly before being shipped to Fort Haddox, Lily, on instruction from the lady, had taken the gem-encrusted trinkets and thrown them off a cliff, into the Gantic. Better that, than they land on the necks and fingers of her husband's mistresses.

When Lady Swellbrook had not disclosed the location of a hiding place (where Heron imagined the jewelry to be) he had flown into a rage and threatened her.

"The lady's servant is mistaken, good fellow," Heron insisted. "I have only the deepest affection for my dear aunt."

A brave fellow would have barked Privet down and called him to duel by this point, but Heron was anything but brave, most especially when facing an armed military man with a murderous look in his eye and a fist around the handle of his sword.

Capt. Finchberry interceded. "My apologies, Swellbrook," he said, stepping past Heron and taking Privet by the sleeve. "Accompany me, won't you, Privet?"

Several yards away from the tower door, beyond earshot of the distressed Heron Swellbrook, Finchberry rumbled at the seaman. "Privet, have you now lost what little mind you possess? This is unacceptable treatment of a guest of the fort, regardless of your suspicions. Once again you leave me no choice but to discipline you."

Though he threatened to have Privet tossed in the brig, Capt. Finchberry merely altered Privet's assignment. The seaman would remain one of Lady

Swellbrook's two sentinels, but he was now to take on the night duty. The worst of it was that he was made to walk over to Heron Swellbrook and tell him that he was sorry.

Heron took the apology well. "No harm done," he chirped with a charming smile.

Lady Swellbrook's room was not the most convivial of spaces. The walls of dressed stone lacked sheathing and the coat of whitewash, a suggestion of wintry pallor, only added to the chill atmosphere. The furnishings were not much, and the occupant was allowed only a limited portion of firewood per day, and so used it sparingly. Today they had brought her birch, which burnt too fast for the lady's liking. How she missed her home fires of reliable ash logs.

It was after midnight and Lady Swellbrook was still awake, resting by the hearth in a simple white nightgown of cotton, her silvery hair long and loose about her shoulders. She had elected not to use the magically imbued sleep powder, afraid of what dreams might hold. Instead, she went to her door, opened it and stuck her head out, giving her guard a weary smile.

"Seaman Privet, I wonder perhaps if you might care to sit a spell? Some tea and the fire might refresh you."

Privet had stood rigid with a musket over his shoulder for hours. It was proving to be a cool spring, and none too comfortable in that little space. He had thought as much, looking out over the fort's yard and the front wall with its towers and many sleeping cannons, and the Tween beyond. Moored vessels rocked on the shifting water, dark and strangely skeletal with their masts and lines, the softening white of sails furled tightly. The water, just touched with light from the post lantern at the dock, was an amorphous thing of copper and black.

"I should like that, thank you, Lady Swellbrook," he said.

Lily was off sleeping in her own chamber and her breathing could be heard, that and the rippling hum of the flames. The lady's bed, which hadn't been slept in, looked like a big cloth box with its curtains closed. Privet's hostess gestured to a chair by the fireplace, which was an unadorned example of its kind but for a rough lintel set into the stones. The pile of birch branches and splits, heaped by a stodgy old chest of drawers, would not last the night.

Neither said a thing until tea was poured. Privet felt odd being served by a woman who, until some short while ago, had been a duchess. He said a soft thank you.

"Lady Swellbrook, if I may inquire…have you no supposition as regards who might be responsible for the attempt on your life? Is it not plain that your nephew had hand in such?"

"I hardly think Heron has the nerve, truth be told, though his greed is considerable. He hasn't the stuff to heft a pistol, let alone a grenade."

"Might he then have put some more capable creature to the task?"

She looked at the fire. "Perchance."

Privet had been thinking unceasingly on the matter while standing out in the foyer. "What of that Hentwidge fellow, a curious cat that one. He's extraordinarily loyal, they say, and sent, perhaps, for more than penning his histories."

"An assassin? Do you think?"

"If you'll excuse my saying as much, you are something of an embarrassment to the kingdom, and could there not be those in power desiring to remove such a blemish?"

"I hardly think the Kings would sanction—"

"Oh, no, not the Kings, good and decent men that they are, but others? The duke, I mean."

The woman chuckled softly. "*That* fool! Too busy chasing after his mistresses to spare thought for me. No, no, I honestly can't think it. I've been as good as dead or better in his awareness for many a year. He has all that his wretched little heart might desire, and I am forgotten."

Privet nodded.

She looked sad just then, sad and spiteful. But she recovered swiftly and smiled prettily. "I am certain you have heard all as concerns my dreadful transgressions."

"Things are said," Privet replied, looking down into his cup.

"More elaborate and compelling than may be the actual case," the woman speculated. She reached to the simple pewter service on the table at her side, lifted the pot. "Here, have yet another hot cup and I'll tell my awful tale."

More than thirty years previous, the Duke and Duchess of Snoddingshire traveled to the Colonies of West Forest on assignment for King Swanbry the Second, it being before the rule of the twins, Aven and Alder. They were carried across the Gantic on the frigate *Oak Shark,* a swift 28-gun vessel commanded by one of the navy's best, a highly regarded, impressively decorated Post Captain, Linden Quill. He was a handsome young officer of noble manners, and though respectful toward the imperious duke, Quill could not help but find himself attracted to that man's lovely wife.

It was a long trip across the sea, with plenty of opportunities for conversation between Quill and Ivy Swellbrook, the duchess. She found him interesting, warm-hearted, and not a little handsome—an appealing contrast to her husband all around. Both did their best to first deny and then suppress the feelings that were evolving between them.

The Colonies themselves offered distraction for a time. The ship had carried some needed supplies to the colonists and the duke was busy helping the governor with the sort of problems common to a young and developing settlement. He was also required to see that the lumbering interests that had made the continent so desirable to the kingdom of Fellengrey were being properly and profitably managed. He spent a month in each of the established townships.

Blackbirch, predominant in the deep, moody woodlands of West Forest, proved the best of all woods for burning, for gunstocks, for shipbuilding. It was durable, reasonably easy to work and required no paint to withstand the elements. The name, however, was misleading, for blackbirch was an evergreen, spruce-like in appearance, but with black needles. Oddly, for a coniferous tree, the wood was stronger than that of the best hardwoods and burned more like ash than say, spitting, pitchy pine or other softwoods.

Ivy found the new land both remarkable and frightening, for it was a vast and feral wilderness, the coasts ragged with stones, the hilly landscape covered with dark-bristled blackbirch trees. Weakened by the trip, she opted to remain at the mansion of the governor while the duke headed off for the far northern village and the lumber camps on its outskirts. In the afternoon she would walk along the shore with Capt. Quill, tossing bread crumbs to the gulls and sea-moths. One afternoon they kissed at the edge of a dark forest, at the edge of the dark sea.

At length, once the duke's work at West Forest was done, the *Oak Shark* set out for home. The early part of the trip back to Fellengrey was unusually stormy and the commander of the *Oak Shark* was concerned for the safety of those on board. The ship held, but other problems soon arose. The duke, for one, spent half the voyage in a drunken state. As a consequence, he gave the privilege girl no peace. Once, when Ivy commented on his behavior, the inebriated husband slapped her repeatedly, knocking her hat into the gray ocean. In his rage he grabbed her by the hair and threatened to toss her in as well, until Capt. Quill appeared on the quarterdeck in his dark green officer's coat, his high black boots and black bicorne hat.

The young officer drew his sword—a silvery arc that swooshed through the air—and pointed it accusingly at the duke. Without raising his voice, the captain promised, "You will unhand that woman, sir, or I shall be forced to run you through."

The duke was befuddled. "I am a duke!"

"Duke, or king or beggar, no man shall mishandle a woman on my ship."

The drunkard released Ivy, called the captain a bastard, and passed out. In the morning he acted as if he had no recollection of the incident. The captain did, however; it was a moment he would never forget.

"Let us have some more wood. A story calls for a warm fire," Lady Swellbrook said, starting up from her chair.

Privet gave her a kind smile. "Allow me, madam."

Some of the remaining birch pieces were placed on the blackening remnants in the firebox.

Fixing him with her gaze, the once-duchess stated bluntly, "It was but one time. One time alone, and it had to do with hearts as much as flesh. Nothing so sordid as the seamen here are pleased to think—it was as natural as moonlight on water. Linden told me he loved me. And I loved him. I have ever since."

Ivy Swellbrook never saw Capt. Quill again once the ship returned to Fellengrey. There were only secret letters, a love upheld by words and memories. The duke had no idea about any of it, but, eventually, through no act of will, even the letters came to an end.

In the spring of 1717 the frigate *Oak Shark,* under the command of young Capt. Quill, was drafted into the service of crown experimentalists, the famous Coppermast twins. The ship set out into the cold gray waters off Fellengrey for the purpose of testing theories and techniques of weather magic.

Some sort of mishap took place and the ship was thrown dramatically off course. No one ever learned what caused it to stray so far, or what happened to it once it did, but pieces of the *Oak Shark* were found floating in the vicinity of the strange North Islands. All aboard were lost.

Lady Swellbrook stared off into the fireplace, a tear glinting on her cheek. She wiped it away with a trembling hand before it could drop into her tea.

"And there have you my villainous tale, young Privet," she said, a small poignant smile on her lips. "The duke found the letters which Linden had written me, an ancient secret unearthed. And here sit I for the sake of it."

"I am sorry, Lady Swellbrook," Privet said, moved that this woman saw fit to trust him with her private history. "One can ponder only at the injustices of the world. You ought have had better than what was dealt you, and deserve better than this bleak place."

"Kind you are to say. *You* deserve better as well."

Privet gave a short quiet laugh. "So I do. Well, won't be long; months only, then I'll have done this tomb. But, sad shall I be to leave you here."

"And sad shall I be to see you go, Seaman Privet."

Nillsgate, five miles to the south, was the nearest village to Fort Haddox. The healer Mealton Skiggs was called there to stand in for the local midwife, who was mending in bed following a nasty fall from a horse. He left the infirmary in the early evening and returned after midnight, having tended the delivery of a healthy set of twins, who, having been born on the night of the new moon, would enjoy good fortune.

It was Skiggs' habit to move slowly and quietly and he did so now, more than ever, as he entered the gloomy sickroom. There was no sign of the watchman responsible for monitoring the comatose fellow who'd been taken from the mystery boat, and the candles in the wall sconces had burnt so low that their erratic flames blinked off and on like fireflies.

Two rows of beds, lined up along the walls of the long room, showed vague in the dimness; only one was occupied. The covers were pulled up over the patient, loosely defining his shape. The fluttering light gave the lumpy mass the suggestion of movement, as if it were a great mound of clay being shaped by invisible hands.

Skiggs muttered something unpleasant about the lacking guard and made his way for the candle-box on the wall. He heard a low moaning somewhere in the dark, and a sudden tapping noise that caused him to look over at the patient. More than a trick of the light this time, the figure under the covers was shaking, convulsing so violently that one of the bed's legs drummed against the floor. Drawn away from his task, Skiggs rushed bedside and pulled the covers back.

"Blast!" Skiggs cursed at the sight of the guard, who was gagged with a clump of bandages, tied to the bed with lengths of rope.

The elderly healer felt the cold mouth of a flintlock pistol press against the back of his head. He shuddered. A voice he had never heard before spoke. "Here now, Healer Skiggs, turn about, but slow, if you please."

Whibb Penningbrook, his head distended for its bandages, had awaited this night, feigning his coma, patiently counting the days since his capture, *waiting for the new moon.* When the healer had gone off to tend a mother in labor, the seaman guarding Penningbrook took the opportunity to sit down on one of the empty beds. The man was stretched out and snoring in no time, his weapons for the taking.

With his own pistol pointed at him, the guard had been forced to fetch some rope that was on hand there at the infirmary. Penningbrook, taking the coil, went round and around his captive, flintlock in one hand, wrapping the guard like a spider wraps a meal. Then the guard was made to hop over to the bed, where he was gagged, and tied to the frame.

"You seem to have recovered nicely," Skiggs said to Penningbrook with a touch of sarcasm.

"Indeed, sir, thanks in part to your hand. Now, Healer Skiggs, I require further assistance on your part. I need you take me to the duchess."

Lady Swellbrook was charmed by Privet's tales of growing up in field-country. She especially enjoyed hearing about all the different animals that had been so integral to his family's life, the milkers and laying-hens, the sheep and geese and hogs. He told her some of the wonderfully silly things that his family's cats had done over the years, and she told him about hers.

Neither had minded the clock, and there was a steady poring of tea. The birch for the fire was down to very little and a soft freckling of rain could be heard blowing against the windows.

"Do you hear?" the lady asked, "It sounds to rain."

Privet listened. Yes, she was right, he could hear the gentle patter, but another sound as well. It came from outside the chamber's door, down on the stairs. Footfalls, perhaps.

Lady Swellbrook studied him. "Something troubles you?"

"A noise from below—and here sit I, off from my post." Privet got up and was moving toward the corner where he had leaned his musket when a solid knock fell against the door.

Privet's first thought was to move Lady Swellbrook into the adjoining compartment where Lily slept, in case this was the assassin who had tossed the grenade, coming to finish his work. But there wasn't time. The latch clicked and the door swung open and a strange blue light fell into the room.

A tall man in gray clothing and cloak stood in the doorway, pistol in hand, his head encased in a great glowing jar of webs and dead spiders, his clean-shaved face little more than a blur, though still recognizable to the former Duchess of Snoddingshire. She gasped and flew up from her seat, a hand to her breast.

Privet, having snatched up his musket, whirled and clicked back the cock all in one motion, bringing the butt plate to his shoulder. He aimed the heavy weapon at the luminous blue jar.

The visitor's face looked like a thing of wax, though the eyes were open and moving. Privet, expecting something horrible, was about to fire, but hesitated when the man in the doorway smiled.

Lady Swellbrook took a step forward and shoved the barrel of Privet's musket aside before rushing to the strange figure. "Linden!" she called.

Captain Linden Quill held out his arms to meet the woman's embrace, and in a voice like a hissing sea, said, "Ivy."

Neelam Hentwidge liked when things were just a certain way, his inkstand at a particular angle to his right hand, hot tea ready on the left. The candle had to be positioned so that it did not toss the shadow of hand and quill over the paper on which he wrote. He liked comfort too, the warmth and smell and sound of the fire, the cozy feel of his finely embroidered sleeping gown and cap. While the temporary quarters provided for him at the fort were far from ideal, he had done his best to make the place habitable.

The hour was late and he was calling on his memories of the day, conveying them to paper. He documented the grenade attack on Lady Swellbrook and details of the investigation that followed. He noted that no suspects were as yet held accountable.

Done with his documentation, the man shoveled some coals into his long-handled bedwarmer and ran it over the mattress before settling in. He blew out his light, pulled the bed curtains shut and surrendered his mind to the snug darkness.

But Hentwidge's mind was not content to rest. His dreams were uneasy—something was nagging at him. He tossed and turned and awoke before dawn, sitting up and saying to himself, "*The name...*"

The previous day, when he had spoken with the fellows guarding the cell of the man with a jar over his head, one of the sentinels had told him that the stranger from the boat would speak a name in the night. The guard could not recall just what that particular name was, though, and suggested asking the men from the night watch. Hentwidge, now unyieldingly curious about that name, found himself shoving his curtains open and rising from the bed.

He dressed with less care than usual, threw a cloak over his shoulders, and grabbed his cane before going out into the cool spring night. A light rain was falling in the yard, with a sound like the paws of a million ghostly cats.

Here stood Capt. Quill, who was presumed to have died some thirty years before. Privet, while not so surprised as Lady Swellbrook, was perplexed, and unsure what to expect from the armed figure. He kept his musket at the ready.

"You are alive," Swellbrook breathed, her face pressed to the man's oddly beating chest.

"I thought never to hold you again," the captain spoke quietly, his aura of webs trembling in the jar like an unearthly combination of lace and mist.

"And I you. All these years—these many terrible years—I thought you dead."

"Forgive me my silence. I meant not to cause you pain."

The woman stood back and reached a hand up, pressing it against the cool glass of the jar, as if she could touch his cheek through the barrier. She could see her reflection in the vessel, a woman gone gray, a face thirty years older than the one Quill had fallen in love with. "See how I have aged," she said, smiling sadly.

The man touched her cheek, unimpeded by glass. "Your loveliness defies the years."

Lady Swellbrook blushed and turned to look at Privet. Poor young fellow didn't know what to make of the situation. He was keeping an eye on Quill's pistol, keeping his own finger tight against the trigger of his "long."

"Linden," the lady said, "this is my good friend, Seaman Privet."

Quill moved his pistol to his left hand so that he could salute. "Seaman," the captain said.

Privet nodded, "Captain, sir."

"You needn't be concerned, Seaman," Quill rasped, "I mean no threat."

Quill leaned to place his pistol on the floor and slid it off to the side with a shove of his boot. Privet relaxed his grip on the musket, standing it on its butt, while holding to the barrel as if it were a walking stick.

A swarm of questions buzzed in Lady Swellbrook's mind. For instance, "What is your condition, Linden? This jar, and how be it you have so eluded age?"

The man, his voice an eerie hiss from within the luminous jar, explained what had happened to him those many years ago, when his frigate the *Oak Shark* vanished.

His ship was carrying the Coppermast twins into deep water for the sake of magical experimentation. The first few tests had been uneventful, but on one particular day the brothers performed a certain weather magic experiment which, apparently, went terribly awry. From out of a calm sea there came terrible waves crashing upon the ship.

"But, more a horror than the waves were the flocking spheres of queer green light flung out from them. Hissing swarms of balls—no larger than musket shot— sought after us as if powered by intellect. I know not how I managed to evade them. My crew did not, nor did the Coppermast twins."

Privet spoke up, "What did these spheres do?"

The jar swiveled his way. "They passed as a knife through water, unimpeded by wood or flesh."

Privet cringed. "Oh."

Quill continued with his tale. The waves subsided and the rushing clusters of light dissipated into the air, but the craft was crippled and thrown far from her course. Most aboard did not survive the spheres and the watery bombardment. Her sails tattered, her weight listing, the frigate floated into northern waters.

But cruel fate was not done with the *Oak Shark*. An opportunistic pirate ship spotted the injured frigate and came alongside. The scoundrels boarded. Quill and the other survivors tried to fend them off, but, in their weakened condition, were no match for an attacking force. Quill's men were shot down without mercy and he himself took a ball in the chest. Thinking that he was as good as dead, Capt. Quill decided to blow up his own ship.

Assisted by his boatswain (the only other crewman from the *Oak Shark* left alive) the captain rigged a bomb to ignite the forward magazine, where cartridges for the cannons were stored. He managed this, without obliterating himself or his man, and succeeded in killing a good number of the raiders, while bringing ruin to his own beloved ship. The blast was so great that it caused serious damage to the pirate vessel, which was snug in proximity. In all the smoke and confusion, Quill and the boatswain rowed free of the wreckage in the captain's cockboat.

The small craft was heavy with casks of coin that were hidden in a secret compartment. This was Quill's personal fortune, or at least the part that he carried in his travels. His condition was steadily worsening and the boatswain aimed the craft for the only land masses in sight, which, unbeknownst to the pair at that time, were the mysterious North Islands. But, before they could make shore, they were intercepted by a strange red sloop. Red from sails to keel.

The two survivors of the *Oak Shark* were taken aboard the sloop and transported to land. Quill and his friend found themselves moved to a simple domed building of clay and were put into the care of several women dressed in long black robes. The women, two old and two young, were lacking a single hair on their heads. Even their eyebrows had been shaved away.

Quill's chest wound was so severe that they could not prevent him from dying, but, according to the boatswain, just as the man's last breath rasped out of him the women cupped the mouth of a glossy red vessel bearing crude carvings of skulls—a soul-snare—over his mouth. The bottle was promptly stopped with a wad of some pulpy, almost organic-looking substance. Then the women, all the while speaking their curious language in hushed voices, produced a large jar of clear glass and a simple pine box no bigger than a tea caddy.

They opened the box and a mist of blue light rose into the air. It contained spiders, blue glowing spiders. These were emptied into the jar, which was then fitted over Quill's head and fastened snugly at the neck with a thick leather collar that extended down to the upper chest area.

Next, to the amazement of the witness, the women made a deep incision in the captain's belly and carefully inserted the red vessel containing his breath. Within an hour of being sewn shut Quill opened his eyes and asked where he was.

Both Privet and Lady Swellbrook listened to the telling with wide eyes.

Quill told how he had spent a number of years with the people of the North Islands, and then decades alone, back in his homeland. Much as he longed for contact with his beloved Ivy, he had felt that he was no longer a man in the true sense, hampered by the constraints of his new situation, and so hid himself away, not so much as writing. Better he fade like a mist fades to sunlight. "But my heart was constant," Quill proclaimed.

"You might have let me know, Linden," Lady Swellbrook said.

"I am more sorry than I can say, Ivy."

At the time when the *Oak Shark* was lost there had been little formal contact between the peoples of Fellengrey and those of the North Islands. The natives were staunch isolationists. Still, they had saved Quill's life and fixed to preserve the stranger indefinitely with what they termed "moon-life," as he went on to explain. The magic employed: the jar, the spiders, in conjunction with the phases of the moon, sustained his spirit, as well as a functional physicality.

This particular magic, by its nature, was governed by lunar phases. Beginning with the new moon, and throughout the waxing period, Quill was lively and lucid, able-bodied, so long as the jar on his head went undamaged. But, as soon as the full moon turned toward its waning, Quill found himself listless and hardly capable of free movement, like a creature in hibernation, until the new moon wheeled around again.

"Could you, Ivy, love such a creature as *this?*" Quill asked, gesturing to his own head.

The woman gave a little laugh. "I would love you were you the ugliest frog in a pond."

Privet's alarm subsided and he was moved swiftly toward compassion when he witnessed the tenderness evident between the two. Separated by thirty years, and many miles, each had remained close in the other's heart. They made for a strange and poignant image standing there: she, an aged woman, and he, thirty years younger in flesh, a figure animated by enigmatic forces. But love transcendent— more mysterious perhaps than all magics combined—prevailed.

It was only upon learning of the duchess's exile to Fort Haddox that Quill felt compelled to emerge from his self-imposed exile. He had to rescue her. Having kept his wealth of coins, he was able to hire some men and purchased the humble boat, and set out to free her.

But, the captain insisted, it was not the intention of he or his men to resort to violence, unless of a defensive sort. The possibility of danger was there, certainly, which is why Quill made sure to bring a jar and spiders and a soul-snare, in case any of his crew, or Ivy, were mortally injured during her release. No, it was not to be an attack; the boat was simply to steal down the Tween so that Quill could cleverly sneak Lady Swellbrook out, without a gun being fired. But, something went wrong.

Quill, at the time, was in his lethargic waning-moon state, but he had left his men orders: they were to travel to the vicinity of the fort and anchor until the new moon, so that he might preside over the operation himself.

The crew miscalculated, and rather than quietly sliding into a sheltered cove as planned, they found themselves floating past Fort Haddox in full view, in full daylight. One of the young men on board panicked when a guard flew out of the stone guardhouse by the shore and shouted for the craft to stop, drawing a pistol as he did so. Thinking he was to be fired upon, Quill's hireling on the boat let off a shot with his musket, hitting the unfortunate man on the boardwalk, instigating the terrible battle that ensued. And the eventual capture of Quill and his wounded man, Whibb Penningbrook, who, as it turns out, was the son of the boatswain who survived the loss of the *Oak Shark*.

"That would be my extraordinary tale," Quill concluded.

"A remarkable adventure," Privet noted.

With the story finished, the trio suddenly found themselves in silence, but for the weak crackling of the birch fire. It was as if all three suddenly shared the same thought: *what next?*

The tapping of Hentwidge's cane echoed through the stone corridors beneath the fort as he made his way to the brig. Oil lamps were mounted intermittently along the way, challenging the long stretches of darkness that might have passed for the fossilized innards of some long-extinct behemoth. While another man might have gotten himself lost down there, Hentwidge's famous memory had previously mapped the place.

Brassy light from a lamp wobbled on the walls and bars of the brig, and while it was dark there when Hentwidge entered, there was light enough to show him that the four armed guards were absent from their posts. The man, alarmed, slid a thin sword from his cane—a razor-sharp whisper of light—and quickened his pace.

He stopped when he reached the compartment where the mysterious fellow from the boat had been interned, the man with a jar about his head. *He* was gone, but the four guards were stretched out on the stone floor as if sleeping.

Hentwidge tried the door, found it locked. He looked for the key and while he found the weapons belonging to the guards piled to one side, there was no sign of it. Turning his attention back to the cell, Hentwidge noticed that the men were still breathing and called to them, *"Hallo! Hallo!"* until one of them stirred.

The young enlisted man was groggy and could only muster the strength to sit up on the cold hard floor. He blinked at Hentwidge, trying to focus. Hentwidge fired questions at the man. What had happened? Where was the prisoner?

The man, while dazed, answered as best he could. He and his mates had been guarding "Jar-Head," as they called him, when all of a sudden the captive sat up on his bed and stared at them. The light in the jar began to grow brighter and a strange, high-pitched sound came on the air.

The noise increased as the light grew swiftly brighter—brighter and brighter, until the men could hardly see into the cell for the harsh blue glare, and found that their limbs would not move as the will dictated. The last the guard remembered was seeing a shadowy figure standing in the blue aura just on the other side of the bars, that and the deafening shrill that seemed to make a molten thing of his brain.

The other men were rousing now, like sleepy children in the morning rubbing their eyes. Hentwidge maintained the presence of mind to ask about the name that Jar-Head would mutter in the night.

"Ivy," the guard replied. "He would call out the name Ivy."

Ivy, Hentwidge thought. *Ivy Swellbrook, the duchess.* His sword disappeared back into its cane and the stout documentarain turned to hurry back through the labyrinth, leaving the men locked in the cell. He was headed for the tower at the rear wall of Fort Haddox.

The rain had stopped and the eastern sky was lightening beyond the Tween, silhouetting the high front wall and its towers. Hentwidge paid this little mind as he rushed into the front door of the brick barracks building and roused some of the men on the first floor.

"Sound the alarm," he instructed hastily.

He urged several of the men to go along with him, though they were still in their sleep gowns and caps. The men took up arms and followed Hentwidge to the back tower.

It was at this time that the changing of the guard took place, and here and there around the fort, the men reporting to relieve the night watch were making baffling discoveries. The guards being replaced were asleep at their posts. They were up on the towers, snoring and soggy from rain and dreaming soundly in the warmer sheltered places.

While armed only with his sword-cane, Hentwidge led the way, the seamen with muskets following from behind. They entered the ground floor of the tower stealthily, the light of a hand lantern washing over several doors and the bottom steps of the stone staircase. They tried the doors, which were locked, then started up.

The doors to the fort offices on the second floor were locked, with no strange sounds to be heard behind them, so the party continued upward, men's slippers scuffing and hissing on the steps. There was a little foyer at the top, a space just big enough to pace in, its window facing east to the Tween. The guard regularly stationed there at this time, a Seamen Privet, was not to be seen. The door to Lady Swellbrook's chamber was locked from the outside.

"Ready your weapons," Hentwidge said to his gang. The cocks on the flintlock mechanisms were clicked back, ready to snap forward against the striking plates, which would flip back on hinges, exposing the primed pans, and the sparks there would flash through the small touchholes to ignite the greater powder in the barrels and send the balls flying.

The door was unbolted and thrown open and men charged, muskets first, into the murk. The only light came from the most feeble of fires, a sad little fire of birch. It showed a body lying on the floor, a man in a coat of navy sage. It was Privet, wrapped with ropes, a stocking stuffed in his mouth. He kicked and made muffled sounds at the sight of Hentwidge and the rest.

There was no sign of Lady Swellbrook, her attendant Lily, or the man with a jar over his head. Within minutes it would be discovered that one of the boats was missing from the dock, and the Healer Mealton Skiggs would be found asleep, along with a watchman, in the circular stone guardhouse at the edge of the Tween.

An eventful day followed. Boats were sent off in pursuit of the escapees, who, for whatever reason, apparently kidnapped Lady Swellbrook and her hooded servant girl. Or so it was initially thought. But, when Hentwidge spoke at length with Mealton Skiggs, he learned otherwise.

After being surprised by the wounded man at the infirmary, Skiggs, at the prompting of a pistol, brought his abductor to the tower. The night guard Privet was missing from the small foyer, and the survivor from the mystery boat tapped on the door.

The door opened a crack and a hazy blue light showed from within the room. Skigg's captor stuck an ear to the opening and someone on the other side hissed something to him. The man nodded, withdrew, and the door shut, only to open a moment or two later. That tall, mysterious fellow with a jar on his head stood just beyond the threshold, and gestured for the armed man and Skiggs to come into Lady Swellbrook's room.

Privet was lying still on the floor. The healer was taken into a small room off the lady's chamber, where he was tightly wound with bedding, gagged, and wrapped around the head with lengths of cloth that prevented him hearing or seeing. Sufficiently restrained, Skiggs was made to lie on the bed.

Hentwidge asked, "You observed no distress on the part of the lady as regards the presence of her strange company, Healer Skiggs?"

"Indeed I did not. In fact, I rather took there to be something of a harmonious temperament among the whole."

"Which, if true, minds one to the possibility that her accompaniment aboard the stolen boat was something other than forced?"

Skiggs, gaunt, and tall even when sitting, nodded. "Yes, yes, I suppose, Mister Hentwidge. Think it! Perhaps that boat came to the fort for to rescue Lady Swellbrook."

Hentwidge sat back, peered over his spectacles and smiled gravely. "At this point, sir, I am like to think *anything*."

Each of the night guards reported the same thing to Hentwidge. A lovely young woman with loose golden hair had approached them at their posts. She was wearing a dark cloak and carrying a small cloth sack, and when she got near, she flung the cloak wide, revealing only her pallor and curves beneath.

"I must have a kiss," she said to each of them, coming close. Each time she brought a hand up and blew powder out of her palm, into the faces of the sentries. A deep, contented sleep was the result.

This was especially perplexing, as no woman meeting that description could be found within the fort, the only women on the premises being the two privilege girls, Lady Swellbrook and her attendant.

Capt. Finchberry, who was present during the interviews, wondered aloud who the woman could be.

"The lady's girl, Lily." Hentwidge offered coolly.

"I hardly think," Finchberry grumbled. "These men saw a fetching thing, not that beast."

"Do you know her to be a beast, Captain? Have you then seen beneath her hood?"

"Well, no, but..." Finchberry could not think of anything to bolster his point, and so dropped the subject and called in the next guard.

Privet sat down in front of the writing desk where Hentwidge was seated in an office at the rear tower. Finchberry hovered by one window, and Lt. Brittles by another.

"Seaman," Hentwidge said, "would you tell us, please, precisely what it is happened this morning?"

"I shall," Privet said glumly, "but shamed I am for having failed in my duties."

Finchberry rumbled, "There, Privet, you needn't suffer all that. There always be something to outmatch a fella, and that cunning lot outmatched the whole blasted fort."

Privet told how he was overtaken by Jar-Head, how he was bound and gagged, and how he watched helplessly as Lady Swellbrook and her servant accompanied the men of the mystery boat when they exited the room. They took Skiggs with them, a hostage, apparently. Privet recalled the rasp of the bolt on the other side of the door as they locked him in, and the sound of footsteps fading down the stairs.

A few days later Neelam Hentwidge and Heron Swellbrook sailed off from Fort Haddox. It was a warm spring morning and small birds lighted atop the front battlement of the fort to take pieces of bread that Privet had left for them. From that vantage point he watched the naval cutter as it floated out into the silver-gray waters of the Tween, and he smirked bitterly as Lady Swellbrook's nephew, who stood on the starboard side, whipped off his hat and bowed showily to the officers on the dock.

Privet, aside from this momentary amusement, was solemn. Having held history in high regard since a boy, he suffered no small amount of guilt for the account he had shared with the documetarian, Hentwidge. The facts were quite different from the story he had given, the version that the crown records would preserve as true.

A short while later Privet walked outside the walls of the fort and wandered along the rolling green of the ancient ramparts. He wondered if, perhaps, he should feel some measure of regret for his actions, and yet he did not.

It was he who had broken the silence there in Lady Swellbrook's room after Quill finished his tale and the three of them hovered in a long quiet moment.

"Should you wish to go," he had said, addressing Quill and the lady, "I would do nothing to stop you."

Privet did better than his word. He assisted in planning the escape, suggesting which vessel they might take from the dock, offering to accompany them to the boat as a hostage. Lady Swellbrook didn't care for the hostage idea, however, lest there be gunfire and Privet be injured.

The biggest problem would be stealing past the night watch. Lady Swellbrook had a thought: if only there were some way to dust the guards with her sleep-powder. She grinned and went into the adjacent chamber to wake Lily. When the women came into the chamber proper Lily had a look of horror on her face. She had never been seen unclothed by a man before, let alone a number of them, but, if it meant freedom for her lady, she would suffer the task.

Privet described where each of the guards needing sedation was located. The plotting was interrupted briefly when Whibb Penningbrook showed up with a captive Healer Skiggs. Privet quickly got down on the floor and pretended to be unconscious until Skiggs was brought in and stashed off in Lily's little room, his ears wrapped so that he could not hear the final details of the plan being discussed.

Daylight was not far off when Privet allowed himself to be tied by Penningbrook (Lady Swellbrook turned away, not bearing to see him trussed). Thanks and best wishes were exchanged before a stocking was put in Privet's mouth. Capt. Quill paused, saluted, and said, "Seaman Privet, you are a man of noble heart," before striding out the door.

Privet did a convincing job of squirming when Mealton Skiggs was walked out of the side room and to the foyer. Penningbrook was the last one out and he gave Privet a wink as he passed through the threshold. The main door was swinging shut, but before it could close, Lady Swellbrook hurried back in.

She knelt down beside Privet, gently rested a hand on his shoulder, and bent to kiss his cheek. "Goodbye, dear Privet," she said.

He had smiled at her with his eyes.

Privet thought of the kiss now, out alone on the ramparts, and absently reached to his cheek, where cool air off the Tween brushed against him. He had walked the whole encircling length of one of the earthworks and found himself standing over a small mound of brown earth. It was the spot where Lady Swellbrook had thought to bury the little gorse-wing, outside the smothering walls of the fort. Privet turned to gaze out over the restless gray water with its promise of distance. *Something lovely deserves a place less dreary than this*, he thought.

I need only tolerate four days more before I take leave of the Fort, then off I ride for Bloodingsham where I shall board the Bright Heron, *which from that port sails, and take my first tour of duty at sea.*

Privet, sitting on the edge of his bed up in the garret of the brick barracks building, had his portable writing desk on his lap and his goose quill in hand, writing to his family back in East Whittle.

He gave a rudimentary version of recent events at Haddox, and entirely avoided the matter of his involvement in Lady Swellbrook's escape, a crime he would swing for if a letter telling of such were ever opened in the wrong hands.

I hope this bit of scrawl finds all of good health and—

A voice from the next bunk intruded on Privet's line of thought. "So tell, Privy, do you pen a teary avowal of affection to your lady fugitive?"

Privet's features tightened, and while he did not look up, he could picture Fimble's big loutish face and frog-like smile.

"I wager you miss that soggy old cat of hers. Must it not have felt like giving the peg to your very mum?"

Privet set his writing desk aside and stood up. He might have looked menacing were it not for the bedgown and cap.

Fimble chuckled. "What now, Privy, are you to sing me a lullaby?"

Privet did not raise his voice to the man this time, instead he spoke matter-of-factly, "Fimble, if you insist upon goading me, I should be forced to call you to duel."

"Fart off, Privy. Finish your blasted letter to your hag and have out with your candle afore you find it in your arse."

If Privet were thirty and not eighteen, he might have possessed the restraint to resist the barbs. Fimble was well aware of the man's temper, and if one stopped to consider the situation, they would deem it unreasonable to think that Fimble would not be seeking to incite Privet's temper unless he was prepared to meet it.

"Yes, that's a top idea! I'll stick a candle in your arse and set you off like a rocket."

Adrenalin was starting to get the best of Privet now; he found himself taking a step toward Fimble's bed. Fimble, grinning broadly, scooted over to the edge of his mattress and patted the space beside him. "Here, Privy, perhaps you desire something other than a candle up your rump, as does your dear mum, I've no doubt."

Privet closed the distance between bunks. Fimble, moving as quickly as possible, reached under his bed and grabbed for the handle of the unsheathed sword waiting under him. But, when he went to yank the sword out from below, the handle caught on something. He had forgotten about the low wooden box with rope handles, one of which was now snaring his weapon.

"Blast!" Fimble cursed, and he gave the sword a tug, releasing it from the tether while tipping the box in the process.

Privet heard a thump, followed by a sound like wheels on wood, and looked down at his feet to see a hand grenade rolling out from under Fimble's bed. Both men froze in place, each with a look of realization. Privet suddenly *knew*, and Fimble could tell that Privet had figured something out.

"It was *you*," Privet snarled. "It was you threw the grenade under Lady Swellbrook."

Fimble rolled off his bed, half-stooped, and rose holding his sword.

"Here then, Privet, let's not have a fuss. I meant only to kill the birds to teach you a thing about threatening me."

The bunk, and now Fimble's outstretched blade, were the only things separating the men. Privet's sword was hanging on a peg on the wall on the far side of his own bed and he would have to expose his back to reach it. His spindly iron candle stand was closer.

Privet made a quick reverse step, and, without taking his eyes off his opponent, reached back with his left arm and grabbed the candle stand. Fimble's bulk flew, springing onto, then over, his mattress, falling at Privet, the straight blade of his sword swinging down.

Privet whipped the stand around in front of himself, the candle streaking, blowing out, spitting wax as the impact of Fimble's sword clanged against the long iron rod. The impact was enough to knock Privet backward off his feet; he fell across his mattress and rolled sharply to one side. Fimble's next slash found bedcovers rather than flesh, and Privet swung the stand, its tripod of gracefully curved legs catching the lout in the side of the head.

Fimble grunted and grimaced, collapsed against the wall. Regaining his balance, he staggered back a few paces, blinking and shaking his large head. "You little fart!" Fimble rumbled. The moment afforded Privet the chance to trade his candle stand for his sword, the sword that had belonged to Rye Blackbird.

Privet, incongruously clad in his long sleeping gown, moved to the aisle between the flanking rows of bunks and struck a swordsman's pose, his legs slightly bent, his fighting arm outstretched, the sword a steel extension of the arm, pointing like an accusatory finger. The slim blade was thirty inches long, double-edged, the grip smooth dark blackbirch wood from the Colonies. A knuckle bow curved from the shaft to the silver pommel, which bore a handsomely accomplished lion's head.

The other men in the garret were all awake at this point, sitting up in their beds or standing beside them. Privet's friend Willows was there among the rest and he took up his own sword, in case Privet required help.

Fimble clomped barefoot into the center aisle beneath the two slanting sides of the roof, and, taking a duelist's stance, faced Privet. He, too, was dressed for sleep, and how silly the men would have looked were it not for the deadly swords.

With Privet's candle extinguished there was little by way of illumination and not moon enough to show through the windows at either end of the long garret. One flame alone glowed, from a smoky rushlight belonging to a certain homesick fellow sitting on his bunk relying on memory to make a sketch of the love he had left back in New Crown.

The swordsmen regarded each other for what seemed a lengthier time than was actually the case, as reflected firelight smeared shimmering honey on the blades, making the cold steel look warm.

With a hiss of breath and a soft scuffing of slippers over boards, Privet lunged. His blade streaked, a slash of silver on the darkness. Stronger, but slower, Fimble made to dodge. He barked in pain and tottered backward, his arms flung out to his sides, like shuddering wings. His sword dropped to the floor.

"Goodnight, Fimble," a chilly Privet said.

"*Goodnight?*" Fimble had a confused look on his face. He felt like a horse had kicked him. He looked down, saw that a good portion of Privet's blade was buried in his chest.

"Yes, goodnight." Privet withdrew his sword and it was as if a bottle were uncorked. Both men's white sleeping gowns were spattered. Fimble wobbled, made a harsh rasping in his throat and then toppled stiffly backward. His weight thumped loudly and the men in the barracks chamber below mistook the sound for thunder.

Privet looked around the room at the others. No one moved or spoke. He bent down and took up the hem of Fimble's garment, wiping blood from the sword. The blade was honeyed by the glow of the rushlight.

3

The Bright Heron

Ghost Hasten at sea in the year of 1749. The wind and rain were full of phantoms, washing across the wobbling bulk of the merchant ship *Steady Rhino*. Not a man was above deck, in consideration of the occasion, and precautions had been taken, including the strategic placement of face-carved apples and swags of brittlethorn, for warding off damaging spirits.

The *Steady Rhino* was a relic of sorts, tall and stout so far as seafaring vessels go, and certainly not built for speed, though she could handle 500 tons of cargo. Both worn and rugged, she wore open balconies on the stern and boasted a high forecastle reminiscent of ships past. While amply armed, the *Steady Rhino* was never without her escort, the gun-sloop *Night Cannon*.

Painted a midnight black, the 16-cannon tri-master *Night Cannon* was known as a "spice-gun," one of those small, quick fighters hired by independent merchant companies to guard crafts and freight along perilous journeys to and from the Figwort Islands.

Both ships were anchored for the night, out in the wild dark waters of the Gantic. They were halfway between Fellengrey and the exotic locales to the east, some safe miles from Drowning Fangs, the terrible stone spires which, without any land masses proper for many a mile, stabbed up unexpectedly out of the deep water.

Huddled in a dim little cabin aboard the *Steady Rhino*, a black man and his nephew sat wide-eyed, listening to the wind, and the moans and cries that faded in and out of it. Neither the man, nor the ten-year-old, had ever been on a ship before, or so far from their warm green homeland. The damp chill of the air and the alien rocking of the monstrous floating thing surrounding them added to the terror of Ghost Hasten.

Mapdall, the boy, like every third child born to a woman on their home island Cabbadun, had the gift of truth-blood. Contact with a fresh drop of his blood would cause the truth to fly out of one's mouth faster than a finch after thistle seed, whether the subject desired to tell it or not. Thus, all the courts in all the major settlements of Fellengrey kept one of the Gifted on hand to assure that honest testimony was upheld. But, even a gift has its limitations, and the magic was only good until the bearer reached puberty.

Many from Cabbadun rented themselves out to the Fellengrey courts for a year or so, time enough to earn money, the compounded value of which would make them wealthy in their home country. Some reaped additional income hiring out to prove or disprove the fidelity of prosperous men's wives, and came in handy for seeing that captured pirates disclosed the whereabouts of hidden treasure.

The Vers-eh-senians, on the war-plagued continent proper, just east of Fellengrey, used the blood of the Gifted in aphrodisiac magic, though they had little access to the source, honoring a longstanding contract disallowing them from crossing into Fellengrey trade territory, which encompassed Cabbadun and the rest of the Figwort Islands.

Mapdall's uncle, Dallpul suddenly found himself having second thoughts about pursuing his fortune in the land of the "light people." The man, who was a slender forty-two and bald, was dressed in the strange layers of "lights'" clothing for warmth, rather than his thin native robe, and sat hugging himself on his bunk. He had raised Mapdall since the boy was five, when the child's parents and sisters died in an outbreak of "heat wart." Already he missed the warm night-scent of Cabbadun and hearing the comforting hum of harp spiders outside of their hut.

A bluish face blew past the window, bandages or seaweed trailing like a meteor's tail. This was followed by the sound of a woman's weeping, momentarily rivaling the sound of rain trotting over the panes. A strange glow hung in the sky, and Dallpul thought if light could be a dead thing it would look like that.

The only other illumination in the cabin came from a conical lantern of punched tin that hung from the low ceiling. This swayed as the ship rocked and the many spots of light it threw wavered drunkenly over the walls.

"Sing the monkey song, Uncle," young Mapdall said in his native tongue.

Uncle Dallpul smiled nervously and nodded. "Yes, the monkey song."

Something with a chalk-colored face scurried up the side of the ship and bit at the window, the haphazard teeth screeching against the glass.

Uncle Dallpul started to sing in his home language, his voice soft and quavering, "See the monkey in the tree, see how happy is his life. Small, beautiful monkey climbs to find the fruit that makes him strong."

Mapdall thought that he heard sounds in the tight hallway outside the cabin.

"See the monkey swing his tail, it is like a happy snake. Swing, beautiful monkey swing, above with all the laughing birds."

The door to the cabin banged open and uncle and nephew startled. A dark-clad figure stooped through the low entrance, cape dripping rain, pistol pointing. Its face was a hideous metallic thing with a long sharp nose and long sharp fangs. A second figure hovered behind the first, and a third behind the second, each wearing a frightful mask generally reserved for a fancy dress ball.

The first grabbed the boy by the wrist and yanked him off his bunk. "Come along," the man said gruffly.

Uncle Dallpul started up from his bunk and the man just outside the room rushed in, cloak flapping, something thin and silvery in his hand. He punched the dagger up under Dallpul's ribs and shoved him back onto the bunk. A dead woman with stringy wet hair obscuring half her face peered in the window and grinned.

"Uncle!" Mapdall cried as he was dragged out of the room, a hand clamping over his mouth.

The black man was gasping, his eyes wide. The assailant, who was wearing a bronze-colored boar mask, pulled the blade out, said, "Sorry, Uncle," and drove it in again.

Mapdall was ushered above deck into the howling night by the first and third of the masked figures. Several moments passed before they were joined by Boar-face, who had lingered in the cabin. The boy struggled as the man in the long-nosed mask urged him toward the edge of the deck. He pounded at the caped figure with his small fists, and, in flailing, unintentionally knocked the captor's mask from his face. The mask fell into the wind and flew off with the faces of the disembodied dead.

Mapdall took a good look at the face of the man and then a good look down the barrel of the man's pistol, which was only inches away.

"Over with you!" the man barked. The boy climbed over the side of the ship and descended on a rope.

The other two started down as well, until one noticed a dark shape shambling after them, arms waving through the rain, watery ghosts whipping by like ribbons.

"Farts! He lives yet," Boar-face bellowed against the rush of wind and surf. "Four times I stuck 'im and yet he lives!"

He pulled a long pistol from his belt as Uncle Dallpul staggered closer. Boar-face pulled back the cock—click—stretched his arm out and took aim. A finger squeezed the trigger and the cock holding its flint snapped against the hinged striking plate, knocking it back, exposing the open hollow of the little pan so that the spark would ignite the powder there. But it didn't. In all the rainy wind the powder had gotten damp.

"Double farts!"

The man pulled a second pistol, a compact version, from his belt. Uncle Dallpul was only steps away, eyes wide, his bloody hands groping the air. Click—Boar-face thumbed back the cock. This time the prime in the pan caught, flashing through the touchhole to the granules in the barrel. The pistol boomed like the thunder that the rain was lacking and smoke puffed white in the darkness.

Uncle Dallpul stopped, looked down at his chest, muttered something in a language that Boar-face did not understand, then toppled straight back like a man made of wood.

As was often the case, the morning following Ghost Hasten was clear and dry. The sun came up, a molten bubble, dying the Gantic copper, and the sky hung vast and brittle. Chill movements of air flew over the ocean, which, more enigmatic than sky, kept currents secreted beneath its surface. The invisible forces above the water filled the sails of the frigate *Bright Heron*.

Proven in battle, the *Bright Heron* was as handsome as she was dangerous, her plentiful canvas hugging the air and her graceful shape built for speed. Her elm keel was painted an autumnal rust from the gun ports down; the rest of the hull, but for stark black trim, was a warm mustard. Three proud masts, her 118-foot length and 28 nine-pounders made for a worthy guardian of the dangerous eastern spice route.

This morning she was about her patrol, watching for pirates, homebound, and Seaman Privet was up on the quarterdeck to witness the sunrise. Looking out upon the great water he thought of lines penned by the poet Nettles, lines about the sea:

The lover who needs not a heart, whose fangs sleep 'neath her kissing,
like air for wings to make ships fly, on surf above the missing.

Privet was glad for heading home. Not that he was eager to be off the sea, more that he found the Figwort Islands disagreeable for their soggy heat and buzzing pests. Nothing like a civilized place! Certainly they were an exciting locale so far as the eyes and taste buds were concerned: the tropical landmasses ringed with reefs of luminous coral the brooding red of figwort blooms, which delineated the islands mystically in the night; and the food, transformed through the use of spices, brought strange rainbows of flavor to the tongue. But Fellengrey, though clammy and gray in comparison, was infinitely more appealing than those season-less sun-cooked jungles.

Privet, in the muted green of his uniform coat, was enjoying the cool air on his face and the rhythmic dance of light and waves. A black tricorne sat on his head and a black cross-belt made a bold X across the gray of his tight metal chest plate. From these straps hung the sword that had belonged to Noll Slate, or, rather, Rye Blackbird, and a flintlock at either hip.

The identical pistols were handsome things with brass barrels and iron firelocks. They measured thirteen and three-quarters inches from end to end, the heavy barrels falling just short of eight. The trigger guards were silver, as were the bands that held the wooden rammers snug under their barrels. On each weapon the graceful curve of the walnut grip terminated in a silver cap with tapering ears, which was pleasingly decorated with leafy scrollwork.

Privet heard a shuffling sound and turned to see the captain approaching from behind. The man was wearing a dark green unbuttoned officer's jacket over his nightgown, along with a sleeping cap, and slippers. He was carrying a cup of tea.

Post Captain Spurry, at the age of sixty, was a tall willowy figure with a puff of graying red hair perched above his high forehead. He was handsome in an aristocratic sort of way, his long features clean-shaven, his pallor offsetting his stark green eyes. He was one of the oldest officers in the fleet, and was so enamored of the *Bright Heron* that he had turned down the chance to command more-important vessels.

Some few captains desired personal bodyguards; Spurry, having survived a mutiny in his younger years at sea, was one of these. Privet had seemed a good choice for a protector, considering the bravery exhibited in protecting Lady Swellbrook at Fort Haddox. Spurry took further comfort in knowing that Privet would not shy from killing, if need be, as proven by his altercation with a fellow at the fort. And, it ought be noted, Privet was a keen shot with a pistol, though he had never actually fired one at a person.

"Captain," Privet said with alarm, "should you not be at your rest, sir?"

Spurry grinned and, lifting his teacup, gestured at the ocean. "Would you deprive me this lovely sunrise, Privet?"

Privet lowered his tone. "I would not, sir, but your fever…"

Spurry had been sick since leaving the Figwort Islands, stricken with fever, his blood infused with jungle heat. The islands offered exotic illnesses as well as exotic spices.

Ignoring his guard's concern, he sipped his tea, gazed at the water, and spoke wistfully, "Ahhh, my two most favored liquids, tea and the Gantic."

The men shared the view for a moment and noticed something moving in the air. It was a moth, a good-sized pearl-colored example of its kind, a type used for carrying messages. This minded the captain of a story—he was always good for a story, Privet found—and began his recollection of the moth-eclipse of '29, when the pearly insect made a purposeful descent toward the ship.

The moth came close, ducking under the sails of the mainmast and, with rounded wings as wide as tea saucers, landed on the edge of the captain's cup.

"Well, hallo, my beauty," the man said in a rich voice.

A small scroll was tied around the fuzzy gray abdomen of the moth. Privet reached over and gently removed the paper.

"From a ship, you'll find," Capt. Spurry speculated, "there being no isle within manageable range of a carrier moth." Spurry blew a kiss at the moth and said, "Am I not right, my sweet?"

Privet opened the note and read it. His face grew serious and he nodded. "It is as you say, sir, from a ship. The missive penned by a Mister Sniddles, second mate of the mercantile *Steady Rhino*, anchored for Ghost Hasten within proximity of Drowning Fangs."

Privet held the scroll out for the officer to read, but the man shook his head. "I haven't my spectacles, dear boy, tell."

"There's been a murder aboard *Steady Rhino*, sir, and one of the Gifted gone missing."

Of those merchantmen traveling this trade route, some were working directly for the empire and some were independent entities, though prey to substantial taxation. Crimes at sea on either kind fell under the jurisdiction of the King's Navy.

Spurry held his free hand up to the moth so it would climb off his cup onto an offered finger. He took another sip of tea and said, "Well, then, we'd best turn about and have look at this situation."

Sailing on her new course, the *Bright Heron* made good time, for the wind was in her favor. The captain conceded to rest until the ship reached the *Steady Rhino* and Privet was up on deck with the first and second lieutenants, one of whom was cursing after soiling his boot in dung that one of the ship's goats had dropped.

The coxswain and his mate were busy with their navigation equipment, and among the first to notice a ship at full sail on the horizon. The lookout had already spotted it, and assumed it to be the merchant *Steady Rhino* until the distance between vessels grew smaller and he saw the red and black colors of a flag through his telescope.

The man called down from the foremast, "Vers-eh-sen Fortress!"

That had Privet and the rest by the ears. The Vers-eh-senians, old enemies of Fellengrey, presently upheld the peace treaty of 1735, but all were wondering why this great warship was violating trade territories by straying into these waters.

"Alert the captain," the first lieutenant told the second.

Capt. Spurry, upon hearing the news, ordered his lieutenants to ready their cannon crews, but cautioned that a hasty shot could lead to war, stressing, "Should one wild ball fly I shall have the balls of those who fired it."

By the time he was dressed and went above, the fortress (as the massive three-gundeck Vers-eh-sen warships were known) had sent up its bright yellow peace-flag and turned back on its course. This brought a great deal of relief to the crew of the *Bright Heron*, knowing full well that the fortress was a mightier vessel by far.

The lieutenants and midshipmen remained agitated, like chickens rushing back and forth, while Spurry, sharp in his uniform and steady as the masts, stood with one hand on his hip and the other on the handle of his sword.

"You best make off," the captain threatened, squinting out at the departing stern of the Vers-eh-sen ship.

The bulky *Steady Rhino* sat over its own quivering reflection in the deep water off Drowning Fangs. Her spice-gun *Night Cannon* was anchored close by, like a ship made out of shadow in her skin of black paint. Her sails, along with those of the larger vessel were furled, masts silhouetted against the late autumn sun.

Capt. Spurry's *Bright Heron* came alongside the old brown trade ship and a small group of navy men boarded. The party consisted of the captain himself (against the recommendations of his ship's healer), first Lieutenant Fippers, the captain's clerk, Pepperpinch, and Spurry's bodyguard, Privet.

They were greeted by a captain, a man in his mid-fifties, who was round in the middle, with short legs and a heavy-looking head. Bald on top, his gray hair swept down across his ears and the back of his neck. His greatcoat, which fell past the knees, was black, as were the frock and waistcoat beneath, and the matching breeches. A sword hung from the shoulder-belt that crossed his chest and two pistols, one a long black thing, were tucked under the belt that wrapped his waist. Navy men considered this method of carrying a pistol somewhat uncouth.

Bows were exchanged and the man introduced himself as Captain Bramble Oats, of the gun-sloop *Night Cannon*. Capt. Spurry had expected this to be the commandant of the *Steady Rhino*, who, as it turns out, was presently in his cabin.

Captain Quince Oats was singing *The Pretty Maid of Dunklilly* to Cicely, this being her favorite song. Cicely was a rat. Soft and gray and old, the rat, whose health was failing, rested in a circular nest of bedcovers on the bunk beside the man. Her small black eyes were half-closed, but her head raised slightly at the sound of the song.

Aside from a twin brother, Cicely was the captain's oldest and closest companion. Up until recently she had been a fixture on his shoulder, or as a small pointed head poking from a coat pocket.

When the song was finished the rodent put her head back down. Her whiskers twitched and her breath seemed an effort. With a hand that was gentle for its size, the captain stroked Cicely's back. How bony she had become!

Quince spoke softly, "Will you not stay with me, small one? So much have we seen, you and I, so many waves shared, and sunlight and storm."

Cicely wiggled her nose and lifted her head to look at the door just before it sounded with a knock.

Quince made a disagreeable sound. He took his time getting up and going to the door. "Yes?" he said, opening it.

The ship's second mate, Sniddles, stood outside with his hat held to his chest. "Begging your pardon, sir," he said in his high grating voice, "but the navy men have just now arrived."

Quince was dour. "Very good. I'll be but a moment."

The skinny second mate went off and the captain shut the door. He took his greatcoat from a peg on the wall and gazed at his little friend. He hoped that she would hold out until he returned, hating the thought of Cicely dying all alone.

The air was calm and cool as it moved in from the north, the tacit turning of the seasons hardly forceful enough to ruffle a flag. Soon there would be snow, this far from the sodden heat of the Figwort Islands, and rearing gales with armies of waves.

Capt. Spurry was glad for the chill against his brow. The fever had progressed to the point where his dizziness suggested more rocking than the hulking *Steady Rhino* actually provided. He held to one of the scratchy ropes that angled up to support the mainmast and smiled pleasantly as the spice ship's second mate appeared with a man in a cranberry-colored greatcoat and pearl-white silk waistcoat. The man's lacy cravat spilled down like ocean foam. This fellow, stout with stubby legs, had no more hair on top than did his twin, who was the captain of the *Night Cannon*.

After all the bowing and introductions, Capt. Spurry got right to it. He asked the *Steady Rhino's* commandant to relay what had happened the night before. Spurry's clerk jotted down the testimony.

"I was made awake by shots in the night," Quince Oats explained in his heavy voice, "and found wounded upon the deck the grown Cabbadunian. The child was lacking their cabin."

Here the second mate, thin with a pointy face, interjected enthusiastically, "The lad's uncle lingered long enough to say there be three what took the boy. He said also they stole the boy over side."

"Did he recognize the assailants?" Spurry asked, "or say nothing of their look?"

"They bore masks," the second said, pleased with himself for having information to offer to the esteemed navy man.

Spurry nodded pensively. "No witness other than the victim, then?"

Oats managed to reply before Sniddles, "I fear not. All were below, it being Ghost Hasten."

"Of course. Well, then, might we have look at the poor fellow?"

Oats sighed, wishing this business was behind him so that he could get back to Cicely.

A bloody bundle lay on the bunk in a snug cabin at the rear of the ship. Privet peeked in from the suffocating little passage beyond as Capt. Quince Oats peeled back several layers of the shroud, revealing the tragic mess within.

"They did him good enough," Spurry remarked with a frown.

The wiry second mate squeezed past Privet and poked his head in, excitedly noting, "Made a pincushion of the poor savage, they did!"

Oats gave the young man a shriveling look. "Have you not duties to call you elsewhere, Sniddles?"

Sniddles recoiled sharply.

Spurry nodded to Oats, who closed the wrap back over the black man's face.

"Thank you, Captain," Spurry said.

The party returned to the waist of the ship, outside the stern-facing windows of the raised forecastle. It was good to be up in the air again, removed from the gory stench of the corpse's cabin. Privet gazed over at the sleek black gun-sloop *Night Cannon*, studying those men who were about the topdeck. They looked to be ruffians, by his estimation, a raggedy lot, all heavy with pistols and blades.

Spurry dabbed his forehead with a handkerchief. Oats, who stood with his brother, who was all in black, showed earnest concern on his face. "Are you well, Captain Spurry?"

"Quite well, thank you. A touch of fever is all."

Spurry collected himself as Privet moved faithfully to his side, as if to guard him from internal threat as well as external.

Even sickly, the navy officer presented a distinguished appearance, tall and lean in his tailed green coat with its bright gold buttons. His bicorne pointed fore and aft.

Capt. Spurry asked to be shown where the dying man had been found and challenged his own dizziness by peering over the side of the ship to see if there were any markings of particular interest on the hull, something that might tell him about how the Cabbadunian boy was stolen. No evidence presented itself. Afterward, he grabbed onto Privet's arm to steady himself, and took a deep breath.

"I do rather fancy the scent of a spice ship," Spurry admitted with a little smile.

The trader *Steady Rhino* smelled of tar and spices, her hold heavy with barrels of sugar, molasses, nutmegs, cloves, tobacco and winter spice from Mabbaduni and Cabbadun. In addition, there were blaze-moths, harp nuts, and coffee from Mindacabba, the three major masses of the Figwort Islands group represented by the cargo.

Quince Oats's brother, Bramble, captain of the *Night Cannon*, had not said very much, but he had observed the investigation with a keen eye. Unlike his sibling, who was unarmed, Bramble wore sword and pistols, one of the flintlocks bearing a silvery barrel and firelock, which stood out starkly against the smooth dark wood of blackbirch.

Capt. Spurry, in spite of his present lightheadedness, liked to pace when he did his thinking. He did this now for several moments, squinting, hands behind his back. When he stopped, he addressed the twin captains, who stood side by side.

"Gentlemen," Spurry said, "the lad has been taken for profit."

The *Bright Heron's* first lieutenant, Fippers, and Pepperpinch, the clerk, who had been chatting amongst themselves, fell silent. They cast admiring eyes on their commander, both as loyal as can be.

"He is one of the Gifted, yes?" Spurry asked.

"He is," Quince Oats returned.

Spurry continued, "Well, then! They meant not to *slay* the boy, it is clear, or we would have two bodies and two shrouds in that sad little cabin."

The other captains nodded.

"No, no. He was taken to some purpose, which, you will find, has all to do with his blood. His captors meant to deliver him to some party aboard a Vers-eh-sen fortress, for a handsome sum, a sum worth risking their very breath to gain, venturing out and about at Ghost Hasten. But, what better time for mischief of the like, when all others were like to be below in safekeeping?"

"Vers-eh-sen?" the *Night Cannon's* captain exclaimed.

Sniddles popped up behind the twin brothers and echoed shrilly, *"Vers-eh-sen!"*

"Indeed, for this very morn we spied such a ship, in the business of trespassing Empire waters."

Quince Oats scowled. "Are you quite certain, Captain Spurry? A much reckless venture it would be, the Vers-eh-sen making through our territory."

Spurry grinned, "Ahh, but the Vers-eh-senians are extraordinarily fond of their amorous spells, to which the Gifteds' blood is applied, Captain Oats. Few things carry so high a value to their kind. At any rate, the ship was a fortress, without mistake, and were it not for their having a sight of the *Bright Heron*, it might this very moment be taking possession of the lad."

Capt. Bramble Oats, without thinking, dropped his hand to the grip of his sword.

Privet, familiar with his superior's manner, knew that Spurry was working toward something. His estimation was correct.

"I should like to have a look about the *Night Cannon*, Captain Oats, with your permission," Spurry said firmly.

Bramble Oats's face tensed. "I see no cause to search the *Night Cannon*, if I may say, Captain. Is it not clear that the child was hastened away on some smaller craft of unknown origin?"

Spurry stood steady. "I'm not at all sure that is the case, good man. The boy's uncle said only that the boy was taken over side. To where, we know not. The *Night Cannon* would make for the most reasonable destination." Bramble Oats's resistance made Spurry all the more eager to look over the *Night Cannon*.

Oats was becoming agitated, angry, "My crew would be a respectable lot, sir, and there be not one aboard so foolhardy as to risk such a thing as has been done; you may depend upon it."

Spurry took a step forward. "Taking a *small* craft out upon the Ghost Hasten waters would be a fool thing, Captain Oats, more foolish than, say, taking the boy from one ship to that just by its side." Turning to his team, Spurry gave the order, "Mister Fippers, send to the *Bright Heron* for twenty musketeers. We search the spice-gun."

Bramble Oats narrowed his eyes and hissed just loud enough for his twin to hear, *"Bastard."*

Twenty armed men in sage-green navy jackets, worn open over shiny chest plates, and wearing helmets like bowls with lamb chop cheek-guards, boarded the *Night Cannon* along with Capt. Spurry and the rest. Five groups of four musketeers spread out to search the black-hulled protector.

They went down below, with the cold eyes of the crew upon them, kicking through chicken feathers in the manger and sawdust in the carpenter's shop. They visited the galley with its big black stove, and the captain's stores, crammed with casks of island spices, a stock of coffee beans and a barrel of brandywine. They thumped up and down ladders and stairs, ducked low beams in passages where the only light was provided by lanterns. Half-seen rats—distant kin of Cicely, perhaps—darted underfoot.

The men scrutinized the shot locker, and storage compartments that were home to flour or wood, and others containing sacks of biscuits and cheese, or barrels of drinking water. One room was committed to powder and weapons—plenty of weapons.

There was nothing in the long gunroom (with its heavy iron cannons resting on their yellow garrison carriages) to suggest the presence of the missing Cabbadunian boy. Boots were traded for soft felt slippers when two of the *Steady Rhino's* musketmen checked the magazine, where the slightest static spark could set off the stacks of tubular flannel-skinned powder charges and blow the ship apart.

Especially keen scrutiny was given to the main hold, where provisions were tightly packed in a low-ceilinged darkness. The seamen tapped on each container they could access, listening for cries from within, or a telling hollowness. They went so far as to open some barrels and crates, but found nothing out of the ordinary.

One team of men focused their attention on the sleeping cabins and the healer's rooms. Capt. Bramble Oats's was the nicest of the lot, the walls decked with raised paneling and painted a deep, rich blue that was almost a green. He had books and wine and a game of conquest pegs secured there to pass the time, and a hammock as well as a built-in bunk, the hammock for those nights when the sea was restless. When the mattress was removed, the top part of the bunk was found to be hinged, and the men, lifting this, found a storage compartment within, and several items there.

Coinage was stashed, and a jar of winter spice, a powder named for its snowy color (certainly not named for the hot humid Figwort Islands where it originated), which came from ground nuts and had a taste somewhat reminiscent of apricot.

There was something else as well, secreted in a round biscuit box.

"What have you there?" one man asked another.

The vessel contained a large quantity of small dead beetles. They were a metallic blue, and glinted in the light of the windows.

"Blue brews," one of the other men offered, calling them by their slang name and not the long unpronounceable word used by the natives of the islands.

The outer carapace of the insects, when boiled soft and distilled with wormwood, made for a strange euphoria-inducing concoction known as "blue giddy," a substance popular with poets and some artists, and the spoiled, wealthy sons of dukes. It was against kingdom law to smuggle the blue brews from their homeland.

The lead man of the team took one of the beetles to show to Capt. Spurry, who, with his accompanying staff, and the captain of the gun-sloop, was up on the quarterdeck. The musketeer discreetly showed the bug to Spurry, who nodded and quietly noted, "Is it no surprise, under the circumstances, that our good Captain Oats so resisted our exploring of his craft?"

"I reckon not, sir," the man said.

"And the boy, no hair of him as yet?"

"I fear not, sir."

"Very good, Mister Bittergrove."

The musketeer was sent to rejoin his fellows, and Spurry grabbed Privet by the sleeve and tugged him close enough to whisper. "Bramble Oats may just find himself in chains before the fall of evening, my lad."

When all of the ship had been thoroughly gone over the five teams of men reported back. The day was dimming and Capt. Spurry looked more pale than usual, and frequently dabbed at his head. No sign of young Mapdall, the Cabbadunian boy, had been found. Still, Capt. Spurry had a plan.

Three ships hovered near to each other on a calm, dimming Gantic. The water appeared to deepen as the sun moved closer to the horizon and a mysterious azure, starting in the east, began to spread across more and more of the sky. The light made an eerie thing of the gun-sloop's figurehead—a bare-breasted woman with a cannon poking out of her mouth like an incredible tongue. A hushed sloshing of inconsequential waves against the hulls at the waterline could be heard.

The crew of the *Night Cannon* was gathered on the topdeck at the request of Capt. Spurry, the lot of them snared in the intricate shadows of the rigging. This assemblage consisted of the sailors, the fighters, the cabin boys, the shabby toothless privilege girl who doubled as the cook, even the boatswain and helmsman. They were a hard-looking bunch overall, their faces and clothes worn by long voyages at sea, a good many of them (festooned with scars and tattoos) being veterans of bloody exchanges with pirate vessels. They crowded the top of the ship, forming two lines, one portside, one along the starboard, and scowled mutually at the navy commandant and his troops. Capt. Bramble Oats was spared the indignity of scrutiny out of respect, and allowed to stand apart, alongside the navy men.

The twenty musketeers from the *Bright Heron* were positioned up on the quarterdeck. They were accompanied by Lt. Fippers, and had orders not to fire without his word. Capt. Spurry, tall in his dark green jacket, with Privet at his side, addressed those present through the metal funnel of a speaking trumpet. "The Cabbadunian child has here been discovered, aboard the *Night Cannon*," he announced.

Murmurs of surprise came from the crew.

Capt. Spurry held up a drinking glass half-full of red liquid. "I hold in hand the blood of the Gifted. A single drop upon any one of you would elicit the truth. I shall proceed to test all, lest those responsible for the murder of the Cabbadunian man, and the stealing of the lad, step forward to own their crimes."

One of the crewmen, while not aware that the blood in the glass actually came from a chicken, was insightful enough to note, "It is a trick!"

Spurry swung to face the fellow. He walked briskly to where the defiant man stood in the starboard line. "You shall be first," Spurry said with a chill grin.

The captain dabbed a finger into the blood and slowly raised it to the man's face. The man squinted, as if the substance would burn, and Spurry smudged red on a stubbly cheek.

"Tell, seaman," Spurry said, "Did you in any way participate in the murder of the Cabbadunian man aboard the ship *Steady Rhino*?"

The man seemed to hold his breath for a moment, then with a shudder, he spat, "I did not!"

Spurry took a step back and smiled. "He tells the truth," he proclaimed.

At this point Privet observed a certain tension rising into the faces of the rest. Trick or not, they could not tell, but the force of suggestion was in the navy captain's favor. Much as the crew wanted to believe that Spurry was about some trickery, apprehension urged them to take the man's words as true, for one never knew what secrets might fly out at the prompting of truth-blood.

Spurry wheeled flamboyantly and strode back to the start of the line. A young fighting man stood ready. The tattooed head of a crow peaked out across his upper chest where the top of his shirt was open. The captain recited his question and touched the man's cheek with blood.

"No, sir, I did not," was the reply, and so Spurry, satisfied with the man's sincerity, moved on to the next.

The officer continued down the entire row of men, gaining no admissions, then crossed portside, moving his wrist so that the blood swiveled like brandywine in its glass.

The privilege girl, in her dingy skirts and apron, her dark hair windy, though there was no wind, stood with what sad little pride she could muster.

"Good woman," Spurry started.

Privet, hovering close to his ward, was keeping a subtle watch over the others in line. He noticed that a cabin boy, several bodies down, was staring ahead with wide eyes and sweating about his brow.

"Did you in any way participate in the killing of the Cabbadunian man aboard the ship *Steady Rhino*?" Spurry asked as he dabbed blood on her cheek.

The privilege girl, who was really too old to be accurately called a *girl*, replied, "I did not, though I wisht I could say otherwise, for I hates the Cabbaduns, all!" With that she laughed like a braying mule.

The captain took a half-step back and blinked. "Thank you, miss," he said.

Privet kept an eye on the slender cabin boy, whose jacket and breeches were stained with tea and tar, his head terminating in a nest of brown hair that seemed too big for his body. The boy was trembling. Privet gently rested a palm on the handle of one of his pistols.

"Did you in any way participate in the murder of the Cabbadunian man aboard the ship *Steady Rhino*?" Spurry asked the slouching grizzled man just ahead of the lad.

The cabin boy, out of turn, lurched forward, tears gushing suddenly from his eyes, as he cried, "I am guilty! I am guilty!"

Spurry turned, clamped a hand onto the boy's shoulder, and held him steady, "Here now, young man, tell."

"I took the boy, sir, but I lifted no hand against the boy's uncle. I killed no one, sir, I swear it!"

Down toward the end of the line, a man with long dark hair and a pointy beard, wearing a heavy brown cape against the autumn air, broke from line and yanked a pistol from his belt. In that moment, Privet thought, *should have collected their weapons!*

"Fool!" the man bellowed at the confessing cabin boy, and he grabbed the nearest crewmate, a young sailor, by the jacket, stabbing the muzzle of the weapon under the fellow's chin. The armed man positioned the startled chap in front, to serve as a living shield.

Twenty musketeers gave the bearded man their full attention, aiming loaded "longs" his way. Privet pushed immediately in front of Capt. Spurry and filled his hands with pistol grips. He tugged both from their holsters and tipped them so that their barrels briefly faced the sky while his thumbs clicked back the S-shaped cocks.

Privet, Spurry and the guilty cabin boy were standing close to the companionway of the quarterdeck and the bearded man was at the prow. He barked instructions,

"I'll have readied the captain's gig, with provisions, and powder and shot and "longs," or Willowton here should gain a blowhole."

The loud report of a musket sounded and the dark-haired man shrieked, his gun hand breaking in a burst of red. His pistol handle was smashed as well and the weapon dropped to the deck as the man's captive ducked away. Across a length of water, standing on the forecastle of the neighboring *Steady Rhino*, Capt. Quince Oats lowered his smoking musket.

The wounded man staggered back, cursing, and reached for a dagger that hung from his belt. Lt. Fippers was about to give his musket-men the order to fire, when Privet thrust his right arm out and discharged his pistol, a funnel of smoke leaping from the muzzle as the weapon's thunder crashed against his ears. The bearded man jolted back, a look of surprise on his face as an arterial starfish opened wide red arms across his chest. The man sagged to his knees, released a terrible rasping sound, then flopped forward with a thud.

The air was dark and rank down in the manger where the cabin boy, Bellin Bramish, lead some of the naval men. Goats perked up when the group ducked into the room, and pushed against the enclosing rails with their strange and eager eyes. The cows in their stalls, by contrast, registered little interest, and went about chewing. Capt. Spurry petted the head of a sheep as the cabin boy pointed to a spot on the floor.

"There," Bellin said. "He be under there, sir."

Spurry nodded to one of his musketeers. The man, with weapon slung over one shoulder, entered the sheep's pen (the sheep had been kept with the goats at one time, but the goats were not above injuring, or even killing, the sheep). He used his boot to brush aside a mantel of hay, revealing an inconspicuous opening covered by loose boards. The man bent and lifted two wide planks and Privet shone a lantern down into the confining darkness.

A young black boy was on his side atop a soiled matt of hay, his arms and legs roped, a cloth gag wound around his head. Unaccustomed to the glare of the lantern, he could not make out the figures looming above him. He shuddered, thinking these were the men who killed his uncle, now coming for him.

Spurry stepped nearer the hidden compartment and called down, "Not to worry, good woman. I would be Captain Spurry of the frigate *Bright Heron,* here for to rescue you."

Privet turned to his superior, "It would seem the Cabbadunian boy, sir, not, in fact, a woman."

Spurry blinked and bent to get a better look. "Ahh, so it is. Well, then, let's have him up from that reeking pit."

While Mapdall was being cleaned up and dressed in fresh clothing, and given something to eat from the galley, Capt. Spurry and Bramble Oats were in the latter's dining cabin at a heavy table, which was fastened to the floor. There were plenty of lit candles and there was plenty of tea, and seated with them was the cabin boy Bellin, who, in his nervousness and remorse, proved eager to vent the anxiety of his crime through admission. A weight of guilt lifted from him as he described the particulars, at least those particulars that he knew enough to tell.

The faithful Privet exhibited his best posture, hands behind his back, looking forward, as he stood at the back of his captain's chair. Two rigid musketeers were present as well. The clerk, Pepperpinch, busy with his quill, logged the testimony as it came.

Capt. Bramble Oats maintained that he knew nothing of the misdeeds and claimed earnest surprise at finding that members of his crew were culpable, and that the Cabbadunian boy had been stashed on his dear *Night Cannon.* Spurry secretly decided it best to have Oats's integrity proven with a dab of truth-blood, but was hoping to solve the mystery without resorting to such an extreme. There was a certain brotherhood among sea captains that Spurry was hesitant to violate.

Capt. Spurry took a sip of tea then studied the youth sitting opposite. "How is it you came to partake of this dreadful plot, being a promising young buck as yourself?"

"Mister Cumber, sir, came to win me with his talk of great riches assured us were we to deliver the Cabbadun to the Vers-eh-sen ship." Cumber was the man Privet had killed, the one who had sported a mask with a boar's face, according to Bellin. It was Cumber who had stabbed and shot Dallpul, the black boy's uncle.

Spurry nodded. "And the other fellow, who might he be?"

The boy, his pale hands clenched on the table, shook his head. "I know not, sir, for he bore always a mask as I knew him, a frightful thing with long nose and fangs, and I made acquaintance of him only upon the *Steady Rhino*. But, I took it the proposal to sell the Cabbadun to the Vers-eh-senians was of *his* making, and not a notion of Mister Cumber's."

"Hmm." Spurry sat forward, staring back at the strange goat's eye peering up at him from the steam and beige of his tea. He poked a spoon into the liquid and the eye blinked away. *A small clump of old milk, and nothing more.*

It had been noted that the massive Vers-eh-sen fortress did not show as planned, their progress hindered perhaps by the storm and strange forces of Ghost Hasten. When they failed to arrive, the kidnappers stashed Mapdall in the manger. The Vers-eh-sen vessel was, no doubt, on its course to rendezvous, belatedly, when the *Bright Heron* came upon it and scared it off, so to speak.

The cabin boy had nothing more to offer, but he asked, "Am I to hang, sir?"

Spurry's only reply was a sad little sigh.

Capt. Quince Oats sat on the bunk in his chamber gently stroking Cicely's back with one finger until she took her last breath and went silent. He fashioned a small shroud out of a length of cloth and sewed it shut before carrying her to the topdeck in his pocket one last time.

Sunset colors were on the western water and darkness ruled the east. The man walked soberly to the stern of the *Steady Rhino*, whispered a farewell, and gave his small friend to the sea.

He knew that Capt. Spurry, over on the *Night Cannon*, wished to speak with him about what to do with the Cabbadunian boy, but Quince wanted only to lay in his cabin and forget things. While resenting the intrusion on his grief, he gathered himself and swung over to the smaller vessel.

Apparently the questioning of the cabin boy, Bellin, had been completed, for when Quince, in his cranberry-colored coat, arrived on scene, one of the navy's musketeers was bringing the young prisoner up from Bramble's dining cabin.

Quince found himself walking behind Lt. Fippers, who was escorting the black boy toward the rear of the ship for his turn at being questioned. Capt. Spurry and Quince's twin brother, Bramble, were taking some air and a view of the dissipating sunset. Privet was with them. They turned when they heard Fippers and the child approaching. That was when Mapdall got a look at Bramble Oats's face.

Mapdall had seen those features before, when up on the deck of the *Steady Rhino*, while flailing to get away from the kidnappers. The mask, with its awful long nose and awful long teeth, had blown off in the Ghost Hasten wind and Mapdall had gotten a clear view of what was behind it.

"He bad man! He bad man!" Mapdall cried, pointing.

Bramble Oats's face registered surprise, and the boy dashed at him so suddenly that he barely had time to react. Mapdall moved in close and started tugging on one of the pistols at the captain's waist. The weapon snagged in the belt, and while Oats made to move his bulk, and raised a big fist to strike, the boy got the cocking hammer back and fired, pointblank.

The dimness of the hour and the black of Bramble's clothes subdued the color of his blood, but a good deal of it came out, and he toppled back, gasping, before the others could rush to grab the young Cabbadunian.

"He bad man, he bad man!" Mapdall called over and over.

Lt. Fippers got a hold of the boy from behind and snatched the pistol out of his hand (not that it was much of a danger now, with its ball discharged). He pulled the squirming boy back as Spurry and Privet bent over Bramble Oats, who, having sprawled on the planks, went from wheezing to gurgling.

"My brother!" Quince Oats roared.

The stocky figure flew swiftly for his size and fell on the skinny Mapdall like a wave. Fippers was pushed aside. A large hand grabbed the boy by the throat and a large fist thumped hard against his face. The boy collapsed on the deck like a bag of sticks.

"Bastard!" Quince cursed, and he squatted down and punched Mapdall again, even though the child was flat on his back, stunned. Blood from the boy's broken nose spattered the captain's big hand. Quince drew his arm back to strike again, but stopped. His fist hovered in the air, cocked back, with specks of blood on it. Truth-blood on his hand.

Capt. Quince Oats stood up stiffly, staring ahead as if dazed, and his arms drooped at his side.

"I had the boy stolen," the man said like one talking in his sleep, *"I had his uncle killed."*

All eyes and ears turned to Capt. Oats.

"I had the boy stolen," he repeated. *"I had his uncle killed."*

Mapdall, along with the prisoners, Quince Oats and Bellin Bramish, returned to the *Bright Heron* with the navy personnel. Oats admitted having contrived the plot to sell the young Cabbadunian to the captain of the Vers-eh-sen ship and told how he had recruited Cumber, who was known to be a smuggler, and with whom he had sailed in the past. Cumber, Oats explained, had solicited the aid of the cabin boy, Bellin. The *Steady Rhino's* captain also noted that he had *not* ordered Sniddles to pen the note that was sent out on a messenger moth. Sniddles had taken it upon himself to contact navy authorities, thinking that Quince Oats would approve of his taking the initiative. How ironic! The captives were put in the brig, and the boy was made comfortable.

Spurry, reposing in his handsomely furnished day cabin, informed his top officers that the *Bright Heron* would change course come morning and head back to the Figwort Islands to return Mapdall and the body of his dead uncle home. The murdered man's corpse had been put in a barrel of brandywine to preserve it. The *Steady Rhino* was free to return to Fellengrey with its cargo; the *Night Cannon* was free to go as well.

"What of the boy?" Lt. Fippers asked. "An innocent man has died at his hand."

"A tragic mistake. He mistook one twin for the other, as would I in his place. No blame shall upon him lay. The child returns home."

"As you wish, Captain."

Later, while heading for his bunk, Privet passed the cabin where the Cabbadunian boy had been put up (the privilege girl having been temporarily displaced to occasion Mapdall's comfort). A soft, plaintive singing could be heard through the door. While Privet had learned very little of the Cabbadun language, he knew enough words to determine that Mapdall was singing something about a monkey.

Strange dreams followed Capt. Spurry into his sleep. They began, quietly enough, while he sat updating his log by candlelight. He was drained following the day's events, more sleepy than he cared to admit. His extremities felt as if they were immersed in snow, while his head was full of tropical heat, a cruel reminder of the sweltering jungles back at the Figwort Islands. At one point he glanced up from his writing and the fever showed him a vision of his mother. She was lovely with her long red hair and a gently colored gown. She was standing by the banks of the Kipping, in the town where he was born. A fistful of hawks' legs with bloody talons stuck up from her grip like a posy of dripping flowers. Spurry had put down his quill and rubbed at his eyes.

Too tired to finish with his log, Spurry retired to his sleeping cabin. He fell asleep right away, and dreamed of black octopuses shooting across the autumn sky like meteors, and sheep marching along a rural road singing *The Fighting Ship's Lament.* He dreamed of a towering city of stone, and a great monster that rose up out of the sea breathing fire from its many mouths.

It was morning and Lt. Fippers had command of the ship. Capt. Spurry remained in his bunk at the healer's insistence, with Privet sitting at his side. The day was bright and cool and the water, following the bronze of sunrise, was a bottomless blue. A good wind was in the sails and waves threw themselves at the *Bright Heron's* hull, breaking into foamy white.

Up on the top deck, Fippers was by the wheel, conversing with the helmsman who was steering the vessel back toward the Figwort Islands, when a lookout called down from the fighting top platform of the foremast.

"Messenger moth comes portside," the lookout reported.

The man had a look through his telescope and noted the sinuous red ribbon trailing from the large insect. He shouted down again, "Distress tail!"

Lt. Fippers cut short his chat and moved swiftly across the quarterdeck and the waist, onto the forecastle where the crooked black chimney of the galley stove below poked up through the planking like a metal harbor seal.

Fippers unfolded his own telescope, squinting into a fine mist of spray that rode the wind washing up over the ship, the wind that flung his black cape behind him and made the sides of his unbuttoned jacket flutter. He spotted the moth and the long, thin, telltale ribbon. The moth came closer and closer, and finally—as if it could tell that he was the officer in charge—landed on the lieutenant's wrist.

The red ribbon was a universal symbol of distress shared by all the civilized seafaring countries. The note fastened to the moth's leg was encircled by a smaller round band of red that bore a minute image of a hawk holding a sword by the blade. This was the sign of the Vers-eh-sen. Fippers shuddered.

Capt. Spurry was sitting up in his bunk nursing a cup of tea while an anxious Lt. Fippers stood nearby, his hands trembling as he showed his superior the distress note.

Spurry said, "I haven't my spectacles, Fippers, tell."

"The fortress *Oak Cloud,* sir, according to the note, suffered a wave of singular might, and found herself cast among the spires of Drowning Fangs. The ship remains stranded, sir, and takes water, with hundreds of lives under threat."

Spurry was pensive for a moment. It was not unheard of for Vers-eh-sen ships and Fellengrey ships to come to each other's rescue (following the treaty of

1735). Written laws of the sea, and those unspoken, were firm against the crime of baiting a ship with a false claim of distress, but Spurry, who had been to war against the Vers-eh-sen, could only muster so much trust in their regard. His orders reflected this.

"Lieutenant Fippers, have all cannon crew at ready, and all fighters as well. We shall answer this call for help, but heed to caution, lest the Vers-eh-sen be about some deception."

"Yes, Captain, as you wish, sir," Fippers said. He saluted sharply and rushed from the cabin.

Privet stood solemnly, like the toy soldier carved of wood that he had played with as a boy.

Spurry slurped down the rest of his tea, then struggled up from his bed; his red hair was wild following a night of tossing and turning. With a wry grin he said, "Privet, dear lad, fetch this old warrior his sword."

The autumn-colored *Bright Heron* cut swiftly through the waves, its 118-foot length and 34-foot width impressive enough in the realm of men, but a relative speck on the great expanse of the Gantic. There were no gulls to hint at landmasses, no distant ports with chimneys streaming, nothing but a thin line of white haze along the horizon. In time, vague, dark, varyingly sized shapes poked up from this line where the world seemingly ended. These shapes grew and took rigid form as the frigate approached. They were massive spearheads of black stone, terrible teeth reaching up from the ocean's floor, and snared in their bite was a brown ship of imposing proportions, its red distress flag rippling above.

"It seems not a trick," Lt. Fippers, who had the watch, said to a couple of midshipmen who were hovering on the quarterdeck, looking with awe at the scene before them. The damage and peril the Vers-eh-sen ship was experiencing seemed all too real to be a mere ploy to facilitate an ambush.

The *Oak Cloud* was wedged between two of the upright formations. She was tilted to the portside, her tall masts dwarfed by the highest of the fangs, her keel impaled on a shorter fang's tip. Seen through a spy-glass, the occupants on deck appeared small—upright ants, scurrying about.

There was a rush of activity on the *Bright Heron* as well. Men were dashing about; powder-boys were running cartridges up from the magazines, cannon crews readied their weapons. Each of the twenty-eight brass guns contained a nine-pound ball of round shot. Two portable swivel guns, themselves small cannons, were positioned at the fore, fitted to the gunwale, and loaded. Marksmen took up strategic positions, and a boarding party armed themselves with muskets and swords, and pistols and fighting axes. All this as a drumming boy riled the air.

Topmen were in the rigging; they scurried up ratlines like spiders in their webs, furling sails, leaving in place only those needed for combat, should the situation come to blows.

Capt. Spurry came above deck dressed in his dark green jacket, a breastplate underneath it instead of a waistcoat, his bicorne hat facing forward. He had forsaken a cape, though the morning was chill, and stood by the wheel with Fippers, the clerk Pepperpinch, and Privet.

"Run the yellow," Spurry ordered.

The *Bright Heron's* yellow peace flag was run up, to assure the Vers-eh-sen that no hostility was intended.

"A treacherous span of sea," Fippers noted dourly as the nose of the ship aimed straight for the stranded vessel, a misty spray spitting. There were fangs below them in the cold blue water, and now poking up in a row off the starboard side. A sudden fluke of current would see them dashed against the projections.

"Steady and with care," Spurry said to the helmsman.

"She's a monster, sir," the wide-eyed helmsman noted, staring at the *Oak Cloud*, "two hundred foot or better."

Privet noticed that his captain's face was sweating. It was the fever, not fear.

They were now within firing range of the great Vers-eh-sen ship. The fortress's many gunports were closed like sleeping eyes. There were three gun decks, 130 guns onboard, ranging in might from 12-pounders to 32-pounders. Minutes later the dizzying spires of stone towered above the humbled *Bright Heron*. Distant cheers could just be heard from the crew of the wounded ship.

Capt. Spurry turned to the air next to him and said, "Yes, mother, tea would be just the thing."

Privet and Lt. Fippers exchanged bewildered looks.

Spurry addressed Fippers, "Heave to."

Fippers lifted a metal trumpet to his mouth and called out the order. Other voices echoed the command and the sails were adjusted so that the *Bright Heron* slowed.

The Fellengrey vessel could better navigate the treacherous maze of stone spearheads than the unfortunate Vers-eh-sen craft. Smaller and more manageable, and spared the freak wave that had assailed the *Oak Cloud*, she was able to glide within several ship-lengths of the bigger craft, bow favoring the left. Dropping to a crawl, the *Bright Heron* came up alongside. The sun was bright on the winking water and the spires were stark against the blue sky, their tremendous shadows rippling, writhing in the water as if drowning.

The crew of the Oak Cloud shouted down to the lower ship, waiving their hats and dancing. "Fellengrey! Fellengrey!" they chanted merrily. Even some officers, identifiable by their neat black, white-trimmed uniforms, joined in with the gleeful throng.

Capt. Spurry, without explanation, briskly walked away from the men gathered at the wheel and headed for the hatch several yards up the quarterdeck. He went down below with Privet hurrying after him.

"Captain Spurry, sir, are you well?" Privet called.

Spurry stood in the long dim gundeck with its great beams and low ceiling. He looked confused, as did the many men stationed there. They all watched him without a word. A second lieutenant, manning his post, and a musketeer, saluted. The captain strode past these men, halfway down the deck, all heads turning to follow, and stopped at a rack of cannonballs. He lifted one and smiled.

"Have you ever seen such an apple, Privet?"

Privet, who just now caught up with the man, gave the round shot a strange look. "Sir?"

Spurry wobbled in place, waves of heat rushing through his head. His grip on the ball failed and it hit the floor with a good thump. The captain flinched at the sound, which, distorted in his fever-ears, seemed the report of a cannon.

"They fire!" Capt. Spurry boomed. "Run out the guns!"

Privet took the man's arm, "Captain…"

"Fire!" Spurry shouted at the nearest gun crew.

The men stared at him for a moment before responding. They pushed the cannon on its carriage, squat wheels squealing, and knocked open the gunport. The 9-pounder's brass snout poked out into the sea air.

"Captain," Privet said, "They've *not* fired, sir."

Spurry stepped closer to the captain of the six-man gun crew, drew his sword, and pointed it at the fellow. "Fire, blast you!"

Privet barely had time to clamp his hands over his ears. The gun captain tugged on the length of line that triggered the cannon's firing mechanism and a great smoky thunder filled the deck.

Above, Lt. Fippers jolted. He saw a cloud belch out from the *Bright Heron's* side. The ball punched a chunky hole through one of the *Oak Cloud's* gunport doors. Men's screaming followed from behind the perforated wood.

There was confusion among the crew of the Vers-eh-sen ship, a moment when they were collectively stunned. But then they were swift to their stations, and orders were shouted in their native tongue. The men of the *Bright Heron* were perplexed as well, unsure of what to do.

Fippers barked at one of the midshipmen, "Fetch the captain!"

Spurry was still below, wagging his sword at another cannon team, urging them to discharge their gun. Privet got between his leader and the men, warning, "Do not fire, he is mad with fever!"

"Step aside, Privet!" Spurry spat, gesturing with his blade.

A crash came from outside and the ship shuddered. The Vers-eh-sen had shot back. This prompted the gunners to run their cannon out and obey the captain's wishes. The lanyard was pulled, setting off the firing lock, and the cannon bellowed, the deafening burst filling the gundeck, smoke billowing away from and back through the gunport. The nine-foot long cannon recoiled against the thick breeching rope that prevented it rolling too far back.

Now the gun crews set to their awful work, the cycle of firing, reloading, firing. But the nine-pound shot seemed bees attacking an elephant against the three-decker, whose heavy projectiles, fired from 32-pounders, came exploding through the hull in showers of dust and splintered wood.

The light from the open gunports was defined by the haze in the air, tapering rays streaming in. Capt. Spurry saw a figure running toward him through the otherworldly radiance and thrust with his sword. It was a boy, no older than Mapdall, making his way up from the forward powder magazine carrying a cannon charge in a wooden cylinder. The child grimaced as Spurry's blade disappeared into his chest. The round box dropped and rolled and the boy slumped back off the sword and sprawled on the boards.

Spurry snarled down at the body, "Board my ship, eh, Vers-eh-sen swine?"

Privet did not witness this, for he had crouched fetal when a shot from the *Oak Cloud* breeched the wall and crashed through the deck only yards from him. Staggering in the choking air, he tripped over the dead boy, nearly slipping in the blood as he made for the companionway on the heels of the captain.

A hail of musket fire came down from the *Oak Cloud.* Spurry strode boldly out into the morning chill, waving his sword, cursing, balls gouging the deck all around him. Privet poked his helmet up from the opening and looked over toward the wheel, but the wheel was gone, remnants of it scattered. The helmsman's limbs were scattered there too, not far from the bloody bodies of Lt. Fippers and Pepperpinch, the clerk. Musketry had felled them.

A great wave of cannon smoke came rolling over the frigate as a volley of fiery blossoms erupted from the hulking opponent. Little on the *Bright Heron's* topdeck escaped destruction. The chimney to the galley stove was torn away, the belfry was decimated and the fore and mizzen masts, their sails already ripped by high-fired chain shot, toppled. Privet lost sight of the captain for a moment, then spotted him over at the waist of the ship. He noticed that the ship's boats had been smashed.

The Fellengrey frigate was not built for this sort of close, side-by-side combat, and the barrage pocked her hull with terrible craters. Loose tendrils of rope swung down from the crippled mainmast. Spurry sliced through them as if they were the tentacles of a great squid and continued on to the forecastle.

"Captain…" Privet hissed to himself. *His ward. His friend.*

Shadowy figures, obscured by smoke, could be glimpsed on the deck of the *Oak Cloud*. Marksmen were up on mast platforms, picking off targets on the *Bright Heron's* deck.

A musket ball took Capt. Spurry's hat. He turned and snarled and wagged his sword. Another ball followed, better-aimed, and caught the man in the side. His chest plate tempered the impact, but he was knocked sideways to the deck nonetheless. His sword skidded several feet away.

Privet ducked and dodged his way from the quarterdeck to the waist of the ship, stepping over bodies and parts of bodies. Cannonballs roared past, whined past, and struck, tossing planking and splinters up like sparks, splinters like spray from a wooden sea.

Privet was not far behind his captain now. He spotted a musketeer leaning over the gunwale of the *Oak Cloud*, taking aim at Spurry. Privet pulled his twin pistols, thumbed the cocks back and rose from his crouch long enough to fire. The flintlocks banged and smoked and gore shot up from the Vers-eh-sen like the spray of a whale.

The brig below deck had taken enough damage to loosen the bars that comprised its door. One wall was smashed in and smoky light penetrated from outside, through a ragged breach. Capt. Quince Oats shoved the twisted door open and stepped over the headless corpse of Bellin Bramish, the cabin boy, and made his way out into the thick, dark air. He fumbled through rubble until he reached the horrible scene in the gundeck, where there were only a handful of starboard cannons left to fire and the dead and wounded outnumbered those still working the guns. He urged the men to cease action, then followed the dusty funnel of light that streamed down from the aft companionway.

The *Bright Heron's* mainmast went with a terrible sound, tilting off the portside. Ragged sails fluttered and marksmen were thrown from their perch as it tumbled to the sea and splashed. This distracted Privet for a moment. When he looked back to spot the captain, he found the man was standing in plain view at the bow, looking out over the figurehead, which was a glimmering copper-plated Heron with great wings plastered back against the left and right sides of the ship's beak.

The towering spires of Drowning Fang were vague smudges, and the massive *Oak Cloud*, for all the smoke, might have been a hill swelling up from the Gantic. Two figures moved on the hill, not far from Capt. Spurry, taking care to aim. Privet, his pistols spent, shouted to his commander, but the rapt Spurry noticed nothing but the ocean.

Two smoky reports came. One shot missed, but the other caught Spurry in the chest plate, punching a hole through the light metal. Spurry stumbled.

Privet cursed and sprang up the forecastle as the men reloaded. He got behind the swivel-gun and turned it to face the musketeers. The small cannon boomed and a half-pound swarm of shot tore into the Vers-eh-senians and nibbled the railing in front of them. The men shrieked like osprey.

"Privet, dear lad," Capt. Spurry said, his voice straining, "come have a look, won't you?"

Privet, glancing back over his shoulder, hurried to the captain. Spurry pointed to the water, which was blue and bright underneath a ghostly, shifting mantel of smoke.

Spurry smiled. "The Gantic has turned to tea: my two most favored liquids are one and the same."

Privet panted, "Captain, we must seek cover, we be plain targets here."

"I must drink it," Spurry said, and he turned, took a small run and dove off the side, his dark green jacket fluttering like wings as he fell to the sea. Bubbles and an amorphous cloud of blood rose to the surface.

Somehow, dodging heavy fire, Quince Oats had made it to the aft of the ship and ran up the white flag of surrender. The Vers-eh-sen boarded. Oats and the Vers-eh-sen captain, a big man with hair and beard as dark as his uniform, recognized each other. The *Oak Cloud's* captain asked about the Cabbadunain boy he was supposed to purchase from Oats.

Speaking in Vers-eh-sen tongue, Oats lied, "Off to Fellengrey aboard the *Steady Rhino.*"

"A pity," the disappointed Vers-eh-sen captain noted.

All of the *Bright Heron's* important officers were dead, there being only a pair of midshipmen left alive. Privet, along with these young fellows, with Oats interpreting, explained the tragic circumstances, how the Captain, mad with fever contracted in the Figwort Isles, had set events on a terrible course.

The Vers-eh-sen captain apologized for the destruction rained from his warship. Those of the *Bright Heron* did likewise.

The Vers-eh-senians returned to their vessel, which was now in worse condition than it had been when the *Bright Heron* came to its rescue. One might have thought, to look at the *Bright Heron*, that she was beyond repair, which may have been the case. Moths bearing notes and red distress ribbons were sent out from each ship, for there was nothing left to do but wait and hope, and tend the wounded. And send off the dead. Both ships were sinking.

The lumbering merchant ship *Green Maiden*, painted a summery color from mid-hull down, heavy with coffee and blaze-moths from Mindacabba and sugar and tobacco from Mabbaduni, was the most welcome site Privet had ever seen. The messenger moths, fastened with distress notes, had performed nicely!

Somehow the trade vessel was able to fit the survivors from the *Bright Heron* and the many men from the *Oak Cloud* onboard with her own crew. Quince Oats disguised the Gifted child, Mapdall, with bandages before bringing him aboard, so that the Vers-eh-sen would not notice the boy's dark skin color and know who he was. Once hidden away in a cabin, the child was unwrapped and left in the care of the privilege girl, who had also survived the bombardment.

There was a strange intermingling of people during the long journey to Fellengrey. Healers from the vessels that had battled so fiercely worked side by side, mending their injured and a Vers-eh-senian sailor, having mastered a quantity of Fellengrey words, tried to teach Privet a bawdy song about a milk maid.

One could hardly take a step without bumping another body, the ship was so packed with people, and the decks below were paved with snoring lumps by night. Quince Oats found a snug little spot off the galley.

It was late and he was dreading his dreams, but close to sleep nonetheless, when he heard a small noise. An eye opened. There was wood all around him, unpainted plank walls and ceiling and board bed beneath. Such had been his life for many years, a world of floating wood. *Just the creaking common to a ship,* he thought. But the sound came again, and he took the source to be a fissure where the wall met the floor.

A tiny gray face with a sharp nose and black eyes poked from the split. Oats grinned.

"Here, pretty, don't be shy," Oats said, fishing in his pocket where there was a chunk of dry cheese.

On a certain evening, up on the poop deck, Privet stood gazing out to sea as Capt. Oats and the captain of the *Green Maiden* traded tales of their exploits under canvas, stories about pirates and storms and a ghost who was fond of setting sails on fire. The *Green Maiden's* captain was an ambitious young fellow who dressed handsomely to boast his success. He spoke of building a smaller, more fleet ship of costly blackbirch wood from the Colonies, and pushing farther east, expanding his fortune by joining the Chiddidin trade.

At one point the men speculated about Quince Oats's fate.

"I shall hang for my crimes," Oats said, stonily, "suitably enough."

Privet, who had only been listening to this point, interjected, "Perhaps our good courts will bestow some measure of leniency in consideration of certain facts, it being true that your courageous deeds put halt to the bombardment of the *Bright Heron.* And have you not made efforts for to keep the Cabbadunian boy cloaked against the awareness of the Vers-eh-senians?"

"I have," Oats said humbly.

"Well, then. Perhaps, if there be yet mercy in the world, your acts of nobility will weigh against your crimes."

"Perhaps," Oats said. He felt something move in his coat and took a small piece of cheese from one pocket and delivered it to the other.

The two merchant captains carried their conversation (almost a competition of adventures) down below and Privet was left to his thoughts, and the vast Gantic that had called to him as a boy.

He was having a cup of tea in someone's honor. He took a sip, then, with a sad little smile, looked out across the great water.

4

Love Spell

Privet spent the next two years as midshipman on the frigate *East Falcon* sailing the spice route between Fellengrey and the Figwort Islands. He served under Post Captain Winscomb, a sharp young officer who was quite fond of the ambitious Privet, and perhaps a bit too fond of brandywine. Privet was happy to be applying himself as something other than a personal guard, which, at best, had proved unsatisfying. He turned his attention fully to learning every aspect of sailing a navy vessel, and exceeded all expectations, his own foremost.

It was during this time that bewildering news came to the man. Willows, who had been Privet's closest friend back at Fort Haddox, wrote to tell him that Rye Blackbird had been spotted alive and well boarding a merchant ship off Mindacabba, in The Figwort Islands.

"It cannot be so," Privet had said aloud, reading the letter, which suddenly shook in his hands.

It was common knowledge that Rye Blackbird had been put to death back in 1741 for his part in the mutiny aboard the *Lion Squall*. Blackbird had received *the wet cage*, a form of execution that offered the sentenced an improbable chance of survival. This particular method consisted of locking a person in a large basket composed of metal straps and lowering them into water for ten minutes. If a person survived, they were set free. Blackbird, like many who were condemned to die, was given a choice and chose this form of fatal punishment over hanging.

As the story goes, Blackbird was submerged in the ocean at Dunker's Point, Demmingsfife, the cage being hoisted out after ten minutes. Oddly enough, the door of the metal basket, which had been locked when it was lowered into the Gantic, was found to be open, and the cage was empty, dangling there from the arm of a wooden scaffold.

Blackbird, it was assumed, had managed to get the door open, but apparently drowned nonetheless, for a man's body was found several days later, washed up on a near shore. While hungry sea life and bloating had marred the corpse's identity, it was thought to be the mutineer, for the figure bore a beard not unlike that which the condemned man had worn. Perhaps this assessment had been wrong, if the alleged sighting in the Figwort Isles were true, for the sea was known to spit out bodies that went unnamed and unclaimed.

Privet, having read and re-read the letter, sat on his bunk and took up his sword. Rye Blackbird's sword. He sat with it resting across his legs for some time, and heard himself mutter, "May you be well, Mister Blackbird, wherever you might be."

More news came: a sad letter told him of his father's death from quick-moss in the autumn of 1750; a glad letter told him of his sister Betony's marriage the following spring. She went to live in Upper Noonbury, where the fellow she wed served as a blacksmith's apprentice. His mother, well provided for by what remained of Rye Blackbird's treasure, moved to Hemmings Port to tend her older sister, a spinster who had been crippled in a carriage mishap. The younger twins went with her. Betony's twin, Alba, married a local man from East Whittle and they took over the Privet farm there. Midshipman Privet was glad to know that the dear old house of his youth remained in his family's keeping.

The year 1752 also proved a time of change. While he had only served as midshipman for roughly two years, Privet was encouraged by Capt. Winscomb to try for a promotion to lieutenant's rank. So, he went before the examining board and stood in front of three captains, who went on to question him and place him in hypothetical situations to test how he would react under a variety of circumstances. Privet passed with ease and returned the next day to receive his certificate.

Lt. Privet, who, for the last two years had been based at (or setting out from) East Fellengrey, was soon transferred to a more appealing placement as second lieutenant on the frigate, *North Swan*, whose purpose, as late, was patrolling for pirate ships along the outer coast of West Fellengrey. This proved favorable to the young man, for now he was close enough to visit his family, as circumstance allowed.

"It is a handsome sword, I'll give you that, Privet," Mill Burnshire, the coxswain of the *North Swan* said, sitting in the lieutenant's small cabin holding a glass of wine. Burnshire carried a great nose on his face and bore silvery curtains of disorderly hair.

The sword was indeed handsome, with its straight thirty-inch blade of double-edged steel and a grip of smooth dark blackbirch wood from the Colonies. The knuckle bow curved from the shaft to the pommel, which in this case was a silver lion's head.

Privet and Burnshire had imbibed a bit much and the wine loosened complaints from their mouths. The coxswain's had to do with certain lax members of the crew, while Privet's had to do with a navy-wide command passed down from the admiral of the fleet. All officers would commence to carry swords bearing blue blades fashioned from superior steel imported from the North Islands.

"A pity to retire so fine a weapon," Privet muttered, saying nothing of the weight of personal value he placed upon it. He sheathed the sword.

Both men sat quietly for a moment. Burnshire gazed off. His eyes, which were a rich, intelligent brown, wore heavy lids. These were heavier than usual, getting more so with each glass of wine.

Burnshire lifted his drink and said, "To swords!"

"To swords," Privet echoed, raising his glass.

Lt. Privet had heard tell that there was love magic to be found in the old part of the city, high above the sea, up a perilous set of stairs that innumerable feet and centuries of salty rain had worn to a slippery grey.

There, overlooking the waves, the houses were tall and weathered, with steep-pitched roofs and faded paint. The streets were narrow for the nearness of the buildings and there was something about the air that was both damp and comforting, a certain ghost for the nose that told of close-knit generations, and the danger that was never far when people settled near an ocean.

A fine drizzle was coming in off the Gantic when Privet stopped to catch his breath. Not even halfway up and he was winded. The stairs rose in a dizzying line before him, to a horizon of shadowy structures. There were no banisters to grab onto and the crudely cut slabs of granite were slick beneath his feet. Only love, or something along those lines, could have made the young man consider venturing further.

He thought of the innkeeper's daughter in New Crown, her pale round face, her great green eyes, her hair a fluid mystery of nocturnal shades. He thought of her laugh and the soft scallop-colored breasts that leaned to gravity when she bent to place food on the tables. Suddenly he was moving again, up and up and up the ancient stairs, until at last, he reached the top.

It was true what they said about the old half of the city—it might as well have been an altogether different world from the more recent colony below. The architectural styles had been outmoded for more than two centuries, the houses high and thin with tapered windows. While simple in frame, the structures bore embellishing details that featured graceful curves and delicate patterns.

Privet stood and collected himself. He was young, as mentioned, and handsome enough, with warm brown eyes looking out from under his officer's helmet. His uniform reflected the recent increase in trade with the North Islands, for the lightweight breastplate beneath his dark green jacket was the shimmering blue of imported "sea steel." His breeches, boots, and the scabbard containing his new blue sword, were black, but not quite so dark as the hair on the innkeeper's daughter.

The lieutenant set to looking for a brick-colored house with a wreath of brittlethorn on the door. The dwellings were tired things and Lt. Privet saw more scrawny dogs than people. Those upright creatures that were about were cloaked against the weather and, characteristically reticent, peeked rather than stared at the stranger. Slick cobbled veins wove between the houses, taking him through a maze of shadows, until he found the place he sought. It was modest in its anemic paint, two and a half stories tall with thin windows and a projecting entry arch bearing worn carvings like webs and tusks. A big tangled wreath of thorny vines was nailed to the batten door. Privet straightened, despite his aching legs and back, and knocked.

Two old women greeted the lieutenant when the door was opened. They were the Deerfield sisters—twins, as were the majority of folks in Old Crown. The women, Privet soon found, spoke each word simultaneously, as though two mouths shared a single mind.

"Yes?" they said.

Privet removed his helmet, which was like a bowl with lamb chop sideburns, and held it under his arm. His hair was auburn, swept back over his ears and tied in a neat little tail.

"Good afternoon, ladies. I am Lieutenant Privet of the frigate *North Swan*, on her way to Westheath, and anchored for repairs in the port below."

The women were pretty old things, gray haired, gray-dressed and leaning forward with great interest. They shared a blush at the sight of the sharp-looking military man.

"Ohhh," they cooed, "please come in, Lieutenant."

It was dim and comfy inside and a nice fire heated the parlor against the day. The place smelled of bergamot and old linens.

"Tea?" the sisters asked, seating Privet in the best chair.

"Thank you," the man said, smiling.

Once tea and jam cakes were on hand the officer got down to business.

"It is told in the town below that you gentlewomen have a singular mastery in the ways of love magic."

The women, seated side by side on a settle, smiled and giggled, "Is *that* what they say?"

"Indeed. And so I have come to ask your help with a certain matter…"

Privet went on to describe the troubles his navy ship had encountered while traveling up the coast from Hemmings Port. The craft shook as if it had taken a cannonball, and a hole appropriate to such an attack was suffered on the starboard side, yet no firing was heard and no source of an attack was to be seen. In fact, no remains of a projectile were found in the damaged section of the craft.

Thus, the *North Swan* had been under restoration for a number of days, during which time Privet and others from his crew had frequented The Salty Hag, an inn not far from the docks.

"I have fallen in love with the innkeeper's daughter. She is a flower in a field of weeds, the most fetching lass I have seen in my days. I will not leave to sea without her hand."

The sisters, delighted by the man's profession of affection, looked to each other and smiled before addressing their guest.

"We would be happy to help you win the heart of this woman, Lieutenant Privet."

And so the man sat in the humble little parlor while the twins clattered about in the near kitchen. They might as well have been preparing a great meal for all the noise, and the smells that followed reminded him of exotic spices he had encountered in his years traveling the sea to distant lands. The old women even hummed in unison. Their light and pleasing voices floated in to where the man sat sipping his tea.

The lieutenant was not one, generally speaking, to turn to magic, having witnessed a tragic misfortune when he was quite young. Two half-grown neighbor girls in his home village, intent on seeing visions of their future husbands, had concocted an oracular brew and filled a wooden washtub with it. In order to witness apparitions of their future loves, it was required that each girl submerge her head under the liquid for ten seconds. But magic was a fickle thing, and the hasty twins, rather than take turns with the head dunking, poked under in the same instant. The magic found this disagreeable, for some inexplicable reason, and when the sisters withdrew from the tub, their faces were obscured by a thick connecting tube of tissue as long as a man's forearm, a bridge linking their heads together. All that remained of their features was a single misplaced eye, set off at one side of the anomaly, the dark pupil flittering like a fly under glass. With their faces sealed within this fleshy mass, the girls were incapable of breathing, and fell to the ground, where they writhed, conjoined, until dead. From that point on, Privet had avoided magic whenever possible.

At length the sisters glided in from the kitchen, beaming, one holding a small bottle in her hand. The young officer felt a chill down his spine. He took the jar and held it up to view, but the contents were obscured by the green of the glass.

"Just a sprinkle will do," the Deerfield sisters cautioned in unison.

Privet stood up and asked what the women wanted for compensation, and, unassuming creatures that they were, they told him to part with whatever petty amount he saw fit. Privet gave them a handsome fifty-moth piece and their eyes bulged.

"Thank you, Lieutenant," they sang, "you are indeed a generous man."

It was not long before dark, and Privet still had the daunting climb down those terrible steps to look forward to. He put on his helmet, bid goodbye to the ladies, and stepped out into the drizzle. From that vantage point, high in Old Crown, he could see the roofs of the contemporary buildings below, and the jagged rocks that stabbed out above them and the silvery Gantic Ocean. His wounded warship was anchored down there, and from this height it appeared to be no more than a toy.

The Salty Hag was host to a good crowd that night, with nearly every table full. Crewmen from the *North Swan* accounted for much of the patronage, and they were welcomed warmly by the proprietor and the local folk who frequented the establishment. Lt. Privet was there with the rest, seated in a corner under low beams, with the sound of a fiddler competing against the many loud voices. He drank from a mug of chestnut-colored squall, while watching the innkeeper's daughter, Hazel, as she tended tables. With so many customers on hand, the lovely young woman relied on the assistance of another serving maid, a red-headed little thing with a cinnamon constellation of freckles.

Unfortunately for Privet, he had wound up on the wrong side of the tavern room, the half *not* being tended by Hazel. He would have to wait for another night to try out the mixture that the Deerfield sisters had supplied him with. Even so, he enjoyed watching her as she moved about, her dark hair whipping, her green eyes smiling. She was lovely in a long plum-colored skirt that rippled about her legs like a fluid, and her pale scoop-necked blouse more than hinted at her feminine charms. All the other sailors watched her too, and wanted her, but Lt. Privet grinned a secret grin, knowing that she would soon belong to him.

"Lieutenant…" a man's voice intruded upon Privet's reverie.

He looked up and saw the uniformed Captain Moorsparrow of the fighting class *Swift Cannon*. He was accompanied by a well-dressed, attractive middle-aged woman with piled amber hair.

Privet was quick to his feet, quick to salute.

"Sir," he said.

"Might we join you, good fellow?" the handsome older officer asked.

"Of course. Please." Privet was confounded by the appearance of this man. He'd had no idea that the venerable *Swift Cannon* was in the vicinity.

The captain and his wife sat down at the small round table. The officer was bearded, his straw hair tied back in a tight knot. A gleaming blue breastplate with silver inlays of stylized sharks was visible between the dark green halves of his dress coat. The elegant Mrs. Moorsparrow looked out of place there in the simple tavern, adorned as she was in pearls and lace and the fine white material of her dress.

"Well, what's good to drink?" the senior officer asked with a smile.

"The squall is fine. It's all I've tried, truth be told," Privet replied.

"I should like some wine," the missus said dryly.

Lt. Privet, less tactful than usual on account of drink, was quick to ask what it was that brought the respected naval officer to New Crown.

"We were transporting Prince Fenny up to Drumford for the wedding of the duke when we came under fire," Moorsparrow explained, his manner turning serious. "A ball, or *something* clipped our mainmast and took two of my men with it."

Privet sat forward and nearly spilled what was left of his squall. "Heavens!"

"Queer thing it was. We heard no shot, we saw no smoke, but the lookout spotted a red sloop—red, of all colors—headed off north-west. While I was dead set on seeing the prince safely ashore, *he* insisted we give chase. Thus, we pursued the thing for two days, only glimpsing it here and there, as if it were a ghost. Got as far as this dismal rock and lost her entirely in the fog."

The captain's wife sighed, "We had a horrid time of it, winding about those silly little islands off Nellyhaunt…and *such waves!*"

"Sounds dreadful," Privet sympathized.

The captain studied the younger man. "I hear tell your ship has endured an attack not dissimilar to mine."

"Quite the same," Privet noted. "No noise from a cannon, no smoke. We never even saw what it was fired upon us. What of the prince, Captain, would he be on board still?"

"We've secreted him away on shore tonight, better that, than leave him vulnerable on the *Swift Cannon*, should this mystery craft return in the night."

"Ah, yes, a wise precaution." Privet thought for a moment, then asked, "Tell, is the King not better?"

The expressions on the faces of his company answered Privet's question. Even the chilly blue eyes of the captain's wife showed a flicker of concern. The King, Aven, and his twin, Alder, had both fallen ill several months back, when spring blooms were on the boughs. Alder, the elder of the twins by a matter of minutes, had passed away as the haying season was coming to an end, and now the remaining brother appeared to be failing.

"He seems no better," Moorsparrow noted with ominous restraint.

"And the healers know not what ails him still?"

The captain shook his head.

"*I* think they were poisoned," Mrs. Moorsparrow said directly.

The man hushed his wife and fished a small clay pipe out of his waist-length jacket. He filled the bowl with a pale powder blend comprised of the finest ground moths' wings and tamped it down with a pinkie. Meanwhile, the red-haired serving lass had made her way over and occupied the captain and his wife long enough to allow Privet a good long look at the winsome Hazel. *She* was moving buoyantly through the crowded tables on the other side of the room, her skirt a plum-colored breeze, her hair a shifting banner of night, as her smile—which turned to meet his—grabbed him by the heart and shook it like a dog's toy.

Seen in daylight, the *Swift Cannon* did not appear as swift as its name implied. It was a massive 100-gun, three-masted warship, and one might have imagined a number of smaller, quicker vessels overtaking a lumbering craft of this kind were it not for its impressive firepower. The ship was the best that the Royal Navy had to offer and many a skull beneath the sea could sing its terrible praises.

It was a majestic vessel to be sure, and handsome in spite of its bulkiness, the greater part of the sides a honeyed color, the lower third black all down to the keel; green and gold neatly defined the trim. The docks of the port looked frail and skeletal with this ship anchored there, dwarfing the smaller merchant transports and the frigate, *North Swan*.

There was fog out on the open water and the sky was gray, although a silvery sun could be glimpsed above the high cliffs, over the precipitous buildings of Old Crown. Lt. Privet stood at the base of the incline, where the long stone staircase met flat earth before making its steep ascent. He was looking down the shore to where Prince Fenny, a young man dressed in a fine russet coat, and black breeches, was tossing bits of bread to sea moths. Privet walked over to join him and nodded at the two musket-toting guards that hovered nearby.

"Good morning, Prince," Privet said, and saluted.

"Lieutenant."

Fenny had mild, clean-shaven features and his blond hair was pulled back into a tail that hung past his shoulders.

"I see you've some friends," Privet said, nodding toward the moths.

"Lovely, aren't they?"

The moths were the size and color of pewter dining plates.

"Yes," the lieutenant realized, "I suppose they are."

Fenny, like his father, exuded benevolence. How sad, the naval officer thought, that the patriarch was failing. At least there was some comfort in knowing that the King's twin sons would be sharing the crown, for together they embodied what made the man so effective and endearing. Fenny was conscientious, blessed with his father's compassion, while Treadson—presently off on an ambassadorial mission in the enigmatic North Islands—had inherited King Aven's savvy and assertiveness.

Observing the gentleness that Fenny extended, even to simple scavenging insects, Privet found it entirely understandable why a mighty warship had been appointed to transport the fellow to a wedding. He was a worthy heir, and with an increase in pirate activity as of late, the kingdom might have been reckless to trust Fenny's well-being to anything less.

The prince moved nearer to the surf, out where the partly submerged boulders were slathered in drippy tendrils of seaweed. He leaned forward to toss some bread crumbs to one of the moths which, not as quick as the rest, hadn't been able to grab any. The young man nearly slipped off the granite projection on which he was balanced. Lt. Privet's heart flinched and his body tensed, ready to spring out onto the stones to save the prince, but Fenny regained his balance and turned to smile. For a moment, Privet had felt that the whole of the kingdom, and not just that one young man, had been endangered.

The repairs to the *North Swan* were coming along nicely, though the ship was still some days from returning to duty patrolling the western coast for pirates. This gave Lt. Privet more time to prepare. He asked the cook, who was handy with scissors, to trim his hair, and he saw to it that one of the cabin boys ironed his uniform and polished his breastplate. He did, however, shine his own boots, idiosyncratically trusting no other to do as good a job of it as he.

The cook was a stout balding man with a full white beard and a laugh like a seal's bark. He stood in the lieutenant's cabin holding a small green bottle up to the fading light of the window.

"A love spell, eh? I wonder what might be in it?" the cook, Holdren, said.

Privet was busy knotting a lacy white tie around his neck; the ends, which resembled moth wings, hung down against the blue of his chest plate. He grinned and shrugged.

The older fellow put the bottle down and wagged his head. "Love," he grumbled, "makes a man more dizzy than does a wild sea."

"Worse things to be than dizzy," Privet returned lightheartedly.

"And a *woman*," Holdren said with a scowl, "is what a man agonizes over *not* having when he has none and then is agonized *by* once he does."

"Why, that's rather bleak," Privet said, pleased with the way his tie looked in the looking glass on the wall.

"I'll take the sea," the cook said. He looked out the window, and added, "no less mysterious, and no less dangerous, but a mite more quiet."

Privet turned and headed for the door, clapping his friend on the arm as he passed. "Wish me luck!"

New Crown was pretty in the soft pinkish light that preceded the dusk. The round brick houses, with greenish fern-stone shingles on their conical roofs, looked homey and inviting. Lt. Privet walked from the docks, dapper in his uniform, with his sword at his side. His boots made a confident sound on the cobbles, the texture of which was accentuated by the slanted light. He gazed back at the pier, at his ship, and the larger *Swift Cannon*, which was staying on to protect the damaged vessel until the repairs were finished. Both were silhouetted against the western sky.

With one hand on the handle of his sword and the other in a pocket, holding a small glass bottle, Lt. Privet arrived at The Salty Hag. The wooden sign was squeaking on its chains as a cool breeze came in from the sea. The sign depicted a crone's severed head dangling upside down. The terrible visage sported actual hair, pale lengths taken from horses' tails. The hair moved in the air like wrack in rhythmic surf.

This structure, and nearby establishments such as the blacksmith's shop and a bakery, were rectangular in shape, unlike the many cylindrical houses of New Crown. All the buildings were brick of course, and an end wall of the tavern supported a leafy mesh of ghost eye, a vine which at this time of year bore small bluish berries that glowed when it rained. Laughter and the warm luminescence of candlelight greeted Privet as he entered through the main door.

A good crowd, Privet noted, standing in the little foyer, peering into the tap room. That was to be expected, with two military ships anchored in the harbor. The crews took turns alternately manning their vessels, and visiting the town, which had little more to offer than this particular place. The lieutenant looked from one side of the room to the other until he saw *her*.

Hazel floated through the tables in a long fluid skirt the color of heather blossoms. She was lovely with her pale round face, her great green eyes, her hair a fluid mystery of nocturnal shades. Her loose white blouse had voluminous sleeves, and a scooped neck that allowed generous breasts to follow gravity's sway.

A warm weight flooded Privet's head at the sight of her and he thought to himself, *worse things to be than dizzy.*

Once again, the innkeeper's daughter was sharing her duties with the little red-haired lass, and while all of the tables on Hazel's side of the room were occupied, Privet was not discouraged. He walked straight to a table where some of his crewmates were seated and, rather than exert rank and demand that they move, offered each of the men a silvery twenty-moth piece. The men, while a bit bemused, gratefully relocated and the grinning Lt. Privet sat down alone.

Hardly a moment had passed when the officer looked up to see Hazel coming toward him, ethereally soft in the pipe smoke and candle glow. She was smiling at him. Privet, who up until that moment had been steeled and determined, suddenly felt as if she could see the little bottle right through his pocket. He tried to return her smile, but his eyes were filled with apprehension.

"Evening, sir," Hazel said in her pretty voice. "What will you be havin'?"

Privet forgot to breathe, forgot how to speak.

"Sir?"

Privet straightened, cleared his throat and managed a word, "Squall."

Hazel repeated the word then spun to head for the bar, glancing over her shoulder and holding his eye for a moment.

The lieutenant wondered if the spell, while still contained in its bottle, could already be having an effect on the young woman. Such a look she had given him just then! She held his gaze even longer when she returned with his drink, flicking her dark hair back, leaning so close that he could practically feel the heat of her bosom.

"Here you go, sir," she said.

"Thank you, miss," Privet said, and he gave her a coppery ten-moth.

"How very kind of you, sir," Hazel said, taking the coin—a handsome overpayment—and curtsying.

Left to himself, Privet got about his plan. He slipped the little bottle from his pocket and eased out the cork. Inconspicuously, he angled the vessel to tap a pinch of the contents into his dark squall. *Just a sprinkle will do,*"the Deerfield sisters had told him.

Right at that moment a drunken fishermen came staggering along. He was towering and loutish, with a wild red beard that obscured his body from chin to sternum. The man bumped the edge of Privet's table and the bottle of mysterious powder jarred, emptying into the drink.

"Farts!" Privet cursed.

The oaf stumbled away and Privet quickly tucked the empty bottle back into his pocket. For a brief moment he considered taking the liquid out and pouring it in the street, not knowing what it might do if taken in such quantity. Employing magic had been against his better judgment, after all. But when he looked and saw Hazel moving here and there with her dark hair and her green eyes, he found himself rooted to his seat. He would go forward with his plan. Now all he need do was hail the young woman, complain about the quality of his squall, and ask that she taste it (so, as far as the ruse went, he might prove to her that it was not worthy to serve). He was waiting for Hazel to move back toward his table when...

"Good evening, Lieutenant." It was a man's voice.

Privet looked up to see a handsome bearded fellow in the dark green coat of a naval officer. The man's frilly necktie spilled over a sky blue breastplate with silver shark inlays.

"Oh, um, good evening, Captain Moorsparrow."

The refined Mrs. Moorsparrow was there as well, dressed as if she were attending a grand ball rather than visiting a port town tavern. Privet stood to salute the man and bow to the lady. When the captain asked if they might join him, the lieutenant grit his teeth.

"Why, please do. I should be glad for the company," Privet lied.

The lieutenant felt his face frozen in a smile, felt his head nodding, heard his own voice saying casual nothings, all while desperation trembled through his innards. Hardly a second passed that he wasn't glancing at the enigmatic dark of the liquid in

160

his mug, or turning here or there to glimpse the innkeeper's daughter, who had yet to come by to take an order from the man's guests.

Only once did Privet perk his ears with interest to something that Captain Moorsparrow said, when it was mentioned that locals on a fishing boat had briefly caught sight of a strange red vessel out by the Kellingrey Shoals. Privet would have pursued the topic further were it not for Mrs. Moorsparrow and her annoying cough.

She had been sitting there like a portrait in her pearls and lace and fine cream-colored dress, nibbling a handful of ghost eye berries she'd picked off the vines growing on the outside of the tavern, when one of the things got stuck in her throat and set her hacking. Her ordinarily composed face became a red grimace and she shook so hard that her neat pile of amber hair began to unravel. Impulsively, she grabbed Privet's mug of squall and brought it to her lips, gulping half of it down before the lieutenant could even cry, *"No!"*

The drink relieved the woman of her blockage. She put the mug down and sat back, sighing. Captain Moorsparrow, who looked rather embarrassed by the commotion, turned to his wife and growled out of one side of his mouth.

"Are you quite well, my dear?"

Mrs. Moorsparrow did not respond. She was staring across the table at the lieutenant.

"I say, dear, are you in fact well?" her husband persisted.

Privet grabbed the mug and looked in it to see how much of the potation was left. There was not much to see. He flicked his eyes back to the captain's wife, and saw her icy countenance melt away. Her eyes, still fastened on him, were feral with desire and her parted lips seemed to plump around her teeth as she shoved her chair back and got to her feet.

"Well," Privet said, pushing his own chair away from the table, "I best be getting back to—"

Mrs. Moorsparrow launched herself upon Lt. Privet, clamping her mouth over his before he could get another word out. She kissed him with fervor, moaning, hands like a vice squeezing the stunned man's face. The captain, bellowing curses, sprang up, sending his chair toppling, and rushed to drag his wife off of Privet.

"What, are you mad?"

Mrs. Moorsparrow struggled to get free of her spouse, thrashing, reaching her arms out to the other man. The room had fallen silent—but for the woman's beastly growling—and the captain, seeing some of his crew in the bewildered crowd, called for assistance.

"Remove her to the ship!"

The two men who came forward looked hesitant to be involved in the matter, but responded dutifully. They took the woman by the arms and dragged her through the barroom. As she disappeared out the door, she could be heard calling, "I love you! I love you, Lieutenant Privet!"

Privet, meanwhile, rose from his seat and faced the enraged husband. "Terribly sorry, Captain."

"Sorry! What's all this, Privet?" The older man was gripping the handle of his short-sword.

"There was a love spell in my squall, sir, but not meant for Mrs. Moorsparrow. I swear it was intended for another."

"You lie," the captain snarled. "You've wanted my wife from first you set eyes upon her!"

"Not so, sir, honestly!"

The thin blue length of the captain's sword hissed free of its scabbard. He slapped the side of the blade down on the table, pointing the tip at the lieutenant.

"I call you to duel, Privet. Disgrace me this way, will you? You, sir, are a swine, fixing to steal a decent woman from her husband. And from a fellow officer, at that! I'll see you dead."

Privet tried to explain, but the captain marched briskly from the room, leaving him there in a hazy sea of gaping faces. He felt numb just standing alone in the middle of the room, and when he noticed Hazel gawking with the rest, he wished that he could vanish into the smoky air.

It was the afternoon following the unfortunate incident at The Salty Hag, and much had transpired in a relatively short time. First off, Privet had rushed to the captain's

Scott Thomas

quarters upon returning to the ship the night before to explain the particulars to his commanding officer (before the man heard twisted versions of the facts from lesser sources). Captain Langham appreciated Privet's straightforwardness, and believed that the man had no intention of beguiling Moorsparrow's wife. Still, he thought it best not to interfere, not wishing to chance the potentially uncomfortable politics of opposing an officer of like rank, especially when that officer was the commandant of the greatest vessel in the fleet. While secretly disappointed, Privet knew that it was a rational stance to take, all the more so for the presence of the prince. It would hardly have made a good impression on the royal heir if two of his captains were at each other's throats in a time of danger, when an unknown enemy might be lurking out in the fog.

Following the meeting with the captain, Privet retired to his cabin. He slept little, and in the morning climbed the many stone steps to Old Crown, where he again paid visit to the Deerfield sisters. He explained his predicament, and asked if they might come with him to speak with Captain Moorsparrow, to substantiate his story (how he truly had planned to win the love of Hazel, the tavern keeper's daughter). He offered them a handsome sum for their testimony, but the old women declined.

"But why?" Privet asked.

The sisters looked to one another, then back at the lieutenant, and said, "The stairs."

"*The stairs?*"

"Yes," they sang, "we're dreadfully afraid of heights."

The women offered to create a spell potion that, if administered to the captain, would alter the man's disposition toward Privet—a sort of magically induced benevolence. The lieutenant thanked them for the offer, but explained that there would not be an opportunity to get the stuff into the man, who was back on board the *Swift Cannon*. He hardly imagined the captain would accept a drink from him in the midst of a duel.

Privet wondered then if the women might pen a letter to Moorsparrow, something that would bolster his argument, but the sisters could neither read nor write.

163

And so, with no further recourse, Privet returned to his ship off New Crown and solicited his friend, the coxswain Mill Burnshire, to be his "tender." A position of honor, so far as dueling tradition went; this put it to Burnshire to make certain arrangements. He gathered a duel party: a young woman to mourn (if need be), a healer, and a "mercy man" to step in and kill his fellow, if Privet should end up wounded and suffering. This was done efficiently enough, and soon there was nothing left for Privet to do but practice.

Up on the sunny short deck of the *North Swan*, the lieutenant was going through his moves, thrusting and swiping at the cool ocean air. He had the grace of a dancer, and his blade moved with such speed that at times the coxswain Burnshire, who observed from a safe distance, could make out little more than a blue blur.

Burnshire, with his raptor nose, and hair like wild silver shrubbery, applauded his friend.

"Impressive, Lieutenant, if I must say," Mill noted.

Having completed his exercises, the officer sheathed his weapon and walked over to Burnshire. The older man clapped Privet on the back.

"You are a brilliant swordsman, I'll give you that, Privet. But I wonder you didn't choose pistols."

The choice of weapon, as signified in the formal written challenge that had been delivered by a courier of Capt. Moorsparrow, had been left up to Lt. Privet.

"*Pistols*? I heard tell that Captain Moorsparrow is an expert shot with a pistol."

Burnshire chuckled. "Moorsparrow, a good shot? He'd not hit the side of his ship were he ten foot from it. No, no, good fellow, Moorsparrow is a swordsman. The finest swordsman in the King's good fleet."

Privet, who *was* a keen shot with a flintlock, wagged his head and groaned.

Captain Moorparrow arose early on the morning of the duel. His wife—who was still under the care of the ship's healer and only starting to shake off the effects of the love spell—was asleep, and so he moved quietly about their cabin, putting on his uniform and chest plate. Satisfied with his reflection in the looking glass, Moorsparrow took his violin case from a cabinet in the wall and started out of the room. His scabbard bumped the doorframe as he was leaving and the woman on the bed, disturbed by the sound, muttered, "*Privet...*" The captain cursed to himself and locked the cabin door from the outside before climbing above deck.

Though the sun had yet to rise above the cliffs and houses of Old Crown, the sky's tawny haze told the captain that the day would not be bright even when the orb cleared the horizon. Still, it was as lovely a morning as he had ever witnessed. Alone but for look-outs and guards, the man stood on the stern, took out his violin, and played the mournful *Crossing at Wintbridge* to the inexplicable pewter sea. He played the tune twice, then once again, in case this was the last time he would have a chance to.

There was little activity on the opposite side of the pier, aboard the frigate *North Swan*, which was anchored in the shadow of the dwarfing *Swift Cannon*. Sentries minded their posts, and look-outs monitored the dusky sea where a slash of expanding fog haunted the horizon. Below deck in his cabin, the sleepless Lt. Privet sat penning farewell letters. He wrote to his mother back in Hemmings Port and his sister in Upper Noonbury and his favorite cousin down in Blackbirch. He even, for a moment, considered writing a wistful proclamation of love to leave for the tavern keeper's daughter.

That sad business done, the man paced in his chamber as daylight strengthened; he could hear movement here and there in other parts of the ship, and eventually there came a knock at his door. It was the coxswain, Mill Burnshire, and the cook, Holdren (who had brought a breakfast of sausage and potato pie). Burnshire took possession of the departure missives, promising to deliver them if need be. Privet hardly sampled the food, even though sausage pie was his favorite choice for breakfast. It was time to dress.

Privet was sharp in his uniform, with his black tricorne, the double breasted coat left open to reveal the chest plate, the frothy lace of his necktie overlapping pale blue metal. He had shined his boots so well that it looked as if the lower halves of his legs had been dipped in a starry night.

The officer had spoken little, and remained silent all the way over to the neighboring *Swift Cannon*, where the duel was to be fought. It was the prince who had suggested holding it on one of the vessels, not wishing to incite a morbid fuss among the locals. Better this business between officers be treated in a decorous manner, he thought. A coin had been tossed to decide which of the two ships was to host the combat.

The morning air was cool. Gulls circled beneath a drab sky and the sea had a deathly color, darker than the clouds, though distant fog was edging closer and closer to the shore. There was light enough for the masts and rigging to cast web-like shadows across the raised rear deck where three small groups of people were gathered.

Mill Burnshire walked ahead; he and the lieutenant bowed politely as they passed the duel party of the opposition. Capt. Moorsparrow stood tall with hands behind his back, handsome in his woodsy green uniform, the bicorne hat worn crossways on the head, his sword at his side. He looked all the more dangerous for the contained defiance in his eyes, unwavering as he nodded his head ever so slightly to the men. Privet could have sworn that Moorsparrow smirked.

Next the coxswain and the lieutenant passed Prince Fenny and two armed guards. The young heir acknowledged the fellows from the *North Swan* with a tip of his hat and remorseful eyes. One of the wardens gave Privet a pitying look.

The third group consisted of the duel party that Burnshire had assembled. There was the tall gaunt healer from the *Swan*, Polton Juniper, holding an ominous leather satchel filled with bandages, herbs and amputation tools. Next to him stood the "mercy man," whose identity was hidden behind the impassive black features of a metal mask. This fellow—likely a crewman from the lieutenant's own ship—was authorized to intercede with his flintlock pistol and put an end to Privet, should the duelist find himself in an irreparable state. The last of the three was a young woman in mourning black, her long skirt and veil shifting as a breeze whispered in from the Gantic. It was her duty to weep and pray, and sprinkle dead spiders over his eyes, if conditions required. Privet wondered if it were his lovely Hazel behind that veil, but the wind flicked aside her concealment and he saw that it was not. A simple local girl he had never set eyes on. *Better a stranger mourn than no woman at all*, he thought.

166

Agents of the duelists, the two tenders met at the center of the raised deck and spoke quietly. Moorsparrow's representative was Lieutenant. Barrow, a bulky little fellow with a peg leg. Violence could be avoided if Privet were willing to pay a hefty sum to his challenger, or if he were willing to throw down his sword and beg for mercy. Burnshire informed Barrow that Privet was prepared to do neither, so the tenders stepped aside and signaled for the duelists to take their positions.

Moorsparrow removed his hat, handed it to Barrow and smoothed back his straw-colored hair, then strode to the center of the deck and stopped. An arm's length of air separated the men. Privet waited for the order to come, swallowing until his throat went dry, his eyes flicking toward the slightest suggestion of motion—a gull's shadow passing over the planks, a line of rope wavering in the breeze, the flutter of his opponent's cravat.

"Swords!" the tenders called at last.

Moorsparrow's weapon hissed as he drew it from his scabbard. It was handsome with its straight thirty-inch blade of double-edged blue steel. The grip was stag's horn with a knuckle bow curving from the shaft to the pommel, which in this case was a gold skull screwed into the hollow handle, entombing a human tooth. A good luck charm of sorts, the molar was a trophy taken from the first man that Moorsparrow had slain in a sword fight.

Privet unsheathed his weapon as well, and while it too had a thin blue blade, it was less showy than the opponent's. The grip was wood, the cross guard and ball-finial simple and silver.

The men touched blades in a metallic kiss, then each took several steps back, their eyes intense and locked. They waited for the final word, legs slightly bent, backs straight, swords held out straight as if dowsing for each other's blood. The order came at last, dulled by the drumming inside ears.

"Engage!"

Privet saw nothing but a blur of dark green and a whipping blue streak as Moorsparrow sprang and thrust. The tip of the captain's sword made a terrible scraping noise as it carved a line across his chest plate—the sound caused the onlookers to cringe. A small piece of the lieutenant's tie was sliced off and fluttered like a moth. The man found himself stumbling back, slashing blindly at the charging foe. Swords clanked and rang and made swift whispers in the air.

Somehow Privet avoided taking another hit, though it was apparent that the captain was now focusing his attack above the chest plate, his swooshing blade so close that the lieutenant felt a breeze on his face. Another swipe sent Privet's hat spinning through the air.

Regaining his balance, Privet ducked into a defensive stance, nearly crouching, as Moorsparrow continued with his bold and relentless assault. Privet ducked and stabbed, the tip of his blade glancing off the lower half of the other's chest plate. Alarmed, the captain pranced back and remained still, poised cat-like with his sword out-held. His eyes were a menacing squint.

Though the morning was chill, Privet felt waves of heat rushing though his head, and his heart was bouncing against the inside of his chest plate. It seemed Moorsparrow was baiting him to make an advance, but Privet took advantage of this momentary peace and tried to catch his breath. The day was no brighter, but there were still faint shadows, and Privet dropped his eyes to the deck to note the angle of his own as he turned his back to the captain.

Moorsparrow's shadow preceded him, keying Privet to spin and meet the sudden dash. Blue streaks flashed in the air—the lieutenant's tactic failing as his jab was deflected with a parrying stroke. Snarling, his coat fluttering behind, Capt. Moorsparrow slashed a spitting wound down the side of Privet's sword arm. The younger man winced and nearly dropped his weapon. He swiped back in time to thwart another hit and danced sideways, pursued by a flurry of strikes. He dodged some of these, repelled others, but was not quick enough for the master swordsman Moorsparrow. A quick lunge pierced Privet in the cheek. The initial impact felt like a punch, then came searing pain and he saw red crickets leaping away from his face.

"Oh, dear!" the prince gasped, watching from a safe distance.

Privet staggered backward, flailing his steel from side to side. Graceful and composed, Moorsparrow glided forward, and with a flick of his blade swatted Privet's sword free of the bloody hand that held it. The weapon clattered across the wide boards of the deck. The lieutenant stood stunned and dripping, not daring to turn his head long enough to see how close his sword was. Moorshadow grinned coldly and took a step closer, raising his blade to the level of the lesser officer's eyes.

"Farewell, Lieutenant," the captain murmured.

A soft hiss came on the air, just before a great invisible fist punched the side of the *Swift Cannon*. Privet toppled onto his back and his opponent slid sideways, as if the deck were ice. The ship rocked so violently that those witnessing the duel were tossed. The women screamed and the men bellowed and before the ship could steady itself, another impact blew a hole in the hull.

Moorsparrow waved his sword in the air, "We're under fire!" he called. He shouted orders to his crew, suddenly unmindful of the wounded Lt. Privet.

"A red sloop," the lookout called down, pointing into the fog, which by now had closed the distance between horizon and shore.

The prince was clinging to the railing and staring out into the thick haze. His guards pulled him away and were urging him toward the aft hatchway when a boulder of wind came soaring and shattered one of the armed men. The prince was pummeled by red spray and sharp bits of broken chest plate. The surviving warden tugged the young prince down as another swoosh of air flew over the deck.

Privet pulled himself up and squinted into the mist. He glimpsed the red sloop for a second—like a wound opening in the fog—and then it was gone. He noticed the ruined guard's musket lying on the deck and picked it up, taking aim. When the sloop reappeared it was much closer, so close that he could see figures standing on the deck, figures in long black cloaks. Then, like a ghost, it vanished.

The *Swift Cannon* began to shake again, but this time it was from the firing 42-pounders on board, and not the invisible projectiles from the attacking craft. Portside cannons were roaring, coughing great clouds that blurred into the fog. Plumes of water shot up out of the Gantic where the round shot hit.

By now the crew of the neighboring *North Swan* was aware of the situation, and men were running to their posts. There was nothing for them to do, however, for Moorsparrow's great warship stood between them and the mystery vessel.

Despite his pain and the dizzying mist in his head, Lt. Privet held to his spot atop the high rear deck, sighting along the barrel of the dead guard's musket. He thought he saw a red blur in the fog, and then again, even closer. He clicked back the cock and waited until he could get a clearer view, which, eventually, he did.

The sloop was red, sails and all, and the bald women in their long black cloaks stood out starkly against the crimson of their vessel and the pale smoky air. There were round wooden barrels between them, and the women were plucking things out of them—skulls it seemed, though at such a distance it was hard to be sure—and holding them above their heads. Privet saw one of the women hurl a round object his way. His finger found the trigger.

The musket kicked and clapped and the woman, struck by the ball, spun back and fell as the red ship slipped from sight once more. The skull faded also, as it became a ferocious ball of wind that blasted into a gunport beneath where Privet was standing. The *Swift Cannon* shuddered.

The impacts now came in a flurry—it felt as if a giant were kicking the side of the craft. Ragged craters were blown into the gundecks, where agonized cries could be heard. The ship was being destroyed.

"Privet!"

The lieutenant turned and saw Capt. Moorsparrow standing with a pistol in his hand. The captain cringed as another explosion shook the ship.

"The prince! Where is the prince? We need move him off ship before she goes under."

"He's below," Privet said, pointing to the hatchway where the guard had taken the heir.

"Blast!" Moorsparrow cursed. He rushed off into the pungent cannon smoke that the breeze had blown back over the deck.

The air hissed and a mighty force slammed into the side of the ship just feet away from where Privet was standing. The railing snapped and boards flew and the man was knocked flat back. His vision went dark momentarily, and his ears were ringing when he found himself lying there, looking up at the sky.

"Strange," he muttered.

Gazing into the blurry air, the young officer noticed small gray objects overhead. They were above the masts, and hardly bigger than dining plates from what he could tell. Winged creatures, Privet concluded, moths the color of pewter, and they were carrying small white sacks, and flying over the *Swift Cannon,* down into the mist where the red sloop hid.

The aft hatch banged open and Moorsparrow came up, pistol first, followed by Prince Fenny and his guard. One of the unseen meteors whistled by and everyone on deck hunched down for a moment. The skull-wind missed, however, and while the men waited for more, none came. At length the captain called for his gun crews to cease firing. It grew still and quiet.

Women's voices came floating through the mist, through the gun smoke, as the red sloop floated out of the vapor and hovered off the portside of the towering warship. The bald women in dark cloaks were calling over to the *Swift Cannon.* Capt. Moorsparrow hurried to the side of his crippled vessel and aimed his pistol down at one of them.

"Die, you wench!" he called.

"Wait." Prince Fenny said, grabbing the officer's arm, "Listen."

The red sloop was now clearly visible and drifting closer, the large grayish moths lighting on the ropes and watching impassively with eyes like juniper berries. The words of the women could be distinguished, the same words repeating like a chant.

"We love you! We love you! We love you!"

Fenny recognized one of the people on the mystery craft, but this individual was not a bald woman, though he too wore the long black cloak. It was a clean-shaven young man with boyish features and blond hair pulled back into a tail that hung past his shoulders. It was his twin brother, Prince Treadson, and he was chanting along with the rest.

A fine drizzle blew off the Gantic into Old Crown, but Privet was comfy and dry, sitting in the humble parlor of the pretty, old Deerfield sisters. A nice fire heated the room and the place smelled of bergamot and old linens.

"Tea?" the sisters asked.

"Thank you," the man said, smiling.

Once tea and jam cakes were on hand, the sisters, who always spoke in unison, sat down with their guest.

"What a terrible man, that Prince Treadson," they chimed.

"Indeed," Privet said. "Seems he'd been thrown together a bit too closely with those folks of the North Islands. Ahh, but he's always been a hungry one, and with Fenny dead he'd be the singular heir. *That* was his intent in attacking the ships, it would seem."

"Strange magic those women of the North Isles have," the sisters said, "and not so nice as the kind we're like to cast. A shame he got in with that lot, but what a dreadful man to want to do away with his very twin."

"Well," Privet said, "he'd have made to kill poor Fenny whether he was in with them or not, I should think. Some claim he even poisoned the Kings."

The afternoon moved along slowly, the wind freckling rain on the windows, good oak logs keeping a steady blaze in the firebox. There was more tea and more talk.

"What of the moths and the spell?" Privet asked at length.

"It was your doing, in a sense," the old women said.

"*My* doing? Do tell."

"Well, when you paid visit and asked us to act on your behalf, after that dreadful business with the love spell and the captain's wife, oh, didn't we feel just awful? And we so wanted to prevent that nasty duel."

"Hm, yes." Privet absently touched his bandaged cheek.

"But we knew you'd not be able to pour a drink of love potion in the fellow, and so we got thinking. Perhaps there was another way to get a spell to an intended person."

Privet sipped his tea and nodded.

"Powder," they said together. "We thought to try a love spell as a powder. We'd never done such a thing, you know; our love spells were delivered always in liquid form...powders sprinkled into liquid, and administered as such."

"Yes, I recall."

The women sat forward, enthusiastic, eyes gleaming in the hearth-light. "We weren't even certain it would work, we must admit, but we meant it for you, initially. Unfortunately we weren't quite ready with it in time to stop the duel, but thank the gods we had it in time to put an end to that dreadful ship battle."

The carrier moths had dropped small sacks of powdered love potion onto the deck of the red sloop. The bursting clouds of dust had indeed delivered the spell to those on board.

"So," the Deerfields asked, "what becomes of the princes now?"

Privet said, "Well, that rotter Treadson is in dungeon at Castle Wickheath and is like to hang. Fenny will be king when his father's time comes, and a fine king he will make, I believe."

"And you, Lieutenant?"

"I'll be at New Crown for some time. They've ordered my ship to stand guard for the *Swift Cannon* while she's under repair. As for Captain Moorsparrow, he has now accepted that the spell his wife drank down was not, in fact, intended for her. He's apologized heartily, and now can't seem to do enough for me. Perhaps one day we shall even sail together."

"How nice. Then we'll see you again?"

"Yes, I believe you may."

Evening was closing in when the young officer set out to leave. It was still damp and the long line of gray steps heading to the newer half of the city was slick and precarious. The sisters, hunched under a single umbrella, had insisted on escorting him there, though, fearful of heights, they did not venture too near the cliff edge.

"Well," Privet said, "I'm off to the inn. There's something I need say to a certain young woman there."

One of the sisters grinned and produced a small bottle of love potion from under her shawl. She held it out.

"Thank you, but no. I think I'd rather take my chances."

Privet smiled, tipped his tricorne and started down the long, precipitous ribbon of stairs.

Fine drizzle drifted in over the dusk sea as Privet made his way to a rectangular building of brick. A wooden sign hung on squeaky chains—a hag's severed head dangling upside down. Pallid hair culled from horse tails draped down from the wooden head, shifting in the damp breeze. The sign was all the more ghastly for the bluish glow radiating on it from a leafed net of vines growing on one end of the inn. The plant was ghost eye and the small bluish berries gave an eerie light whenever it rained, or, as the moment proved, when it was drizzling.

Privet entered the inn and removed his tricorne, mashing it under one arm. Mad little birds were in his heart as he stood looking across the many tables, most of which were taken up by navy men from the *North Swan* and *Swift Cannon*. Love put the birds in his heart and made his blood race in his veins, made his brain feel heavy and cloudlike all at the same time. He stared through pipe smoke and the warm flickering glow of candles to where a young woman served tables. It was Hazel, the innkeeper's daughter.

She had captured his eye the first time he found himself in The Salty Hag, and ever since he had watched her, aching. She was a poem, quite simply, a poem of flesh, her face soft and white, her eyes a magnificent green, her hair the black of night and its mysteries. She floated about in a long plum skirt, the curved neckline of her white top offering a glimpse of the pallor and fullness of her charms. Privet had to have her as his own.

The lieutenant found a little empty table in one of the corners and waited for Hazel to approach. Even sitting down he was dizzy, but he was determined; tonight would be the night when he made his intentions known. He had rehearsed the words he would say a hundred times, but when Hazel floated over and stood waiting, a hovering poem of flesh, all the lieutenant's words were gone.

"Sir?" the young woman said to the man who stared up at her mutely.

Privet heard himself say, "A mug of squall."

Hazel smiled sweetly, putting painful flowers in his heart. "Squall, sir," she repeated, and turned to go.

Privet cursed himself. *Fool!* He stood up swiftly, called out, "Miss?"

Hazel stopped and turned, her dark hair whipping. She stepped back to the table and smiled patiently. "Sir?"

Privet puffed his chest out and breathed, "There is no beauty I have seen in my travels upon this wide mystery of a world compares to yours."

Hazel's eyes flared a brighter shade of green, her smile as eager and pretty as a smile could hope to be.

The Deerfield sisters lived up in Old Crown where steep narrow buildings of a bygone architecture stood stoically against the elements, overlooking the pewter Gantic. Plain in shape, the houses bore faded paint and decorative features that were elegant in their rounded lines and frail repetitions.

Privet found himself cozy in their parlor, the house a warm refuge from the chill of ocean air. Comforting smells of tea and boiled vegetables added to the hominess, as did the jam cakes the hostesses served, and the hearty fire burning in its box.

The women were twins, like most of the local inhabitants. They were pretty ladies, frosted on top, both dressed in gray and sitting on a settle. They spoke every word together, as if a single mind and a single tongue were shared by two. The sing-song manner of their speech had a charm all its own, and Privet could not help but be delighted by their company. The women had become unofficial advisors to the young officer as regards his nervousness over matters of romance.

"I kissed her," Privet reported happily, smiling as he lifted his tea for a sip.

"Ohhh, how lovely!" the sisters cooed.

"She seemed not to mind," Privet said, lowering his cup. "In all honesty she seemed rather pleased."

The sisters both sat forward, grinning, crinkling their eyes. "How very splendid! And should she not feel so, you being a charming young fellow, an officer?"

Privet beamed. "They are rather taken with navy lads hereabout."

As soon as Privet's cup was empty it was filled again and the sisters, fixing him meaningfully, spoke in something of a hush.

"Do you, Lieutenant, mean to ask her hand?"

Privet sat back and grinned. "Both hands, in actual fact, and everything else that she has."

5

Providence

They walked by the sea and kissed by the sea and watched sunsets of ghostly copper. All the world around them seemed a poem. Rime was on the heather and gulls the color of clouds hung low above a steely Gantic. The season's cold proved a contrast to the warmth within hearts. Winter and love were in the air.

Lt. Privet and the tavern keep's daughter, Hazel, whispered promises, as those in such situations do. Bold proclamations of enduring affection. Privet held his dark-haired charmer by the waist and said, "Will you marry me, Hazel?"

"Yes, Hale, I shall," she returned.

The tavern keeper, Tulling Gorse, along with his wife and two daughters, lived in an ancient house that made Privet think of a home where, as a boy, he had visited an elderly relative back in East Whittle. The Gorse house, which had been in that family forever, was one of the few tall, narrow structures of its type still standing in the new part of the city and would have fit better up in Old Crown. White, with a newer roof of pale fern-stone slates, the wooden house occupied a knoll presiding above fields and orchards. The upper windows lent a westerly view out to sea.

Privet ventured to the Gorse abode on The Eve of Bees, one of those festooned and honorable days of the year when traditions were indulged. Legend held that the sun darkened and died one terrible winter's dusk and a little girl, seeing her family's despair, snuck out into the night snow and prayed until she froze to death. Hearing her prayers, and seeing her sacrifice, half the bees of the world flew up into the dark sky and joined in a great circle amongst the cold stars. The summer heat within them turned them into a great ball of fire—a new sun was born. Thus the winter fanfare for this warm-season insect.

In some tellings (more common to East Fellengrey) the bees flew up to the black ball of the sun and feasted on it, taking what heat was left within before creating the new sun. At any rate, The Eve of Bees was a celebration of the winter solstice, the light regaining after the longest dark of the year.

The innkeeper invited Privet to the family feast, whereat the young officer designed to ask the Gorses for their daughter's hand. The house was humble, but homey, and trimmed for the holiday. Smells of cooking decorated the air. Intertwined black and yellow ribbons were strung above doorways, black and yellow cloths put on the tables. A fine carving of a bee sat on the mantel of the best room's fireplace.

Men gathered in this parlor with pipes and gin punch, and a great roaring hardwood fire, while the women busied themselves in the kitchen. Mr. Gorse, his brother and their aged father delighted in Privet's sea tales and marveled at his blue-bladed sword, once they persuaded him to show the thing. These three local fellows, while having always lived by the ocean, had not spent much time upon it.

Tables were set up and candles placed on them. A windy snow was at the windows and the women, all pretty in their own right, carried in the food that the men had been smelling. Privet sighed at the sight of Hazel, who was lovely in a sage-green gown with lace trim at the square neckline.

Tulling stood once all was in place, and recited (more than sang) a brief seasonal song, "May darkness now pass—all sing praise to the bees, for the new sun is born to bring life to all beasts."

A scene of merriment and gluttony followed. They dined on cider-basted goose, turnip (seasoned with nutmegs) and warm mashed apples. There were robust sausages, and leek soup sprinkled with thyme, and shelled prawns heaped in a steamy bowl of melted butter.

Next came the desserts: small cakes made in a metal form that shaped them as bees, a boiled pudding flavored with winter spice, and pears (having been preserved in wine) served hot and strewn with cinnamon. After eating, and a period of digestion, there was song and more punch.

The tables and chairs were cleared, a fiddle was brought out, and Hazel's uncle played, the humble parlor transformed into a ballroom. Privet and Hazel spun, beaming, candlelight gleaming on the circular brass brooch the young woman wore to signify the sun.

Off in a corner the parents spoke quietly to one another as they watched.

Mr. Gorse, who was beaming, said, "A fine lad he is! *An officer.*"

Mrs. Gorse, who was not smiling, replied, "Yes, and like to have plenty a lass in towns along the coast."

"Oh, shush. He's a respectable sort."

Hazel's younger sister, who was enamored of the dashing navy man upon first sight, had to settle for dancing with her grandfather, who kept stepping on her toes, *"Grand!"*

Hazel, in a hush, asked Privet, "Have you the courage to ask them?"

Privet, a bit giddy from punch, was indeed less nervous about the prospect of begging Hazel's hand than he was initially, though his anxiety was far from cured. "Courage enough? I certainly have, young miss!"

"Then when do you ask?"

"Soon enough." Perhaps another cup of punch would lend the proper amount of fortification, Privet thought to himself.

When the dancers had had their fill of dance the room was put back to order and tea was brewed. Talk was quiet now, as seemed appropriate to the lateness of the hour. Hazel's sister, Lilac, who would rival her sister's beauty given a few more years of maturation, questioned Privet exhaustively about the exotic Figwort Islands.

Privet nibbled nervously from a bowl of fiddle nuts which had shells shaped like full-hipped women without limb or head. Looking to the tall clock in a corner, he realized that he best make his request of Mr. and Mrs. Gorse before the evening progressed to a close. He waited for a pause in conversation, got up from his seat and stood very formally, very stiffly in his dignified uniform, before his hosts. But, before Privet could speak, a knock came at the door.

"Who so late?" Mr. Gorse asked, getting up with a grunt.

Tulling walked from the room and when he returned he was accompanied by a seaman with a sprinkling of snow on his shoulders and a hat held under one arm. Privet recognized the man as a crewmate from the *North Swan*.

The young fellow said, "I beg pardon for the intrusion, good folk. I bring word of sad news, newly arrived. King Aven has died."

A collective gasp flew up from the revelers.

The seaman continued, "Lieutenant, sir, I am asked to hasten you back to ship, for we sail come morning. The *Swan* shall return the prince to Royal House."

Privet rose, collected his hat and cape and thanked his hosts. Much as he wanted to kiss his beloved goodbye, he could do no more (considering the company) than lightly take her hand and bow. Hazel gave him a sad smile and the young officer disappeared out into the snowy night.

A wispy snow fell over the capital city of Demmingsfife, onto the long black funeral procession that edged through the quiet streets from Royal House to Crown's Rest. Mourners crowded the route, many weeping softly, rich and poor alike huddled in the cold, united in their grief. Six black horses sprouting six black plumes pulled the ornate funeral carriage ahead of a parade of marchers and vehicles so long that it took four hours for all to traverse the two mile route.

King Aven was interred at Crown's Rest, the cemetery where his royal relations were entombed. Artisans had worked around the clock to prepare a stone sarcophagus with a cover that bore a three dimensional carved likeness of the King with traditional death-spiders over the eyes. His wooden box, a glossy thing of blackbirch with silver trim, was placed in this impressive container, which was positioned in the stone crypt where his brother, Alder, had only recently preceded him.

The twin Kings, perhaps the most beloved ever to rule Fellengrey, were dead at the hands of Prince Treadson, who, prompted by the blood of one of the Gifted, admitted to poisoning his father and uncle. He had sailed back aboard the *North Swan* along with Prince Fenny—although Fenny did not spend the trip in irons—in a cell. The coronation that followed several days later was a solemn affair, rather than the joyful event one would have liked such a thing to be.

Treadson's public hanging drew a massive crowd, despite dreary weather, and proved profitable to vendors selling food, and effigies of the villain for the burning.

One merchant offered a child's toy gallows complete with a dangling miniature Treadson with clattering wooden limbs.

Lt. Privet's mother came to town for the event. Following the morbid spectacle, mother and son escaped the crowds and walked the sandy stretch of beach beyond the mammoth mercantile buildings along Brittlegate. An icy rain pattered on the woman's umbrella.

They talked about the state of the kingdom under the rule of King Fenny. Both felt he would do a fine job of ruling, but there were others who were less confident, those who feared that past enemies on the continent might see Fellengrey as a weakened beast and move against her. The relationship between the empire and the North Islands was certainly in question.

While Treadson, under the spell of truth-blood, made it clear that his scheme to gain the crown did *not* involve the rulers of the mysterious islands, there was trepidation on the part of Fenny's advisors about becoming too friendly with people in that part of the world. While the northerners were not great in number, comparatively speaking, they had terrifying and powerful magic at their disposal.

"Better they be friends, than enemies," King Fenny noted, and while he decided to limit trade between the countries for the time being, he did not eliminate it, as some suggested.

This worked to Privet's benefit, for the Admiralty withdrew its order that all officers carry blue blades forged of North Island steel, which allowed Privet, once again, to carry Rye Blackbird's lovely sword at the hip.

Fenny was very impressed by the spell utilized by the Deerfield sisters to overcome the red sloop and wondered if the ladies might consider working with the kingdom's military to some capacity. But the sisters remained resistant to having their magic applied to martial purposes. While disappointed, the gracious Fenny respected their decision.

The conversation moved to lighter topics as the lieutenant and his mother made their way along the shore, half-heartedly looking for interesting tidbits strewn at the water's edge. Mrs. Privet collected a palm-sized flat stone, which in color was a mild green speckled with rust spots. The younger Privet stooped to examine the abandoned carapace of a crab.

Mrs. Privet smiled to hear her son talk of his beloved Hazel, never having seen him in love before. It pleased her to hear that Hazel came from honorable, humble people, and didn't he gush about her beauty!

"The most lovely woman my eyes have fallen upon," he said. Then, after a brief pause and a grin, added, "But for you."

Mrs. Privet, still pretty, still rounded, and nicely dressed, chuckled and swatted her son playfully on the arm.

The gray water rolled back, exposed smooth, glistening stones the color of charcoal and milk. Something winked amongst them. Privet, holding his mother's green stone in his right hand, scooped with his left.

It was a pearly shell, no bigger than a walnut, with a shape that made Privet think of a curled up napping cat.

"Oh!" Privet quickly opened his hand and the shell dropped into the foam that came rushing at his boots.

Mrs. Privet looked concerned, "Hale?"

The man chuckled. "It stung me, I think."

Stung might not have been the best word to describe what he felt, for while there was a sudden sensation, he could hardly have called it pain. He turned his palm over and looked at his fingers. There was a rosy glow where the shell had made contact.

Mrs. Privet bent to view the shell, but heeded her son's warning not to touch it. When she righted herself, she said, "Ahhh, it would be a peace-shell."

Privet said, "*A peace-shell?*"

"I once saw one, in picture only, in a book. It's been many a year now, but I'd like to say they were thought to be magical in some way."

Privet frowned. "Oh, lovely, then I'm to turn to a smelly goat."

His mother laughed and swatted at him again. "No, silly thing! Nothing unpleasant about them, as I recall."

"Yes, mother, but you *can't* recall. Tell, am I sprouting a beard? Horns perhaps?"

"Not that I can tell, but *that smell…*"

They both laughed and continued along through the rain. As for the peace-shell, the sea whisked it away as if it had never been there.

Hasten Flint grumbled something disparaging about planters as the blade of his plow clanged against another stone. His horse turned and gave him what he took to be a disgusted look.

"It is no fault of mine the field be laden with blasted stones!" the man responded. The horse blinked, turned back forward and trudged on.

At least he could *smell* the sea, if he could not be on it, he reasoned. And there, beyond the stretch of earth where he meant to grow his fortune, stood his cozy stone cottage, and behind the windows that now glowed warmly in the coming dusk, was his love, humming at the hearth. No, he was not the young creature he had once been, and he was glad for the companionship and willing to set root, for much as a man might love the sea, the sea was incapable of reciprocation. He could not say the same of his Holly.

Following their meal they drank tea by the fire, snug from the chill spring night. Holly was a pretty green-eyed woman with a rich flow of red hair and cheeks that rounded when she smiled. She was a decade younger than Hasten.

"Tell of Chiddidin again," she said, "and the tiger."

Hasten leaned forward, his eyes twinkling in the firelight. Even sitting he appeared tall and sturdily built, a man nearing sixty, with wild gray hair and a wild gray beard and a face that weather had not been kind to. He might have been handsome without all that pewter shrubbery, for the features were good, the eyes raptor-keen and dark as treacle.

Holly grinned as he told his tale, looking at him, then at the fire and back at him again. She had been so lonely before Hasten came along, childless, her husband dead going on three years.

Flint was nearing the end of his story. "So, open the door, I did, but there was no cabin boy—it was a *tiger*," Hasten said dramatically, "with flames just shooting from its mouth and its nose and its farts."

Holly was frightened and delighted.

Before they retired to bed, Hasten retold the tale of a sheep (its five heads facing out like the spikes of a star) that did nothing but eat, and a ship, with a figurehead at either end that could not decide which way to go.

The south-west coast of West Fellengrey was hilly and windy, and green now that spring had come. Birds, and the scent of blooming trees, were in the air. A breeze drifted in off the Gantic as a chill tide nuzzled into the many small inlets common to the area. Some of these coves were furtive hollows tucked in the shade of enclosing trees, others shaped quiet water with irregular banks of hodgepodge stones.

Hasten and Holly lived in a remote region on the outskirts of The Spinnings, which were comprised of Spinning, Spinning Tower and Lower Spinning. Their nearest neighbors were two miles away, which seemed not to bother them. Farther down the coast one found fishing villages, but here, between the sea and the verdant farm country of Spinning Tower, the land was rocky, so few planters had been tempted to settle. But then, few planters were as stubborn as Hasten Flint.

After days laboring in the fields, Hasten conceded to accompany Holly on a picnic, seeing as the weather was fine and the days were growing longer. There would be time to fit some more work in after indulging a bit of rest. The woman packed a hamper and they walked beyond the pastureland where their modest flock of sheep grazed, walked until there was no path to follow and broom bloomed gold in a wild meadow and the smell of the sea was close.

It was a spot where they had picnicked before, and once even made love. A high, round hill dappled with wildflowers, facing out to deep water on one side and rolling green countryside on the other. Smaller hills hunched around this greater rise, sheltering old abandoned tin mines.

"I'm minded of a poem by Nettles," Hasten said, studying the woman as she sat at his side in a humble gown of pale yellow, her red hair free of its day cap, dancing about her face.

"Which do you mean?"

"*The Cooper's Seventh Sister.*"

"But I am not a cooper's sister."

Hasten smiled. "That be not the point. The poem concerns a fetching woman seated by far-flung fields. You *are* that."

Holly blushed, her smile accentuating round cheeks.

They ate and drank wine, and in time, Hasten, lulled by the mood of the day, lay back in the grass and dozed. Holly stretched out beside him and rested a hand on his chest, just to feel his heart beating. She thought she heard distant voices at one point, but the wind did strange things in the hills, and so she dismissed the notion.

Holly gazed off, breathing softly, but perked when a day-moth flit low over her head and skimmed the spent food hamper. She rose on an elbow for a better look, being interested in all things wild. The day-moth was of a type she had never seen before, good-sized, the wings a pale salmon color, each bearing a mark like a splotch of ink. It continued on its way, down the hill, to where shorter hills rippled toward the sea. The woman rose to follow.

"Here, now, beauty, slow up, won't you?" Holly said, smiling as she hurried after.

The slope lent her speed and she ducked into a small birch grove which straddled the sides of two grassy mounds, an inadvertent tunnel. Bright young leaves were on the branches, fluttering as if they wanted to launch free of their tethers and join the pursuit of the insect.

Holly could hear the surf and the voices of gulls as she came out from the shady birches into bright sun. The earth dropped sharply toward the glaring waters of a bay, around which bristly spruce and larch jutted up, shaping to the shore, defining small coves. A ship was in the bay.

The day-moth veered off to the right, and Holly, still pursuing, found herself on a level expanse alongside a knoll, one side of which bore the stone-lipped mouth of an old tin mine. Two men, in the process of carrying a wooden trunk through the low opening, stopped and turned to stare at her with surprise. After several heartbeats one of the men smiled a wide toothless smile and said, "Hallo, sweet!"

The day-moth flitted up over the knoll out of view.

"Holly?"

Hasten woke, uncertain of how much time had passed. Not very much, he imagined, seeing as the sun was still high in the sky. Holly, however, was nowhere to be seen. Perhaps she had wandered off to gather a posy.

A moment passed and the man heard a sound that made him think of a woman's scream, but the birds were making such noise that he remained unalarmed, thinking that he was mistaken. Then the report of a gun came bouncing among the hills. This put Hasten on his feet.

The contours of the land conveyed sound in a curious way, confusing the listener as to the source. With his blood rushing inside, Hasten Flint rushed off in the direction he *thought* the shot had come from. Armed only with a dagger, he descended the steep embankment and negotiated a pair of smaller hills and found himself in a craggy cove.

A soft mist was on the water and it blurred the firs along a jutting strip of land that delineated the far side of the cove. Minor islands arced up like the backs of stationary whales and a two-masted gun-sloop, its hull painted a somber gray, was sitting in the bay. Certain trees had blocked his view of it when he spied the water from the higher hill. A small boat came into view, headed for the larger craft.

Hasten knew where to go to get a better look. He headed south, passed through a patch of short scrubby pines, and jogged down a slope into another cove, a rough concave of staggered stones. Holly lay on her back by the water on a modest patch of beach that was more pebble than sand.

Hasten bellowed, "Holly!"

He ran to her, saw that her eyes were open and unblinking, saw the blood saturating the torso of her gown, saw the terrible hole between her breasts where a musket ball had gone in.

"No! No!" Hasten fell on his knees. "Return to me, Holly, return…"

Hasten shook her by the shoulders, but she did not return. He got up, whirled around, and dashed into the water, arms flailing in the air as he shouted at the small boat.

"Bastards! Bastards!"

There were four men in the boat and they were rowing steadily for the sloop, which was flying the plum and gold of Fellengrey (the two halves of the country represented as a stylized moth's wings). Footprints in the damp sand suggested what had happened. Men had tried to force the woman into the boat so as to take her onto their ship. She had resisted, fought, probably struck one so hard that he shot her in anger.

While they were now out of range, one of the men in the rowboat fired a musket round toward the shore. The projectile dropped into the sea before reaching Hasten.

"Come back, you bastards!" he called as the clammy mist came thicker over the water, turning the ship's sails into ghosts. He pursued them into the bay, for unlike most men who sailed the seas, Hasten Flint, whose actual name was Rye Blackbird, could swim like a fish.

The rowboat reached the safety of its mother ship. The man in the water, his face wet with tears and salt water, swam until exhausted. Barely retaining the strength to swim further, he turned and paddled back to where Holly waited for him on the shore.

On a calm morning sea, in the early summer of 1753, the frigate *North Swan* was sailing northward off the coast of West Fellengrey, some ten miles from the fishing village of Casterwig. Captain Langham was in his dining cabin taking breakfast with the healer Juniper, along with coxswain Burnshire and the ship's best lieutenant, Privet. Sunlight from the windows filled the chamber which, with its paneled walls painted a serene white, hardly ever seemed dark.

Langham, a steady man of middling proportions, who was characterized by a dignified gray beard, sat at the head of the table in a white shirt that was as loose as his breeches were tight. A painting of his wife and twin honey-haired daughters hung on the paneling behind him, near where his ready steward stood.

"The King and The Halves," Langham said, customarily honoring the ruler and the two great islands that comprised Fellengrey.

"The King and The Halves," echoed the rest, before having at their repast.

The breakfast these men indulged was altogether different from the humble fare the bulk of the crew received. The main course was a hearty egg and bacon pie, accompanied by toast with marmalade, and cheese speckled with sage and minute constellations of crushed pepper.

When the meal proper was done there was more tea and the captain filled a long white pipe. A knock came at the door before he could light it.

"Yes?" Langham called.

A midshipman entered. He was not quite old enough for facial hair, though he looked sharp in a short jacket the color of bay leaves. He saluted.

"A ship appears off starboard, sir."

Privet, who was examining the tingly fingers of his left hand, looked up. Was it his imagination or was there the faintest luminosity, a ghostly nimbus around each of the fingertips that had touched the peace-shell?

Langham smiled pleasantly, said, "Well, let's have a peek," and got up from the table, plucking his bicorne from a hook on his way out. Privet and the coxswain followed him to the quarterdeck where the ship's oldest midshipmen had the helm.

It was Hibbits, who, never having conjured the confidence to try the test to become lieutenant, seemed destined to that lower rank for life. His companion, a lovely lamp-tail bird from Cabbadun (the hind feathers of which glowed coal-orange in darkness), sat on the perch in a cage at the man's feet. Its song fluctuated from low drawn out whistles to series of high twitters.

The captain looked through his telescope and saw a smallish two-masted ship, her sails set, the long frontal barb of the bowsprit pointing south.

"A sloop, I think," the man said, turning to Burnshire and Privet.

The three proceeded up toward the front of the *Swan*, passing under great towering sails like flattened clouds and the complex, seemingly chaotic system of lines and shrouds that comprised the rigging. They passed shirtless men, who, on hands and knees, were scrubbing the deck with raspy blocks of sandstone. Up at the forecastle, looking out beyond the figurehead, which was a gracefully rendered wooden swan, the men had a better view. Still not sure what to make of the craft, the captain called to the lookout positioned atop a platform partway up the foremast, "Colors, Mister Stibbs, does she bare colors?"

"Fellengrey colors only, sir," the man shouted back.

Privet asked, "A pirate, sir?"

"We soon enough shall see. Have men to their stations, Mister Privet."

"Yes, sir."

Gun crews were put on alert and marksmen climbed to their high platforms. Other uniformed fighters made sure that their weapons were in good order, checking the state of their flints, and seeing that flash-pans contained dry powder in case the ship turned out to be a pirate vessel and they were compelled to board.

The *North Swan* approached the unidentified ship at a cautious speed. With the distance closing, the other vessel was seen to be a ship-rigged gun-sloop, her hull painted a somber gray. This shortened distance also allowed the crew of the *Swan* to note an apparent lack of activity aboard the other craft, whose visible cannons showed wooden plugs still in their mouths.

Privet, seeing the guns with stoppers in place, noted, "Apparently they mean not to fight."

One of the musketeers in the fighting tops announced, "Dead men all about the deck!"

Langham squinted through his scope and wagged his head. "What's all this?"

Once the *North Swan* drew close enough, a boarding party swung over onto the sloop (which was found to be named *Swift Shark*) and discovered a terrible scene. As the marksman had noted, there were dead scattered on the deck, proof of a brutal struggle. Capt. Langham, with Privet close by, led the way, both with pistol in hand, stepping over and around the hacked and ball-torn bodies.

Lt. Privet, having reached the middle section of the craft, bent down next to one of the men, who, aside from musket damage, was missing his arm from the elbow down. The severed arm, and the long graceful pistol it had been holding, lay several feet away. Privet looked up at Langham with an inquisitive expression.

"She seems not a merchantman," the captain observed, "and the men, by their look would be pirates, I should think. Sailors of the common sort being not so armed as these."

"For all their weaponry they failed in defending their ship," observed Privet, standing, frowning down at the blood that had gotten on his fine black boots.

They made the quarterdeck, helmeted musketeers in their sage-green jackets and gray breastplates close behind. Dried blood suggested that several hours had passed since the slaughter took place, though here and there the deeper puddles were still wet at the center.

There was nothing to suggest that another ship's guns had been used against the *Swift Shark*, and all ten of the sloop's cannons were unfired. Not even the swivel guns mounted on the rails of the raised poop had gotten off a shot. The question on everyone's mind was *who* had done this?

"Pirates against pirates," Privet suggested, standing by the wheel, which was speckled with gore. "Or, perhaps a mutiny, or the crew fighting amongst themselves for treasure."

The captain pulled thoughtfully at his beard. "That may well be the case, Mister Privet, seeing as no one took the ship as prize, but left her adrift."

They went below where a musty silence held sway, a silence that yielded only to the intermittent creaks and groans a wooden sea vessel was wont to make. Their footsteps sounded too loud in close air. In such tight, low-ceilinged confines the "longs" the fighters carried were awkward, even without bayonets attached.

The ship was in reasonably good repair overall, but not what a navy man would have thought of as tidy, though some of the disorder had to be attributed to the fighting that had taken place. Empty drinking jugs of heavy clay were seen here and there, and one, on the gundeck, rolled back and forth as the ship rocked, its sound like rumbles of thunder.

Crewmen's hammocks were still strung from the ceiling between the cannons and a concentration of bodies in the immediate vicinity suggested that the men had been sleeping when their ordeal began. Langham, now equipped with a lantern, moved forward in a crouch, clutching his cocked pistol in one hand. He ducked beams where rammers for the cannons were fastened, his lantern's light washing unevenly over the numerous sagging chrysalises, now vacated, where the sailors had, no doubt, dreamed of women as they rode the night sea.

"See there!" the captain hissed, pointing with his flintlock.

One of the hammocks showed the bulge of an occupant. The rounded white of the cloth was soaked with dark red in spots and the wounded shape, obscured beneath a blanket, was trembling. Capt. Langham moved slowly, stepping closer, his weapon ready. As he drew nearer he noticed a number of low moans issuing from the lump beneath the blanket. When he stood an arm's length away, he quietly set the lantern at his feet and, with his free hand, reached and peeled back the cover.

A wild-eyed man with hollow cheeks and chattering teeth smiled through his bushy beard. "Come back to finish us off, eh?"

The wide-mouthed brass barrel of a blunderbuss pistol poked out from under the blanket and disgorged into Langham's face. The captain's hat flew off and the back of his head ruptured, a fast red cloud dispersing, drops of all sizes pattering on the plank floor as his body collapsed.

Privet howled like an animal and thrust his pistol out, but his hand seized up, shuddered, and lost its grip on the pistol, which fell with a thud. Two musketeers opened up on the hammock and the occupant jerked with a cry, fresh red joining the blood that had already stained the white cloth supporting him.

Privet would ponder the strange failure of his hand later, but now he found himself on his knees with the hand on the shoulder of his dead captain, who lay on his side, his legs half bent. The fighters came over and stared down with pained faces.

"Orders, sir?" one of the men asked, and for a moment Privet didn't realize that the man was speaking to him.

When Privet looked up he said, "Should further survivors be found, shoot them dead."

No other survivors were found, and whatever treasure the pirates may have had aboard was missing. The dead numbered forty-six. Someone had taken blood and drawn the simple outline of a bird on the floor of the captain's cabin. The resident of that compartment, and a woman he had apparently been in bed with, were both sprawled on the wide planks dressed only in their own blood.

The words the wounded man had spoken before shooting Langham suggested that the combat had *not* been between crewmembers, but grief on the part of the men of the *Swan* took precedence over any speculation about who had attacked the pirate sloop, and why.

Capt. Langham's body was removed to the *North Swan* for one last voyage, his corpse wrapped in layered sheets that were soaked with wine to preserve it during the journey back to Fort Wrenning. Privet, having previously been promoted to first lieutenant, took charge of the ship for the meantime. That evening he sat alone in Langham's dining cabin at the big table, feeling an intruder as the dead captain's wife and two pretty blond daughters stared at him from the wall.

Back in Fort Wrenning, Demingsfife, the *North Swan's* new base, Privet received a letter from Hazel.

When do you again come to New Crown? she wrote, which was her way of reminding him that he had yet to ask her hand of her parents.

Privet, in an apologetic response, gave her as much truth as he had. He could not say. In his letter he told of Capt. Langham's awful demise, and how pirates were still quite active in the waters off West Fellengrey, and how his duties, while a welcome weight, were particularly pressing at that time. Further: *When next we sail, the* Swan *shall be at the command of Post Captain Litch, who I have seen only in printed sketches.*

Demmingsfife, crowded with buildings and lives, was an incongruous garden on Remembrance Day, the capital city decked with flowers at every turn of the eye. It was an annual commemoration of those who had passed from life, a tradition which, in ways, harkened back to ancient solstice rituals. Baskets of blooms, both wild and cultivated, offset the austere buildings of brick and stone and lent perfume enough to intoxicate bees.

The sun at this, the longest day of the year, had come to represent the enduring force of spirit, and so masses gathered in places where the orb rose above structures positioned to mark the astronomical event. One of these, The Spear—found at King's Rest—was a tapering tower of granite blocks with a conical cap aligned to the solstice sunrise. The arch over the eastern entrance to Burial Hill was another. The sun, for a matter of minutes, hovered within the open stone curve, silhouetting the graves and statues amassed there.

A solemn parade of official carriages made its way from Royal House to the heavy stone bridge scaling the River Shrike at Fifth Crossing. The slow, steady water, which divided the city into halves, floated a colorful fleet of blossoms toward the sea. Horsemen of the Royal Guard, notable for their pumpkin-orange coats, rode ahead of the King's procession, stopping when they came to the river's edge.

A coachman scurried down from his seat atop the handsomest carriage, unfolded the steps and opened the door. King Fenny stepped out and acknowledged the crowding onlookers with a reserved smile appropriate to an occasion that encompassed both celebration and mourning. His features were mild, clean-shaven, and the blond hair not hidden by his hat was tied in a tail that fell to the middle of his back. Emptying from the other vehicles, in a dignified order, were Crown officials, men close to the throne, high-ranking military men among them.

Fenny looked all that a king should, a white plume spurting from his black cocked hat, the rest of him decked in a fine amber-colored suit, the stiffened skirts of his coat flaring at the hip. His waistcoat was trimmed with delicate embroidery featuring moths and ferns, and the cravat at his throat was like a gush of mist.

Fenny's mother, Violet, and his aunt—widows of Kings Aven and Alder— accompanied him to the middle of the bridge, where deferential pedestrians parted to accommodate soldiers and their wards. The two royal widows wore gowns of mourning black, and, like the young King, carried baskets of flowers.

There were roses—wild and bred—and scenting clusters of honeysuckle. There was cheery yellow iris and the timid pink of dog rose. There were daisies, simple and white, and gaudy blooms of bog-lamp.

Joined by others from the procession, Fenny and the ladies took to plucking flowers from their baskets and tossing them over the wall of the bridge into the westward Shrike. Others on the bridge, and along the banks, also rained flowers into the water.

When their baskets were empty, Fenny and company started back for their carriages, pausing along the way to greet subjects of the empire. The young King was already very popular with the masses. They reached the end of the bridge and were stepping onto the cobbled walkway when a tall woman in mourning black stepped forward carrying a posy, foxglove with bells of lusty purple, bunched together with shade-thorn, its petals a ghostly blue.

"King Fenny!" the woman called, rather huskily.

Fenny turned to her, smiling. The woman, who stood slightly higher than the King, wore a black cap with white lace trim and a black widow's mask, an impassive face of shaped and hardened cloth opened only so that the eyes and nostrils could be distinguished of the wearer's features. Masks of this kind had largely fallen out of fashion since the late '30s, though some older ladies still insisted on wearing them in public. If this was an older lady, she was a healthy example, for she suddenly sprang at Fenny, jamming her posy into his midsection.

The King grimaced and when the woman pulled away blood spilled down his waistcoat. Fenny's mother screamed. The assailant turned to dash into the throngs gathered at the river, but one of the Royal Guard pounced and brought the woman down. The posy dropped to the paving stones, a silvery dagger clattering out from amidst the vegetation. The blooms of broken shade-thorn scattered, and two drops of blood showed like wet rose petals.

It was a chaotic scene. In seconds the King was obscured by a swarm and shouting filled the air.

"I'm stuck," Fenny, who had collapsed, said weakly, looking up, seeing a blurry circle of faces hovering over him.

"Get him to the carriage!" the admiral of the navy called.

Women were shrieking and voices from the crowd hollered, "The King is killed!"

Orange-clad guards pushed through the throng. "Make way!" they cried, as several men lifted the King and carried him toward his vehicle.

Meanwhile, other guards bound the wrists of the attacker, who was dragged through a forest of jeers. One of the officers tore the mask away, revealing the clean-shaven face of a man.

A grim quiet fell over the city as the dusk sky, darker for clouds delivered by an east-blowing wind, loosed a soft summer drizzle. While the day had been warm, it was now chill by the shore where several warships anchored off Fort Wrenning. Word of the terrible incident at Fifth Crossing had flown through Demmingsfife, and soon would pass across the Tween to East Fellengrey, and then spread beyond, like the drizzle.

The best healers were called to tall and sprawling Royal House, called to a chamber on the second floor where a slender young man lay in a great curtained bed. His condition was poor, his organs damaged and much blood lost. Healing herbs and healing spells had been applied but a killing magic, as indicated by certain carvings on the dagger's blade, had been administered through the wound.

"Hours," Herringfield, the top healer, spoke softly to those that flocked around him when he came out of King Fenny's room. "Days, perhaps."

Fenny's mother, Violet, a slender, gracefully aging woman with pale hair and eyes of fragile blue, stifled a sob. The King's favorite advisor, the chronically pensive Spindles, touched her elbow while a serious-faced ancestor, rendered in oils, watched from his frame on the wall.

"All methods fail," Herringfield, a stout fellow with white waves at either side of his barren pate, reported glumly. "At best I shall make him last some small time longer, but repair seems not an option, I am ever sorry to say."

There among those who were close to the King, and important to the kingdom, was a bespectacled fellow in his thirties, just arrived back from Fort Wrenning. He was Crown documentarian Neelam Hentwidge.

Clad smartly in a spruce-colored suit, Hentwidge was a plump specimen with a calm, boyish face and light hair drawn to a neat knot. He leaned on a cane wherein a dormant sword, a razor-sharp whisper of light, slept.

The advisor, Spindles, a tall, lean man of forty-eight, with dark eyes and hair, noticed Hentwidge and moved to his side. "Have you learned something, Hentwidge?" he asked.

The documentarian had been to the fort where the would-be assassin was being detained. He had been present when the man was questioned, the questioners making use of truth-blood supplied by one of the Gifted.

All eyes and ears turned to Hentwidge.

"A lone madman, only," Hentwidge said. "Better that than conspiracy, I suppose. One of The Pails…"

Spindles groaned his disgust. The Pails were a fanatical religious sect devised by Ember Pail in the late 1600s. In accordance with the madman's writings, adherents were required to kill another person annually. The King must have proved an especially appealing target for the attacker.

Hentwidge, the best read and arguably the most intelligent of the lot, had arrived in time to hear the healer's dire assessment of Fenny's condition, and now matched Spindle's pensive look. Peering over his spectacles, he offered, "While I desire not to incite hope beyond a reasonable measure, there is, known to me, some certain thing which may prove cure for the King's injury."

Words flew from the mother of the King, *"Of what do you speak?"*

Hentwidge turned to the woman, replied, "Have you heard of something called the Winter-ash?"

Oh, the Winter-ash is blooming
 When the oak leaves are brown
 See her crimson blossoms dangling
 All when the snow is on the ground.

These were the opening lines of the folk ballad *The Winter-ash*, relating to a peculiar bit of botanical history, the complete verses of which could be found in *Fenwhittle's Compendium of Old Western Island Songs*.

Many years previous a young woman in the Drowned Horse Islands received word that the fisherman to whom she was betrothed had perished at sea. One winter evening the maiden, mad with grief, stripped off her garments and smeared herself head to foot with ashes from the hearth. She took a dagger and walked off into the cold white fields, where she opened her wrists and lay down.

A slender tree grew on the spot where the woman had died. It was like a young ash in ways, the bark grey-green and smooth, the leaves similar to those of an ash, but this was no ordinary tree. Curiously enough, in the midst of winter when other plants were bare of leaf and bloom, the branches of this lonely tree drooled tendrils of bright red flowers. From a distance it looked as if the naked tree were bleeding.

The Winter-ash, as locals named the tree, was more than simply a thing of lore. There was record of it having existed. The naturalist Lavender Gallows traveled to see the rare tree and even made watercolor studies of it. Writing about her visit, she noted that the branches, as well as sporting lovely red blooms, bore frightful dagger-like thorns. The flowers smelled like blood.

Haverly Shellings, Crown Botanist during the reign of King Weldren, also paid visit to the Winter-ash. He took cuttings from the tree and was intrigued to find slender gray female hands growing from the soil where he had planted his samples. The hands were of ordinary size, he wrote, though they remained as closed fists until the first snowfall of the year. Then the hands opened, as if blossoming flowers. When spring came the hands withered and rotted to the bone.

After studying traditional techniques used by the locals of the Drowned Horse Islands, Shellings went on to apply the strange healing properties of the tree in several successful experiments, some of which were quite dramatic. He documented his findings.

Besides being known for its thorns, off-season blooms and smell of blood, the Winter-ash possessed inscrutable powers specifically capable of reversing the damage caused by daggers and other bladed instruments.

Royal House was a rambling stone structure, several structures interconnected, more accurately, added onto here and there as years and rulers came and went. There were numerous rooms and offices, an abundance of servants to see that all ran well, and a profusion of armed soldiers about the grounds and in turrets. One of the sitting rooms in this maze-like construction was a stately setting with paneled walls that were painted a solemn green one might find haunting the waters of a shallow cove.

Violet joined the men gathered there. She tried to retain her composure, as was expected of females in the royal family, and sat with hands clenched in lap, unconsciously rocking at the edge of her seat.

Hentwidge had the floor, precise, unrattled creature that he was.

"It remains an uncertainty whether this tree, in fact, exists still," the documentarian said, pacing slowly, his cane punctuating against the floor. Hentwidge possessed an uncanny memory, recalling which of the islands in the cluster of the Drowned Horse group had hosted the anomalous tree. It was the largest of the lot, Small Island. "We shall require the swiftest vessel on hand. What have you, Admiral?"

A gray gentlemen with a face comprised of interesting angles, made stern by tremendous eyebrows like the horns of an owl, Admiral of the Fleet Marshbloom cleared his throat and sat forward. "*North Swan* would fit best our need, Mister Hentwidge. She's a fine, fast vessel, and a top captain takes her command at next sail. Penshoal Litch; do you know him?"

"Mm." Hentwidge acknowledged the name as if it were a pesky insect trying for a bite. "Right, then! I leave required arrangements in your capable hands, good Admiral."

Hentwidge bowed gracefully to the men, turned and bowed specifically to Violet, then strode determinedly for the door.

The advisor, Spindles, called after the man, "Where are you to, Hentwidge?"

The documentarian paused in the doorway, turned, peered over his spectacles and said, "To pack, for I am going on the *Swan*."

The 28-gun frigate *North Swan* spanned 118 feet with a width of 34. She was a warm mustard color from rails to hull, the hull night black down to the rich brown keel. Her ample sails filled the air above, reaching high over the decks, bowing as they took the wind. A figurehead, a white swan, its wings plastered back against the upward arc of the ship's beak, pointed to the cool expanse of the moonlit Gantic.

The capable crew of the *North Swan,* sharpened by regular drilling, could go from peace to fighting in a matter of minutes (they'd been clocked at six). They were quick to move from docking to sailing, as well, and had taken little time in getting her out into deep water, leaving Demmingsfife and their home bay behind.

Unfortunately, this hasty mission deprived the new post captain of the formal ceremony that would have honored his taking up the reigns left by poor deceased Capt. Langham. Thus, Capt. Litch met his crew bit by bit as he made his way about the ship, not having been afforded a proper assembly of the men. He seemed especially approving of the privilege girl, who, in fact, was prettier than most.

Lt. Privet had been below tending to various duties when sail was set and only now made his way through the companionway, up to where the ship's new commander stood at the wheel with coxswain Burnshire, midshipman Hibbits, and Crown Documentarian Hentwidge. The pretty lamp-tail bird was at their feet, singing in a cage, its tail feathers radiating a warm light.

Turning to face the sound of boots approaching on the deck, Capt. Litch smiled. Seen both in the light of lanterns and the moon, and vaguely under-lit by the radiant plumage of the bird, he was a dashing fellow in his early thirties, clad in a woodsy-green officer's coat with a lacey cravat against a blue breastplate. Black breeches and boots and scabbard for his sword. He was almost pretty for a man, but for the somewhat misshapen nose, which had been broken some years before. He wore a captain's bicorne hat (worn crossways) from which spilled long golden hair, the same color as his thin mustache. The robin's egg blue of his eyes was offset by a birthmark in the shape of a pear—a russet thing small enough to fit in the cap of an acorn—positioned near the outer corner of his right eye.

Privet had already raised his hand in salute before he recognized the other man and his blood turned to ice. When Privet's arm fell back to his side, it hung like an empty stocking, and he was unable to take the hand that Capt. Litch offered.

"Ahh, you would be Lieutenant Privet," Litch noted, having met the other two lieutenants already, "who is to be my new right hand."

Privet could not find his tongue and his mind was a combination of hot white light and memories from childhood. He recalled a boyhood day in early winter, when this same man and two of his friends stopped at the Privet farm, how this man improperly set after his sister Alba in the dovecote. He remembered Noll Slate (Rye Blackbird) pummeling the villains with a sauce pan and sending them off. He remembered this man's triumphant return with lawmen, Black Guns that surrounded the house and took his dear friend Slate (Blackbird) away.

Litch chuckled. "A shy fellow, eh?"

Privet lifted his hand numbly, but only offered a pale squeeze compared with the hearty pressure of the captain. Litch did not immediately release his grip, and said, "I've heard only the best about you, Privet. One day, I desire to think, you should be captain of *North Swan* and I captain of the *Swift Cannon*. But, in meantime, we've a King to save, yes?"

Privet heard his own voice, a weak, disembodied thing, replying, "Yes."

Litch finally released the lieutenant's hand and, addressing the small group, said, "Well, here's good luck to us, one and all!"

The bird at their feet was alternately whistling and twittering. The glowing tail made a small pool of light beneath the creature's perch and spread a web-like shadow of the cage's bars. Capt. Litch looked down at the lamp-tail and grimaced.

"Dear! Such maddening racket! How's a fellow to think?"

Litch, in one swift motion, bent, scooped the cage up by its top, half-spun and hurled it over the side of the ship. The cage splashed into the water below.

Hibbits, who had the wheel, gasped, let go of the handles and rushed to the rail of the ship, looking into the great expanse of moonlit water that was like silver glass. A small splotch of orange light showed briefly, and grew smaller as the cage sank.

Capt. Litch glowered, his face a sinister thing in the moonlight, and the light of the nearest lantern. "Crewman," he sniped, "return to the wheel, sir—and best you do so swiftly—or you shall be tossed to follow your silly bird."

The light in the water was gone. Hibbits, who had never summoned the courage to take the examination that could elevate him from midshipman status, could not now summon the courage to howl fire at the new captain. Trembling, his head down, his eyes brimming with tears, he returned to his post.

Mill Burnshire's heavily lidded eyes flew wide and Hentwidge, in contrast, betrayed his inscrutable expression by *narrowing* his at Litch, but quickly regained composure. The captain, who stood straight and smug, gazing at the sea before them while humming the old marching favorite *Seven Heads on Seven Poles*, had not noticed the look of disapproval.

Privet felt a terrible heat rise and race within, and without thinking dropped a hand to the handle of his sword, or rather, Rye Blackbird's sword.

The route to the Drowned Horse Islands was fairly straightforward, a matter of time and distance, really. Hopefully the healers back at Royal House would be able to sustain the King until the *North Swan* could return. Hopefully the Winter-ash still grew on Small Island, and hopefully Hentwidge could be trusted to recall the magical techniques he had read of, the steps required to apply the healing powers of the tree. This last concern needn't have been a concern at all, for Hentwidge's memory was as good as they come.

Lt. Privet hardly slept. The sea was rough and his hammock rocked back and forth in the creaking darkness. What snippets of sleep he gained were infiltrated by strange dreams: a dovecote full of gurgling lamp-tails, a ship sailing underwater manned by bones, a bird with severed hands for wings, sinking in a sea of silver and tar.

Some time after midnight the *North Swan* passed over a Wet Ghost, an area where a ship had gone down, and the watery screams and strange breezes inhabiting the place did not help the man's rest any.

At times Privet simply lay in his hammock thinking, staring up at the ceiling that he could not see. His thoughts were about Capt. Litch, and they were not pleasant thoughts. He had seen ink sketches of the man before, but hadn't recognized him, for Litch's head was always positioned so that the pear-mark near his eye was turned away from the artist's quill.

In the dark of Privet's quarters an almost imperceptible bluish light hovered around the fingers of his left hand, the one that had picked up the peace-shell.

Morning came to the *North Swan,* a stiff wind propelling her, waves leaping up at her sides as the great rolling water—all that could be seen, but for sky—made a small humble thing of the three-master frigate. Clouds like anvils and bed gowns cluttered the west, where the moon had gone, and the sun peeked over the opposite edge of the world, causing a glare of bright colors on the sea.

The morning light came with the cry, "All hands!" and the ship came to life. The boatswain, aside from having charge of the ship's boats, and the sails and rigging, saw to it that the men in the gundeck were roused from their slumber. He sent his mates to prod the hammocks of the sleepers, who, after dressing for the day, went above to wash and scrub the deck until breakfast. Breakfast was watery gruel.

A more appealing meal was served to the small group of men in the captain's dining cabin. A splendid lamb pie was accompanied by smoked herring and flat, roughly triangular cakes called griddle-oats.

Privet had been invited to this event, much to his distress. He sat quietly with the other important men from the ship, just prodding at his plate. Capt. Litch had wished for an opportunity to sit down and get to know the key members of his crew, though *he* did most of the talking. He noticed that Privet wasn't eating.

"Tell, Privet, do you find your meal unsatisfactory? If so, I shall revoke the cook's girl privileges for a month."

Privet looked up. His auburn hair was long enough to tie in an orderly knot at the back of his white linen neck stock. He tried to smile.

"The food is quite satisfactory, sir; it is only that the unruly sea troubles my stomach," Privet lied.

It was true that the wobbling of the craft added a challenging dimension to eating, nearly tipping coffee and making plates slide now and again, but Privet had a sturdy stomach when it came to weathering a ship's motion.

Hentwidge said little while eating and worked on his meal with a surgeon-like concentration.

Capt. Litch sat back in his chair. Unlike the others, he had not donned his uniform coat for the occasion and wore waistcoat and shirt. He grinned.

"Ahh, relieved I am to hear it, Privet. How terribly sad I should be to clip the cook's wings so far as our ship's girl goes. She's a spirited creature!"

Litch had sampled the privilege girl in the night. Privet, who sat just to the right of the captain, flinched when the man clapped him on the back.

"Is it not so, Privet?" he asked.

Expressionless, Privet turned to the man. "I cannot say, sir."

Litch frowned a little. "Dear fellow, you deprive yourself the privilege girl?"

Hentwidge sighed, finding the topic rather vulgar.

"I choose not to indulge, Captain," Privet said.

Now Litch smirked. "Do you care not for women, Privet?"

"I care quite well, sir, but I am betrothed."

Litch chuckled, "Ahh, the lieutenant is in *love*."

It sickened Privet for this lecherous man to hear anything at all of his private business, his Hazel, worse yet to speak in regards to her. Privet's right hand tightened on his knife.

Litch said, "I too am in love...with any woman who lies still long enough!" He laughed a sharp, annoying laugh and once more clapped Privet on the back.

The *Twelve Cats*, a two-masted sloop of 10 cannons, was floating in the middle of nowhere. The crew of the *North Swan* crowded the starboard side to have a look at her, the lot of them rolling back, a human wave, when the ocean hurled her rollers.

Capt. Litch grabbed one of the web-like shroud lines for support as the ship pitched to one side. Privet, squinting against the spray, reached up to hold onto his hat. He fumbled his telescope and it hit the deck with a clang and rolled.

"Farts!"

Litch managed his and scrutinized the other vessel, starting at the figurehead, which showed twelve feline heads arranged like a cluster of grapes. She seemed whole enough, but there were no signs of life. He peered up the *North Swan's* foremast to a lookout in a platform above him. From his high vantage point the man could see what the others could not.

"Report, sir, if you would," Litch called.

The lookout yelled back, "Looks to be bodies about the deck, sir. Blood and bodies."

There was also blood on the fore topgallant, the highest of the front mast's sails. Someone had taken blood and drawn the outline of a bird, just like the one found in the captain's cabin of the pirate ship *Swift Shark*.

Privet turned to Litch and shouted above the hiss and slap of water, "It is much the same as the sloop we found off Casterwig when Captain Langham was killed."

The boatswain asked the captain if a boat ought to be dispatched for boarding, but Litch, who was known to be a shrewd fellow when it came to running a ship, dismissed the idea, not wanting to lose any of his men to the turbulent seas. Specifically, "There is no gain in dangling my crew before providence like so much fish bait."

The *Twelve Cats* was left bobbing and listing, sails furled, crew presumably all dead, the wild gray Gantic rearing and roaring.

Mill Burnshire, who, a little while later joined Lt. Privet on the *Swan's* stern, watched the tottering vessel shrink to the size of a toy and noted, "We are mad, the lot of us—men who would ride the sea."

The *North Swan* sailed through the night. The Gantic had spent her fury for the time being and brushed quietly against the hull of the ship. The ocean was dark, as big and simple as the sky, both just touched with precarious beads of light.

A candle braved the darkness in Privet's cabin where the coxswain was visiting. A wine bottle had been emptied and a second would not last much longer.

After a fellowship of disparaging words about their new leader, the men grew quiet and reflective, until Burnshire offered, "I saw once a most curious thing."

Privet, even with sleepy eyes, could not match his friend's heavy lids. He tried to sit up attentively in his chair.

"Tell," Privet said.

The silvery thicket about Burnshire's face was drying, after the dousing the waves had delivered earlier, and seemed to grow up around the man's head as they talked.

"I was midshipman on the *Spirited,* some years past, transporting, as it were, the Kings, their wives and their little ones. They were off to a funeral for some duchess in the south-east of East Fellengrey. Well, there stood I on deck and the young prince Fenny, no more than five years upon the earth, was at his mother's side until he noticed something flopping about the planks."

"A fish!"

"No, not a fish, but a moth the color of a fish. Some poor sea-moth, injured in a way one can speculate only. Sad creature was short one wing. Well! Our little Fenny wandered from the Queen and found himself a knife…"

Privet *was* attentive now and sat forward on his seat.

Burnshire continued, "The boy took this knife and cut a piece from the purple tail of his coat, a piece in common with the shape and size of the big moth's wing. Not a soul but I looked on as Fenny gently took up the moth and held the new wing to its body, hunching his head down to kiss where cloth met insect."

Privet was rapt the way he had been as a boy listening to the stories told by Rye Blackbird.

Burnshire finished his tale, "Fenny raised his hands and the moth fluttered into the air and made off over the sea beating a silver wing and a purple wing."

The candlelight showed a tear in one of Privet's eyes. "Is this a true story, Mill?"

Burnshire smiled fondly. "In my heart it is."

Dead pirates were everywhere on the *Mighty Badger*, a merchant vessel that had been converted to a raider. She carried 16 guns, and a crew of 50, 49 of whom were deceased. She was discovered shortly after dawn on the second morning of the *North Swan's* mission. The pirate ship, with no one at the helm, had run aground on Moss Float Island—minor, unoccupied, outermost of the Drowned Horse Islands. A party from the *North Swan* had rowed out in two ship's boats and boarded the beached craft.

Neelam Hentwidge stepped over a body. He poked a fragment of metal with his cane, peered at Capt. Litch and noted, "It would appear the boarders made efficient use of hand grenades."

"And muskets and blades as well," Litch remarked.

Lt. Privet had just made a similar observation in regards to grenades, looking down the buckled mouth of the quarterdeck ladderway where the ladder below was shattered, like the men who had been climbing on it.

The ship was tilted to one side, wedged on the rocky shore, trails of blood on the deck complying with the slant. The crew had put up some kind of a fight, though they were likely caught off guard, the majority of them sleeping from the looks of things and the way they were dressed. Not a single cannon had gotten off a shot. It was a slaughter more than a battle.

More dead were below in the cramped darkness and whatever stolen riches the vessel may have had stored were missing. Even the animals from the manger had been taken. Pirates raiding pirates?

Hentwidge stood at the forecastle with Litch and scanned the horizon for a culpable ship, but saw only the *North Swan*. He pointed his cane at the red outline of a bird drawn on the deck and said, "It appears *someone* is most intent upon the killing of pirates."

The lone survivor was found cowering among the bodies of his mates. He had survived by playing dead. His name was Hilt Larch. The pirate, his dark, lank hair matted with gore, crawled out from under soggy corpses, like a lizard with his belly low to the planks, his arms trembling. Larch never imagined he would be glad to see navy men aboard his ship.

The guest took tea and Litch requested coffee (his preferred beverage) as they sat in the captain's dining cabin aboard the *North Swan*. When a messboy brought Litch a cup of watery tan liquid the man frowned his pretty face and carped, "I like the wind dry, my women moist, and coffee dark as a Cabbadunian's arse. I'll have it *black*!"

The young servant apologized and hurried the offending cup away.

Regaining his charming smile, Litch turned back to the pirate and said, "Continue, if you will, Mister Larch."

The raggedy Hilt Larch went on with his telling. Privet and Hentwidge and Litch's clerk were seated around the table as well, listening. Hentwidge was dismayed to find his trip to the death ship had cost him a broken fingernail.

Cupping his tea with shaky hands, the pirate, who was a man in his early thirties, and dressed as a common sailor, said, "They'd stole up alongside us in small boats—might well have been invisible! 'Round midnight, or there 'bouts, I heard screams and shots up on deck. Next I know bombs is goin' off and there's smoke so thick a fella couldn't hardly see his hand."

The captain asked, "How many invaders would you say there were, Mister Larch, how many did you see when you made to the upper level?"

"Oh, no better than thirty I wants to say."

The man told of chaos and horror. The crewmen of the *Mighty Badger* were swatted down as quickly as they rushed above. Then, after the best of the defense effort was overcome, the attackers skulked through the lower decks finishing off those who had sought to hide.

"A queer thing," Larch said, narrowing his eyes in recollection, "even lacking lanterns, and with no great moonlight to speak of, the boarders was like they could see on a clear bright day."

Hentwidge offered coolly, "They *could* see perfectly well in the dark, for they each had a quantity of *this*—"

The documentarian reached a hand over the table and dropped a palm-sized clump of bluish moss, a small mess of brittle tendrils.

Litch and the rest leaned forward to look at the stuff.

"What would it be?" the captain asked.

"I found it on the poop near to some blood. It would seem one of the boarders took a wound and lost it."

Litch was impatient, "Yes, yes, but what *is* it?"

"It would be a rare, mystical moss found growing in the most remote of jungle shadows among the Figwort Islands. The locals call it Deel-plee. Those who sell it on the sly call it 'owl tuft.' When held against the tongue in one's mouth it enhances the senses extraordinarily, even allowing for vivid vision in the darkest of circumstances."

Privet conjectured, "Such a thing would allow a lesser quantity of men to overtake these pirates, whose crews are greater in numbers. Striking in the dark at late hours, sneaking alongside in small boats."

"Precisely," Hentwidge said.

Litch's new coffee arrived at last. He eyed it and nodded before shooing the messboy off, then turned to the storyteller. "A dreadful circumstance, Mister Larch. I should quite like to find these elusive raiders, though there be an element of the ironic, for they spare the navy the task of taking these scoundrel vessels. No affront intended. But, a pressing mission binds me presently. Since I have no proof of crime known to me as regards *your* doings, you shall remain a free man while on this ship. But no folly shall be tolerated, you understand?"

Larch smiled a grateful toothless smile. "Much obliged, Captain. Thank you, sir! I'll not be a trouble, you can rest on that."

"Very good." Capt. Litch now looked to his crew, rubbed his hands together and said, "Well, gentlemen, we near our destination. Who shall accompany me to land?"

The Drowned Horse Islands numbered thirteen and were arranged in a rough horseshoe with the biggest, which the *North Swan* approached, located at the rear curve. Small Island loomed up from the Gantic like a great lump of verdant pudding. A slow, steady approach brought the frigate between the two parallel rows of six islands before it anchored in the bay. One of the ship's boats was lowered over side.

The day was fine with a blue sky, pleasant temperatures and a soft breeze. Gulls spun over the shore making their gull noises and pewter sea-moths were scouring among the rocks and mud where water met land. Here and there, amongst the hills, the thatched roofs of villages could be seen, though the buildings, for their modest size, appeared more distant than was actually the case. They looked as if they might be swallowed by the clouds of deciduous green rearing about them.

Capt. Litch stood at the fore of the narrow barge, hand on hip, handsome in his dark green coat and blue chest plate and black bicorne. He looked the noble figure he imagined himself to be, steadfast about his glorious mission. He wore a pistol in a hip holster—a weapon he had braggingly shown to the others in the landing party—a long thing with shiny blackbirch stock and ramrod, the barrel and firelock (and the rest of the metal parts) fashioned from gleaming blue sea-steel. It was beautiful in the way that a spider's web is a killing work of art.

The tide was out and the smell of the mudflats hung thick in the air. With the water low the boats could only float so close to shore and the men had to wade through sucking brown muck and indiscriminate pools. Hentwidge, with coat, waistcoat and breeches the color of bricks, had donned boots for the occasion.

The landing party trudged along. Capt. Litch was at the lead with his six musketeers, who, he had remarked, were wanted in case there was need to shoot down a few of the "stumps," if the locals were to raise protest against their partaking of the rare Winter-ash. Privet and Hentwidge followed behind.

Burnshire, the coxswain, had requested the captain's permission to go see some dear old friends who lived there on the island, but the captain had refused, snarling, "We are here about the urgent business of saving our King, not to pay visit to the wretched little natives. You will remain on the *Swan*."

Not far off the land proper a small woman in small, simple clothes was up to her thighs in the mud, tugging at a rope that was around the nose of a spotted cow, which seemed enormous next to her. She was red-faced and exasperated, a woman of middle-age with graying strands fallen from her day-cap. She noticed the men coming toward her and a look of hope came to her face.

"Good sirs," the woman said in a miniaturized voice, "my cow has got free of her pen and be stuck in this awful mud. She should drown for certain come the tide. Could you not help an anguished woman?"

Litch, with hands on hips, looked down at the farmwife and smirked. The top of the woman's head was just on level with his lower ribs. "Tell, good woman, do you know the Winter-ash?"

The woman in her distraction had to pause a moment, as if any words *not* about her cow came in an alien language. She did not respond quickly enough for Litch's liking.

He raised his voice, "The Winter-ash, you silly stump, do you know where is the blasted Winter-ash?"

The woman would have taken a step back were it not for the mud that half-swallowed her skirts. She blinked up at Litch then pointed to a path that wound up and away from the sea.

"There a ways, past orchard and pond, in a field by seven hills."

"Thank you!" Litch said, his face softening somewhat as he suddenly wondered what the woman's reduced form might be like minus its garments. Perhaps like that of a girl's he mused.

The captain, and the men in sage-green coats carrying "longs," marched on (if one could call their strained squishing steps marching). Hentwidge slipped a coin into the woman's little hand as he passed her. She was marveling at it when she noticed that a handsome lieutenant was trying to free her cow.

"Ohhh, thank you, sir! She's my best milker, sir and horrible would it be to lose her."

Privet smiled and grunted, tugging first at the lead, then shoving from behind. "Not to worry, missus, I'll have her out smart enough."

"Oh, she's stubborn something awful, sir, and regular to be found by the water when she makes from her pen."

Privet grinned, either that or he was grimacing as mud squeezed up his sleeve. "One would think a cow escaped might head for a nice field rather than a mudflat."

"She's greatly fond of seaweed, sir."

Privet chuckled. He was hunched down pulling at one leg then the next, his uniform paying dearly for the kindness. The spattering mud, he found, had a taste the same as its smell. He had made progress, loosening the front legs, when he spotted a pair of black boots and breeches on the other side of the cow's belly. One of the others in the landing party had noticed his effort and come back to help, he presumed. He stood up.

A flustered Capt. Litch had one hand on his hip and the other on his holster. "Come Privet! Let's not be dallying all day about a foolish cow—there's a King to save."

"But I've almost got her—"

The blast of Litch's pistol, held close to the side of the cow's head, drowned out the rest of Privet's sentence. The massive beast collapsed and rolled onto its side, all legs now free. Privet moved back just in time to avoid being crushed. The little woman put her hands up to her face and shrieked, tears leaping.

"There!" Litch said. "Let's be about our task."

The captain stomped moistly for dry ground and Privet, his face a hot red, bared his teeth. His temper, while not what it was when he was a bit younger, flooded him, the wails of the Small Island woman beating the flames. He drew his own pistol, clicked back the cock and took aim at his superior's back.

"Bastard!" Privet hissed, but when he went to squeeze the trigger his right hand would not work. He felt a tingle of light radiating from his left hand. It was clear to Privet that the magic (or what he now regarded as the curse) of the peace-shell he had handled would not allow him to act in violence against others. What use was he now, he thought, a sea-warrior who could not war, nor even claim revenge?

The men from the *North Swan* traveled along an earthen track, past an orchard and past a pond and into a field ringed by seven green hills. A warm summer smell was about the place, a vegetative essence touched with brine. Sunlight, being somewhat angled now that noon had passed, lent shade, which added texture to the splay of grass and wildflowers. A single tree bearing a proud leafy plume rose from the center of the field: the Winter-ash.

The men approached the tree and stood quietly around it. It was much like a common ash in ways, the bark grey-green and smooth, the leaves similar to those of an ash, though frightful dagger-like thorns jutted from the branches. A mild wind gave lazy motion to the leaves.

Capt. Litch eyed the documentarian and said, "Well, have at it, Mister Hentwidge."

Hentwidge adjusted the spectacles on his nose and stepped forward. He reached up with a knife and cut some small branches loose, careful of the thorns. He bent forward and kissed the trunk for each cut he made, as was the custom with locals partaking of the tree.

"Poor fellow could do with a visit to the privilege lass," Litch joked, elbowing Privet.

Privet imagined taking one of the tree's thorns and doing something unspeakable to Litch.

Hentwidge felt a great sense of satisfaction having found the tree, having taken from it, knowing that it was the final hope for the failing King Fenny. If only they could get back to Demmingsfife in time to make use of it.

Privet was writing to Hazel, the paper honey colored in the glow of a candle.

I have forgotten not our bit of unfinished business, and when next in New Crown, when next I stand before your good parents, I shall ask for your hand at last.

The lieutenant spared Hazel some of the unpleasant aspects of the mission, saying little about the new captain, not mentioning how it was poisoning to have to serve beneath Litch. He gave few details about the horrors on the pirate ships and said nothing about the killing of the cow and how the poor little Small Island woman had screamed and cried. The letter was, in one sense, a diversion from these things, a way to remind himself that there was sweetness and beauty somewhere, good things waiting for him.

Finished with his letter, a restless Privet dressed and went above. Dawn was not far off and light was gaining from the east, the night's clouds bundling off into the south-west. The wind was soft, the sea quiet. He chatted briefly with the third lieutenant, who had the watch, then made his way to the forecastle. He gazed at the Gantic. It was vast, immune to the love and hatred of humankind.

Noise came on the air and gave Privet pause. As a man who made a life of the sea, he never mistook musket shots for thunder; they were two different animals in the ear, each unique in the way that it traveled in the great openness of air and water. There was only one conclusion: what Privet had just heard was the sound of a musket.

Minus the customary drumming that would stir the crew to battle-mode, the many aboard the *North Swan* made to their posts quietly, careful not to alert the other ship of their approach. The other ship appeared to be a blue-hulled brigantine with two masts, the sails rolled. The *North Swan's* gun deck was cleared, the suspended mess tables drawn up against the low ceiling as boys ran charges up from the magazines, delivering them to the gun crews, who poked the brass noses of their 9-pounders out into the cool ocean air. Uniformed men with "longs" slung over their shoulders spidered up webbed ropes to take position on the fighting tops.

"Well, well," Capt. Litch said, lowering his telescope. "It seems we've come upon our mystery raiders in the midst of yet another ugly deed."

He leaned on one of the chase guns at the front of the ship.

Approaching from behind, the *North Swan* had a view of three small vessels bobbing off the pirate ship's portside. The attackers had moved in close and boarded under cover of darkness and were just now loading their plunder, and apparently some wounded, presumably having finished off the crew.

A boarding party was readied, a helmeted Lt. Privet taking up musket for the occasion. Litch had requested that Privet lead a group of musketeers, rather than stay and supervise gunnery aboard *North Swan*. So, he held the musket by the long smooth stock and checked the shaped piece of flint gripped in the jaws of the swan-neck cock. Dry powder in the pan. A fine weapon, certainly, but it might as well have been a child's stick musket in his hands for all the good it would do him. Cursed by the peace-shell, his musket, pistol and sword were all useless, and there he was, ready to swing into a frenzy of battle with no way to fight back against the dangers that might await. His stomach felt as if it were deflating and a warm dizziness swept into his head.

The opponents, at this hour, had neither of the advantages that had allowed them to overtake the vessels they had thus far marauded, lacking both darkness and the element of surprise.

Hentwidge borrowed Privet's telescope for a few minutes and now passed it back to him, noting, "Just as Hilt Larch observed, there can be no more than thirty of them."

Capt. Litch smiled smugly. "This should prove remarkably easy. Amusing even."

Privet took another look. He read the name of the ship as presented in gold letters below the stern windows. It read: *Scythe of Providence.*

The *North Swan* was closing, close enough to be noticed, and how could it *not* be noticed with its puffed, towering sails announcing it from a distance? Men on the *Swan* observed through telescopes as the trespassers on the 10-gun *Scythe of Providence* began to scurry like alarmed ants and men in the small, single-mast boats scrambled for their oars and to set their sails.

"We are seen," Privet stated.

"More sail," Capt. Litch ordered.

Stocky, bespectacled Hentwidge tapped his cane impatiently on the deck. He gave the captain a dispassionate look and said, "Captain Litch, I hardly find this matter worth pursuing at such time as this. The King is *dying*, sir, and *we* hold the cure. Best we hasten it to him without delay."

Litch kept his telescope trained on the horizon, not bothering to look at the man who was speaking to him. "You needn't worry, Hentwidge, this should take but little time."

The voice of a lookout called down, "Sails ho!"

Litch called back up, "Yes, Mister Stibbs, I, too, see them. Black sails at the masthead breach."

A dark ship balanced on the strange stark line where the sky and the ocean met. Now Litch looked at Hentwidge.

He said, "This will be mother ship to these boats, you'll find. There *had* to be a

213

mother ship, as these three trifling vessels could hardly have hunted pirate ships on their own, most certainly not out here with no land to launch from."

Hentwidge tipped his head down and peered over his lenses. "Captain, you *don't* mean to engage, do you?"

Capt. Litch gathered his boarding party and gave instructions, standing behind the balustrade on the raised poop deck with his blue sword drawn, waiving it to punctuate. The men made up a restless mass, sailors armed with boarding axes and curved cutting swords alongside nattily put together fighters with helmets and breastplates, men heavy with sacks of cartridges, shot, priming powder and patches for their muskets.

"We strike the brigantine *Scythe of Providence* before the black ship draws within range of our guns, or rather before *we* are in range of hers, though I hardly expect they be any better than our nines, and likely less in number."

Some of the men nodded, but then some of the men would have nodded if an officer told them to flap their arms and cry like a seagull.

Litch continued, "We shall come alongside her and deliver a broadside with our port guns, targeting their cannons, lest they make to turn them upon us. We next reload, re-sight and swing across her bow delivering a second barrage down her length from the fore, our aim being to clear the deck of men by employing grape and canister shot from our top cannons."

Following that action, Litch determined to loop back and snuggle the *North Swan's* starboard up to the pirate's starboard (that side's cannon hopefully having been incapacitated by the initial gunnery) and board the brigantine.

Capt. Litch stood there rather proud of himself, and while Privet loathed the man, he had to admit that it was a fine plan of action. Only one person stepped forward to challenge the *North Swan's* leader.

It was Hentwidge, of course. "Question, Captain Litch. Should we happen to sink and die *who* then shall deliver the healing vegetation to save King Fenny's life? These raiders have proven themselves quite effective in efforts past, combating greater vessels and larger numbers of men."

214

Litch smiled his charming smile. "Sink we shall not, good fellow, for we are not mere pirates." With glinting blue eyes he looked upon his men, stabbing his glinting blue blade into the sky with a roar, "We are the Fellengrey Navy!"

The crew cheered, *"Fellengrey! Fellengrey! Fellengrey!"*

Foolish, blind, loyal or brave, the mother ship of the small boarding boats continued on its way, toward the savaged brigantine and the handsome navy frigate *North Swan*, despite the naval ship. The vessel appeared to be a sloop of two masts, and while smaller than the frigate, it made an ominous impression on the eye, being black from topsail to keel (the better for undetected night travel).

Twenty-eight 9-pounders aboard the *Swan* were loaded with round shot and ready to fire, the small swivel cannons mounted on the deck rails primed as well, their gullets containing lead pellets. It was only a matter of distance and maneuvering now as the ship glided into position.

Captain, coxswain and Master Gunner were on the quarterdeck with some of the other officers and the Crown Documentarian. The master gunner, Sprig, was a tall, hollow-faced man of fifty-something with a pitted congregation of burn scars covering the left side of his face. He was to remain with the ship and oversee the issuing of ammunition when the boarding party set off. He and Litch discussed final details, the gunner respectfully resisting the use of grape shot, privately exasperated by the fact that the scatter-type projectiles were even carried on the ship. Grape shot consisted of nine 13-ounce iron balls clustered vertically around a metal column and sealed in a canvas bag.

"One must never use grape in brass guns," Sprig reminded his superior, "as it might some damage cause the bore."

Litch, however, was steadfast, and offered a patronizing dose of appreciation for the man's concern. Sprig saluted and left briskly for the gundeck below.

Two of the small boats, which were painted as black as their parent vessel, and likewise sporting black canvas, were making swiftly away from the brigantine *Scythe of Providence*, oarsmen straining to help in the propelling. The third was waiting, which struck those observing from the tops of the *North Swan's* masts as unwise. Did they not see the powerful frigate coming on?

"Fire!" the cry went up.

Smoky thunder mushroomed from the port cannons of the *North Swan* as it flanked the *Scythe of Providence*. The guns on the upper deck of the navy ship were pointed downward to hit those on the deck of the shorter vessel. Terrible noises replaced the morning quiet, the deafening blasts casting sideways cumulus clouds, the 9-pound balls whirring through the air and clanging into the dormant guns of the brigantine. Wooden sparks spat up where some of the projectiles struck, rails shattering, garrison carriages breaking, chunks of planking flung high. Shattered wood danced in the air.

From their high platforms on the masts, navy musketeers opened fire on the few men remaining within view on the *Scythe of Providence*. Other musketeers leaned their "longs" over the ship's rails and fired as well, smoke puffing out into the greater smoke. Some of the raiders, all of whom wore black, were hit and dropped, while others ducked behind whatever might lend cover. Few shots were returned, fired only from musketoons, shorter and less accurate than longer muskets, though better suited to fighting in the confines of lower decks.

Below in the *Scythe of Providence,* the captain of the raiding party which had massacred the pirate ship's crew, was helping one of his wounded men up a ladderway. He had asked that the third of his small boats remain until he could locate the man, who had suffered a stab wound while down near the galley. Having stayed behind to rescue the bleeding fellow might not have been a very good idea, he now admitted mentally, though he had made a point of leaving none of his crew behind, dead or alive. The captain poked his head up into the smoky air as musket balls rained around him, taking bites out of the deck and thumping into the dead sprawled upon it.

There would be no escaping the navy ship, he knew, realist that he was. Better those few of his crew still on the pirate ship die, himself included, then all those on his ship, *Nocturnal,* which was bravely sailing toward the frigate. He set his wounded companion at the bottom of the ladder, then climbed back up, stuck his head into the smoke and flying musket balls, and, using a small tin whistle, blew a series of notes to the waiting boat. He signaled his men to save themselves and leave.

The looming frigate, only partly distinguishable behind a shifting veil of smoke, continued on past the *Scythe of Providence* after having raked it with cannonballs, and now turned sharply to the left, cutting across the bow of the anchored brigantine. Another eruption of artillery fire—smoke blossoming from brass mouths, light flaring within the wall of smoke, shot howling, plowing down the length of the *Scythe of Providence*, bow to stern.

Much of the destruction was blurred by the wafting smoke and was heard rather than seen. The dead were broken into smaller pieces by the spreading pattern of grape shot and the hail of smaller canister shot, as well as the 9-pound balls of "round." One of the black-clad raiders, hiding behind the corpulent corpse of a fallen pirate, felt something kick him hard and reached down to find that his leg was gone below the thigh. The surprise as much as the pain made him scream. The last thing he heard was the roar of another ball flying his way.

"Boarders away!"

Men of the *North Swan* surged onto the *Scythe of Providence,* their combined war-voices, both cheers and growls, an audible wave falling upon the upper decks of the brigantine. They came leaping off boarding nets and swinging over on ropes, and some even jumped the distance between ships, seeing as their starboard sides were nearly touching.

Capt. Litch led the way, pistol in one hand, sword in the other, and Privet was close behind him, ahead of a team of musketeers. They thumped onto the gouged planks and moved forward, squinting into sulfur mist.

A shadowy figure lurched up from the sprawled dead, the blinding cough of his blunderbuss shaking the air. A fellow beside Privet screeched and dropped his "long," hands flying to his face as he pitched against the ship's rail. Privet instinctively aimed, but his trigger finger refused the mental command to squeeze. Litch stabbed his pistol out and fired—sparks at the pan, smoke and light booming from the muzzle. The man flopped backward with a thud.

Boots pounded as the throng pressed on, the bayonets on muskets pointing the way. Dead pirates were underfoot in crimson pools amidst the rubble. Masts were gouged, rails snapped, the deck pocked. The *North Swan's* 9-pounders had torn and punctured both man and wood and crippled the brigantine's top deck cannons.

The second lieutenant brought his team portside on the *Scythe of Providence* to fire at the last of the three black boats the raiders had used to sneak up on the pirate vessel. The boat, to their surprise, was no longer waiting there by the *Scythe of Providence*, and had slipped out of musket range, heading toward the black sloop.

"I should like one alive," Litch said to Privet as they advanced, ducking damage here, stepping over it there, "that we might come to know all particulars about these pirate-killers."

Privet, his head humming with the din of loud weapons, and the drum of his pulse, could only nod.

Most of the ship's boats had been ruined by the naval artillery, though they were intact enough to lend cover. A figure darted out from behind one of them and threw something.

Before Litch could get the word *grenade* out of his mouth a great smoky impact burst behind him and he staggered forward. Privet lurched by, a blur of dark green, his helmet clattering onto the deck. Someone in the smoke screamed.

"I'll have your blood!" Litch snarled, steadying himself. He saw the man flit ahead, no more than a blink of dark motion. The man vanished behind an overturned garrison carriage.

Litch ducked into a crouch and quickly reloaded his flintlock pistol, ramming a patch and ball down the throat, tipping a flask to pour a dash of powder in the pan. He rose carefully and squinted, the small acorn birthmark near his eye crinkling.

Those who were not wounded by the blast moved up behind their captain and the first lieutenant. Privet had dropped his musket in the confusion and looked down at his empty hands. They were trembling.

Litch hissed, "Privet, *there!* He descends!"

The man, vague but for black clothing, dropped down a ladderway into the deck below. Privet found himself hurrying along in pursuit, hearing his own boots fall and his own heart pounding, even as he felt disembodied from himself, a ghost that only imagined it was rushing after a man who may be carrying more explosives.

Litch went down first, into a hazy dimness. Several beams of light streamed horizontally through punctures made by the navy guns. Privet edged down the ladder, his eyes straining to adjust. He noticed a figure off to one side and spun to see a pirate smeared in shadow and blood, slumped against the wall, staring with dead eyes.

Several musketeers came down behind the officers. They took the better part of the impact when a grenade rolled out of the darkness and exploded under them.

Privet found himself face down, ears ringing, his surroundings choked with smoke. Pieces of the ladder, parts of a musket and half a man's leg were strewn on the floor nearby. He saw Litch lifting himself up, coughing.

They were on a gundeck, more a sleeping deck, really, having far more hammocks than guns, its low ceiling crossed by heavy beams, its darkness interrupted by shafts of light through splintered gaps. Enough light for Litch to see the black-clad man when next he appeared.

Boom! Captain Litch's pistol barked and the man gasped, knocked back, dropping the grenade he was about to toss. It landed between his feet and went off. Thunder in the ship, and rumbles afterward as heavy wood sagged and banged, tumbling debris obstructing access to the ladderway, blocking Litch and Privet and three of the musketeers from the others above.

There were only four cannons, two on the portside, two on the starboard. One of the starboard guns had been smashed by the *Swan's* initial barrage, though the other was whole, like those on the opposite side. Privet managed to dive behind one as gunfire pounded the air, the musketeers opening fire as a figure popped up behind one of the cannons at the far end of the deck.

All three musketeers discharged their weapons, and at that close range hit their target. A long black coat, propped up like a puppet by a cannon's ramrod, fluttered to the ground, perforated.

Litch had not had time to reload his pistol, and before the fighters could drop their spent "longs" and draw their own, the man who had tricked them into emptying their muskets stepped out from behind his cover, a cocked pistol in each hand.

The man wore a white shirt with black breeches and boots. He was tall enough to have to bend somewhat beneath the low ceiling, a sturdily built man nearing sixty, with wild gray hair and a wild gray beard and a face that weather had not been kind to. He might have been handsome without all that pewter shrubbery, for the features were good, the eyes raptor-keen and dark as treacle. Lt. Privet and Capt. Litch recognized him at the same time.

"Blackbird!" Litch spat.

"Rye Blackbird," Privet repeated, astounded.

"So it seems," Blackbird said in his rich voice. He did not appear to recognize Privet, who had been a boy when last they knew each other.

Privet, without thinking, took a step forward, and one of the pistols trained specifically on him. Privet said, "Do you not know me? I would be Hale Privet, from when you went by the name Noll Slate."

A softness came into otherwise dangerous eyes. "Heavens, is that you, my buck? How I have thought on you the many years, nearest thing to a son as ever I had."

Blackbird focused the gaze of one pistol away from Privet and onto one of the others.

A rush of heat behind Privet's face might easily have spilled out in tears. He smiled, of all the mad moments in life, he smiled then.

Blackbird observed, "You are, Lieutenant, as once was I, with the love of the sea in your eye, as ever it has been in mine. What strange whim of fate has brought us here upon this bloody ship?"

"Perhaps," Privet offered, "fate is quite like the sea, vast, and mysterious in its currents."

"I think it so."

His eyes darkening again, Blackbird regarded the others, "The navy be not my enemy. I aim only to take my wounded man here and return to my ship unmolested."

Blackbird took two steps forward, the barrels of his pistols staring at the *North Swan's* captain.

Capt. Litch squinted coolly. "How is it you escaped a metal cage and did not drown at your execution, Blackbird? They say you knew not how to swim."

"I swim as well as any fish, in all honesty, though it be little known, Captain. The cage's lock was easy enough to undo, for I had secreted upon myself a simple needle of steel for the purpose. The executioner was not clever enough to put an end to Rye Blackbird."

One of the musketeers spoke up, "He is one against five, two pistols only—two shots to our five."

"Four," Litch corrected, "for mine has yet to be charged."

"Four, five," Blackbird said, grinning, "it matters not. You will see your captain dead if I glimpse a hand on a weapon."

Blackbird kept one of his pistols aimed at Litch and now pointed at the man who spoke. "You, sir, gently turn back to me and fire your weapon into the floor."

The man looked to Litch. *"Captain?"*

Litch saw what was in Blackbird's eyes.

Blackbird said, "Do as I request *or you and the captain die.*"

Litch, without looking away from Blackbird, said, "Do as he wishes."

The musketeer sighed exasperatedly but complied. He turned, carefully drew his pistol from its holster, cocked it and fired into the floor. Every ear rang from the noise.

"Toss it aside, if you please," Blackbird instructed.

The man tossed the pistol off to one side. It slid under one of the surviving cannons.

"Now *you*," Blackbird said, pointing to one of the two armed musketeers.

"Sir?" the man said to Litch.

"Yes, yes," the captain replied, annoyed, "just do it."

The man turned, pulled out his pistol and fired into the floor. He threw the weapon aside. The third fighter took his turn.

Smoke from the blasts hung in the air. The ship creaked, shifting ever so slightly from side to side as it floated in place.

Privet, without being asked, did as his crewmates had done, turning, firing and throwing his pistol, even though he would never have entertained the idea of shooting his old friend. Not that the spell of the peace-shell would have allowed such a thing, if he had been so inclined.

"Thank you, gentlemen," Blackbird said. He walked up to Capt. Litch, stuck the pistols in his face and pulled both triggers. The pistols snapped empty.

Litch, after flinching, growled, "Bastard!"

Blackbird's face became a frightening thing. He tossed his own spent pistols aside and stabbed a finger at Litch's face. "*Our* business remains unfinished, Captain. I recall well your mischief in the dovecote of the Privet farm, how you bloodied one girl and meant to sully the other. I recall your invasion of the Privet farm, bolstered by Black Guns. I recall my arrest and would-be execution, for which *you* are culpable. These recollections pain me, Captain, pain me greater than the sting of the broken nose I once furnished you, and nothing shall alleviate this pain but your death."

Blackbird turned, walked several paces away from Litch then spun back to face him, drawing his sword—a hiss of silver.

"Defend," Blackbird snarled, his dark eyes flaring with an intensity that Privet had only seen in them once before, those years ago on a snowy day in late autumn when Litch and Blackbird had their first duel.

Capt. Litch looked to his men and snapped, "Kill him!"

Three of the navy men drew swords, the collective sound rasping in the dark confines. Three thin, straight blades, three men converging on Blackbird. Capt. Litch pulled his blue blade from its scabbard, but took a step back, away from the fight.

Privet felt the thrill of battle through his blood, but, looking on, knew not *who* he would fight, if the peace-shell were to allow him that option. There were his crewmates, whom he would have fought alongside against foes of all sorts, and there was Rye Blackbird, a near-mythic figure from the rich, sacred realm of boyhood.

Blackbird stood with his sword held out straight, his right leg leading and partly bent, his spine rigid, free hand at the hip. His weapon had a thin, double-edged blade measuring no more than thirty inches. The grip was rosewood, with straight, simple quillons of steel crossing between blade and handle. The pommel was a metal teardrop.

Privet marveled at the grace—nothing short of beauty—with which Rye Blackbird now moved. With a dancer's precision and a deer's darting speed, he lunged and dodged, more agile than his younger opponents. He moved so swiftly that at times it seemed whole portions of his body became invisible to the eye. His sword sliced through the air, a whisper and a blur and while the musketeers were about him like flies, Blackbird swatted them down. One, two, three thuds as the musketeers' heads fell to the floor.

Three bodies crumpled and gushed. Blackbird stepped over one, sword out before him, pointing at Capt. Litch.

"Shall we?" Blackbird asked.

Litch smiled, "Yes!" and lunged.

Privet, still standing there with empty hands and wide eyes, was alarmed to observe Capt. Litch in action, not having seen the man swordfight until now. Litch's fleet, confident moves made him think of the master swordsman, Capt. Moorsparrow, who, as it turns out, had coached Litch in the art back in the summer of 1745.

Swords clanged and rang as the men came together, eyes locked, blades kissing. They circled each other, gracefully poised in this most gentlemanly of murderous techniques. Litch waited for the right moment and thrust, the tip of his blade tearing the white of Blackbird's shirt, reddening it.

Blackbird recoiled then sprang in turn, a silvery light flashing as he raked the tip of his weapon across Litch's blue chest plate. Litch scowled and made a jab, which would have caught Blackbird between the eyes were it not blocked.

They danced backward away from each other, legs bent, steel pointing, then came together again. Blackbird's back was now to Privet, and Capt. Litch had to be careful not to trip over his three dead crewmen. He was not far from Blackbird's wounded crewmate, who sat with his back propped against the stocky carriage which supported one of the ship's 6-pounders. Weak, and barely conscious, that man held a cocked flintlock pistol in one of his pale hands.

A nimble blur, Blackbird swept forward, the point of his blade clanging against Litch's breast. Litch was knocked off his feet and fell back hard on the deck, just beside Blackbird's injured friend. A look of desperation came to the captain's face, and he reached over and snatched the pistol from the ailing man.

Blackbird was swooping in, a hawk to the kill. Litch did not have time to stand; he simply pointed the pistol and fired. Smoke gushed into the shafts of light pouring through cannon ball craters in the hull, and a clap of noise seemed to shake the brigantine. The ball struck Blackbird square in the right knee and he toppled with a cry. His sword skittered from his hand when he hit the planks.

The older man lay on his back grimacing, groping for his steel, which was too far to reach, his fighting daggers having been used and lost in raiding the ship. Litch stood up, dropped the pistol and, with a dismissive stroke, swung the side of his blade deeply into the neck of Blackbird's man. The fellow's eyes rolled up and he slumped down the garrison carriage.

"Well, well," Capt. Litch said, standing as straight as the low beams would permit. "What have we here?"

The blond man swaggered toward the squirming Blackbird, a blue sword leading the way. Blood was expanding beneath the damaged leg and the horrible, burning weight of pain held Blackbird to the floor.

Litch said, "I suspect you will not mysteriously escape *this* execution, Blackbird."

Privet felt his heart, and all the heat and blood in his body roar up, angry and dizzying, and he unsheathed the sword from his hip, Rye Blackbird's sword. Even in that insufficient light the sharp edges gleamed, shimmered as if the very metal were infused with a restless light. It was handsome with its straight thirty-inch blade of double-edged steel, the grip smooth dark blackbirch wood from the Colonies, with a knuckle bow curving from the shaft to the pommel, which in this case was a silver lion's head. Privet held it up and saw one of his own eyes stare back at him in reflection.

Litch was closing on the injured man, lazily tapping the deck with the tip of his blade as if counting off the final seconds of a life. He was smiling, gloating, cherishing every measured step as he neared the prize. He didn't notice that Privet had stuck the tip of Blackbird's sword into the floor, or that he had removed his belt and tightly knotted it around the wrist of his left hand, from which a soft blue light emanated around the fingers.

Litch stood over Blackbird and smirked down. He brought his sword up to his lips and kissed the side of the shaft. "Let us begin with your nose," the captain said.

Privet bent down, pressed the back of his left hand against the deck and plucked the sword free. Squinting, he brought the sword down on his wrist and the blade clunked against wood. The loose hand lay there, the peaceful light around the fingers dissipating as Privet reared up, stump spattering, and pounced toward Capt. Litch.

"Defend, swine!" Privet sneered, planting his feet, taking the duelist's starting position that Rye Blackbird had taught him those years ago.

"Privet? What are you about?"

"I mean to kill you, at last," Privet said.

Litch was baffled. "Are you mad?" And then his eyes showed recognition as he made sense of it all. The name, *Privet*…the Privet farm those years ago, the girls in the dovecote. There had been a young boy, hadn't there? The brother of the twin girls.

"Ahhh," Litch said, "how fate toys with us, we three, reunited again. Well, then, let's have it done!"

Lifting his head from the floor, Rye Blackbird growled, "Woe to the villain who is fool enough to cross the swordsman Hale Privet!"

They came together with a clash of steel. Privet felt as if the hand of the sword's owner was on the grip along with his own as he parried the opponent's blade, pushing it to the side. He lashed, scored a screeching line down the center of Litch's chest armor. Litch skipped back several steps and swiped in return, his blade glancing off the other. Blue steel flashed, cut through one of the hazy bars of light that slanted into the gun deck. Privet pulled his head to the side, but the tip burnt across his ear, inches above the busy veins at the side of his neck.

The officers clashed again, dark green coats flapping behind them, teeth bared, sword to sword. It was a fight that was a dance, a terrible poetry of limbs and metal. Capt. Litch saw the glare of Privet's eyes, the glare of a blade and felt nothing more than a breeze as Rye Blackbird's sword—an icy streak of moonlight—made an elegant arc.

Privet's strike caught Litch above the breastplate and the villain stumbled back, a gushing cravat of gore at his throat.

Litch wheezed. His sword dropped and he reached to his neck with quivering hands, red ribbons threading through the fingers. He wobbled, and one hand rose to his forehead. Privet could not tell if this was meant to be a salute, or was a random movement of the limbs, as the dying were sometimes known to make. Regardless, it was the last motion Capt. Litch made before sagging to the floor.

It was quiet, aside from the sound of bees that the cannon fire and musketry had put in Privet's ears. Only now did he feel the pain and dizziness of losing his hand, though he managed to cut some tackle rope from one of the cannons and used it to help Rye Blackbird tie off the area above his ruined knee. Blackbird grinned up at him. "Fine swordsmanship, my buck."

"I am the student of a master," Privet returned. "*Your sword…*"

Privet offered the weapon, holding it gently by the blade, and the other man took the handle.

"*Our sword*," Blackbird said.

By the time men from the *North Swan* dug through the barricading rubble and discovered the scene on the gun deck, the black sloop *Nocturnal,* which had turned back on its course, was far from cannon range. The only survivors from the lower portions of the ship were Privet, who had lost a hand in the fight, and a man unconscious from blood loss, a sailor according to Privet, a crewman of the brigantine *Scythe of Providence*, who was wounded in the leg.

Mill Burnshire and the ship's second lieutenant walked alongside the stretcher on which Privet lay as he was carried toward a ladderway on the *North Swan*. The ship's healer, Polton Juniper, awaited his arrival below.

Burnshire said, "Lacking Litch, *you*, my friend, assume charge as acting captain."

Privet smiled weakly. "*Captain Privet*."

The second lieutenant asked, "Orders, sir?"

Privet looked up. "We sail home with haste. Perhaps, if fate proves kindly, we shall find the King still breathing."

The documentarian Hentwidge was waiting for Privet in the healer's rooms along with Polton Juniper. There were lanterns enough to make it bright and the air was a garden of herbal scents. They made the captain comfortable in a chair and then Hentwidge, with his usual meticulous manner, set about a curious bit of surgery.

"Haverly Shellings, Crown Botanist to Weldren, had quite the success applying curious healing techniques observed in his time at Small Island," Hentwidge explained, rolling up his white sleeves and pressing his spectacles up his nose. "*This* procedure, which I shall here attempt, was one of those he himself put to use. It may be your good fortune, Captain, that he recorded the particulars of such experiments. Fortunate also that I quite recall what they were."

"You have my implicit trust, Mister Hentwidge," Privet said.

"As you know, the Winter-ash's healing power works only upon injuries come about from bladed weapons. Be happy your hand was not *shot* off!"

"I'm elated," Privet said wryly, grimacing as Hentwidge and the healer worked on his arm.

A cutting from one of the collected branches of Winter-ash was inserted into the stump, the leaves dangling off the exposed end like flattened green fingers. The wound was then sewn shut and the wrist and the base of the twig were then wrapped in bandages that had been soaked in one of Juniper's healing solutions.

When healer and documentarian were finished, Privet lifted his arm and studied the new appendage. "*A sprig?*"

"Not simply *any* sprig," Hentwidge said with a very small smile.

West Fellengrey rose from the horizon, appeared to float up from beneath the Gantic. Having crested, seemingly, it proceeded to expand and, before long, men on the frigate *North Swan* could distinguish settlements amidst the green of the mass. Closer to Demmingsfife, and there were feats of architecture, the cumbersome mercantile buildings along Brittlegate, the solemn gray of Fort Wrenning, and warships sleeping in the calm water of the *North Swan's* home bay.

A carriage arrived at the navy docks to rush Hentwidge to Royal House, where, to the man's relief, King Fenny still clung to life. Just barely clung. The dapper documentarian, in fine coat and breeches the color of a horse chestnut, and a waistcoat of a similar hue (though embellished with ivy patterns in silken thread) strode into the great building carrying a bundle of branches that had been wrapped in a damp cloth so that they would remain fresh.

Hentwidge, accompanied by royal healers, was led into the King's room. Fenny's mother, Violet, sat in a chair by the bed, eager eyes rising as the men entered and bowed.

"Never have I been so happy to look upon a face as I am yours, Mister Hentwidge."

He bowed, thanked the woman, smiled politely and, dutiful creature that he was, set straight to work. Fenny was unconscious, his breathing faint, his color poor. Bandages were removed so that Hentwidge could access the wound. He plucked thirteen leaves from the branches and held them in his palm. Then, cupping his hands over his mouth, he whispered to the leaves before layering them over the King's stab wound.

"Sorry I am to say," Hentwidge addressed Violet, "but there is nothing more to do but wait."

Rain came in the night, swift off the sea, pattering against the windows of Royal House, but the sky cleared by dawn and the east wore a brief bashful color. Morning brought warmth and the warmth urged the smell of flowers from sodden shadows in the gardens of Royal House and soon there were bees buzzing about their duties, like those inside the rambling structure.

"He wishes for jam cakes!" Violet, in a gown of mellow tones, said excitedly as she flew out the door of her son's bedchamber, nearly colliding with Neelam Hentwidge. The woman made off for the kitchen and the documentarian knocked before entering.

"Good King," Hentwidge said, bowing in the room.

Fenny was sitting up in bed against a pile of pillows. Color had returned to his face. "Dear Hentwidge," the King said, "how very nice to see you. I feel I have slept a year!"

"Far from it, my King."

Young Fenny had mild, clean-shaven features and soft blond hair that hung past his shoulders. He looked tired, certainly, but a spirited gleam had returned to his eyes. "Such dreams I've had!"

Fenny's best advisor, the chronically pensive Spindles, stood by the bed. He looked to Hentwidge and said, "The King requests some measure of appreciation be made the people of Small Island for allowing us to partake of their wondrous tree."

Hentwidge nodded. "How very considerate."

"We shall inquire as to what it is they may be lacking and supply it," Spindles said, "livestock, perhaps, new fishing boats, as may be the case."

"I shall make record," the documentarian said.

Fenny took a sip of some tea which his healer, Herringfield, had provided, then squinted in thought. "What would be the name of this fellow who saw the frigate home in so timely a manner? I might likely have perished were it not for him. And his bravery in battling those marauders ought be recognized as well. What again was his name?"

"Privet," Hentwidge said, "Lieutenant Hale Privet."

6

Marriage

It was cool in Old Crown, a clammy breeze coming in off the Gantic, rippling the water around the *North Swan,* which was moored below off the modern part of the city. Post Captain Privet was comfy and dry, sitting in the humble parlor of the pretty, old Deerfield sisters. A nice fire heated the room and the place smelled of bergamot and boiling turnip.

The officer drank tea with his friends and they talked about the Winter-ash, which the sisters knew of from a song, part of which they sang in lilting unison.

"Remarkable," they cooed together, leaning forward on their settle to have a look at his new hand, which had grown to its present size in a mere matter of months.

The appendage was somewhat smaller and more delicate than a man's, but its gray color and dimensions aside, it functioned perfectly, and was much preferred to a metal hook.

The old women also admired the flat, gold, shark silhouettes on the shoulders of his dark green coat, designations of his new rank.

"Captain Privet, of the *North Swan,*" they said in a sing-song way. "It falls pleasingly upon the ear."

Privet smiled handsomely. "You are kind to say."

Evening was not far off when the sisters walked Privet to the cliff, where a great length of uneven stone steps slanted down to New Crown. The women, who were dreadfully afraid of heights, kept a safe distance from the drop. Privet bent to receive a kiss on each cheek.

"All good luck with your young woman," they said, waving as the captain started down.

The Gorse House, an ancient narrow thing with a roof of pale green slates, sat on a knoll with a view out to sea. The autumn dusk was chill, but it was cozy and warm in the best room, a vigorous hardwood fire blazing. The family and their guest gathered here following a rich meal of many courses, and desserts enough to sate the most voracious sweet tooth.

Privet sat in a chair by the fire with his bicorne in lap, wondering if he had been quite so nervous when faced with a battle. His beloved Hazel sat across from him, fetching with her dark hair and her green eyes and a sage-green gown with lace trim at the square neckline. She gazed at him lovingly until the hour grew late, and then she bulged her eyes at him when no one was looking.

Privet swallowed and nodded. He stood up, his sword bumping the leg of his chair and he blushed. The girl's parents looked up at him eagerly. Hazel's younger sister, Lilac, involuntarily drummed her feet on the floor and reached over to squeeze her sibling's hand, exclaiming in a hush, "*Oh! Oh!*"

The officer cleared his voice, then said, "Mister and Missus Gorse, I should like to, um…"

The father nodded so that one might have thought his neck had gone into some strange, unrelenting spasm.

Privet said, "To, ahh, ask of you your daughter's hand…in marriage."

Mr. Gorse flew up and gripped Privet's hand. "You have our blessing, my boy! May the gods bless you both!"

Privet broke into a great smile. "Thank you, sir! Thank you!"

"You ought not spy, my dear," Mr. Gorse said to his wife as she peeked out the window when Hazel stepped outside to see her captain off.

He put down his book and peered over his spectacles with a grin. "Are they kissing?"

"No, they're weeding the garden," the woman said snidely. "Of course they're kissing!"

Mr. Gorse nodded, pleased, and said, mostly to himself, "*A captain!*"

Mrs. Gorse let the curtain fall back into place and turned to regard her husband with a frown. "Yes, a captain, and like to have plenty a lass in towns along the coast, and be much wed to the sea, more so than ever he should be to a woman of flesh."

"*A captain!*" Mr. Gorse repeated to himself.

Privet took Hazel's hand and touched her palm to his lips in parting. She pressed the hand to her heart.

"We next sail north from Demmingsfife in three weeks' time," Privet said. "I shall marry you then, my love."

Tears did not make Hazel any less pretty. Tears and smiling all at once. "I should miss you, Hale."

"And I, you."

Privet put his hat on his head and turned. Hazel watched him walk back toward the docks, where his beloved ship waited.

Crewmen saluted as Privet made his way across the deck of the anchored frigate *North Swan*. The bay in moonlight was a shimmering vastness, the vessel shifting lazily. Mill Burnshire, the coxswain, was on the quarterdeck chatting with midshipman Hibbits, whose new lamp-tail was singing merrily from the cage at the man's feet.

"Mail has arrived, Captain," Burnshire said, handing Privet a small bundle of missives.

Privet had a distant look in his eye and the silly grin of a man in love. "My thanks, Mill."

Down in his handsome cabin with its paneled white walls, Privet sat and opened his letters. There was one from his mother in Hemmings Port, and one from his favorite cousin in Blackbirch, and one with the name Knoll Blackslate in raised lettering on the wax seal.

Privet opened this one first.

My Dear Buck,

I have returned to my cottage in the Spinnings, and while lonely it may be, I find it a peaceful enough place. It seems not the home my dearest Holly made it to be, but I shall, once more, try my hand as a planter.

I have done with the sea and departed the likes of the crew I assembled to carry out my vengeance. They served well, suffered few losses, and gained a handsome fortune in pirate takings. But, enough pirates have died that I might now find some measure of rest in my heart, as I hope Holly has found her rest as well.

I shall ever be grateful for your kindnesses. I should not be here writing this letter were it not for you. Incidentally, I grow quite accustomed to the wooden leg.

I wish you great joy and comfort in your pending wedlock.

Your much obliged friend,

Rye Blackbird

Privet locked the letter away in a sea chest and retired to his bunk. The moon was gone and from the stern windows he could see far off lightning slashing beyond the great black Gantic, could feel the sea shifting beneath him like the pulse of a living thing. He was hard-pressed to believe that Rye Blackbird would not return to sea one day, and he wondered if his friend also lay in bed at night imagining that distant thunder was the sound of mighty warships firing their cannons.

About the Author

Fellengrey is Scott Thomas's first published novel. His short story collections include *Quill and Candle, Midnight in New England* and *Westermead*. He has seen print in numerous anthologies, such as *The Year's Best Fantasy and Horror #15* and *The Solaris Book of New Fantasy*. His work appears with that of his brother Jeffrey Thomas, in *Punktown: Shades of Grey* and *The Sea of Flesh and Ash*. Scott and his girlfriend, Peggy, live in coastal Maine.

www.ingramcontent.com/pod-product-compliance
Lightning Source LLC
Chambersburg PA
CBHW032042240626
47154CB00003B/1039